双语 精华版

心灵鸡汤

[经典系列]

时光的印记--

徐艳 杨芳译

Traces of the Years

Jack Canfield & Mark Victor Hansen 等 著

Chicken Soup for the Soul

安徽科学技术出版社

Health Communications, Inc.

图书在版编目(CIP)数据

心灵鸡汤:双语精华版.时光的印记/(美)坎费尔德
(Canfield,J.)等著;徐艳,杨芳译. —合肥:安徽科学技
术出版社,2007.9
　　ISBN 978-7-5337-3880-8

Ⅰ.心… Ⅱ.①坎…②徐…③杨… Ⅲ.①英语-汉语-
对照读物②故事-作品集-美国-现代 Ⅳ.H319.4:Ⅰ

中国版本图书馆 CIP 数据核字(2007)第 129495 号

心灵鸡汤:双语精华版.时光的印记
(美)坎费尔德(Canfield,J.)等著　徐艳　杨芳译

出 版 人:朱智润
责任编辑:李瑞生
封面设计:王国亮
出版发行:安徽科学技术出版社(合肥市政务文化新区圣泉路 1118 号
　　　　　出版传媒广场,邮编:230071)
电　　话:(0551)3533330
网　　址:www.ahstp.com.cn
E - mail:yougoubu@sina.com
经　　销:新华书店
排　　版:安徽事达科技贸易有限公司
印　　刷:合肥华云印务有限公司
开　　本:889×1100　1/24
印　　张:10
字　　数:202 千
版　　次:2007 年 9 月第 1 版　2007 年 9 月第 1 次印刷
印　　数:10 000
定　　价:25.00 元

(本书如有印装质量问题,影响阅读,请向本社市场营销部调换)

作为原生于美国的大众心理自助与人生励志类的闪亮品牌,《心灵鸡汤》语言地道新颖,优美流畅,极富时代感。书中一个个叩人心扉的故事,充分挖掘平凡小事所蕴藏的精神力量和人性之美,真率倾诉对生命的全新体验和深层感悟,字里行间洋溢着爱心、感恩、信念、鼓励和希望。因其内涵哲思深邃,豁朗释然,央视"百家讲坛"曾引用其作为解读援例。

文本的适读性与亲和力、故事的吸引力和感召力、内涵的人文性和震撼力,煲出了鲜香润泽的《心灵鸡汤》——发行40多个国家和地区,总销量达一亿多册的全球超级畅销书!

安徽科学技术出版社独家引进的该系列英文版,深得广大读者的推崇与青睐,频登各大书店及"开卷市场零售监测系统"的畅销书排行榜,多次荣获全国出版发行业的各类奖项。

就学英语而言,本系列读物的功效已获广大读者乃至英语教学界的充分肯定。由于书中文章的信度和效度完全符合大规模标准化考试对考题的质量要求,全国大学英语四级考试、全国成人高考的阅读理解真题曾采用其中的文章。大学英语通用教材曾采用其中的文章作为精读课文。

为了让更多读者受惠于这一品牌,我社又获国内独家授权,隆重推出双语精华版《心灵鸡汤》系列:英汉美文并蓄、双语同一视面对照——广大读者既能在轻松阅读中提高英语水平,又能从中感悟人生的真谛,激发你搏击风雨、奋发向上的生命激情!

CONTENTS

目 录

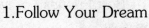

目录

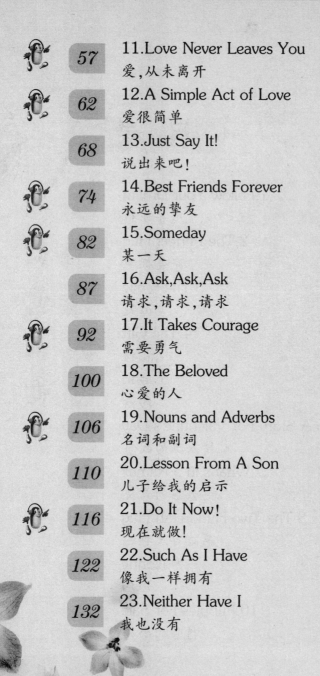

Follow Your Dream
追寻梦想

I have a friend named Monty Roberts who owns a horse ranch in San Ysidro.He has let me use his house to put on fund-raising events to raise money for youth at risk programs.

The last time I was there he introduced me by saying,"I want to tell you why I let Jack use my house.It all goes back to a story about a young man who was the son of an itinerant horse trainer who would go from stable to stable,race track to race track,farm to farm and ranch to ranch,training horses.As a result,the boy's high school career was continually interrupted.When he was a senior,he was asked to write a paper about what he wanted to be and do when he grew up.

"That night he wrote a seven-page paper describing his goal of someday owning a horse ranch.He wrote about his dream in great detail

我有个叫蒙丁·罗伯特的朋友,他在圣·伊丝德罗有一个马场。他曾把他那儿的几间房借给我开展基金筹措项目,提供青年创业资金。

上回在他的马场时, 他这样向人介绍我,"要说我为什么把房子借给杰克,得说一个故事。有个年轻人,父亲是常年奔波的驯马人,来回奔波于马厩、赛马场、农场、牧场,为人训练马匹。因为这样,年轻人的高中学业不停地被打断。毕业那年,他被要求写一篇文章,说说自己将来的打算。"

"年轻人连夜写了整整7张纸,说将来想拥有一个马场。他写得很详细,甚至还画了一张草图,描绘他梦想中那片200英亩的马场,标

经典系列／时光的印记

1

and he even drew a diagram of a 200-acre ranch,showing the location of all the buildings,the stables and the track.Then he drew a detailed floor plan for a 4,000-square-foot house that would sit on the 200-acre dream ranch.

"He put a great deal of his heart into the project and the next day he handed it in to his teacher.Two days later he received his paper back. On the front page was a large red F with a note that read,'See me after class.'

"The boy with the dream went to see the teacher after class and asked,'Why did I receive an F?' "The teacher said,'This is an unrealistic dream for a young boy like you.You have no money.You come from an itinerant family.You have no resources.Owning a horse ranch requires a lot of money.You have to buy the land.You have to pay for the original breeding stock and later you'll have to pay large stud fees.There's no way you could ever do it.'Then the teacher added,'If you will rewrite this paper with a more realistic goal,I will reconsider your grade.'"

"The boy went home and thought about it long and hard.He asked his father what he should do.His father said,'Look,son,you have to make up your own mind on this.However,I think it is a very important decision for you.'

"Finally,after sitting with it for a week,the boy turned in the same paper,making no changes at all.He stated,'You can keep the F and I'll keep my dream.'"

Monty then turned to the assembled group and said,"I tell you this story because you are sitting in my 4,000-square-foot house in the middle of my 200-acre horse ranch.I still have that school paper framed over the fireplace."He added,"The best part of the story is that two summers ago that same schoolteacher brought 30 kids to camp out on my ranch for a week.When the teacher was leaving,he said,'Look, Monty,

出所有房子、马厩和赛马场的位置，最后他还附了一张200英亩的梦想马场上4 000平方英尺的大房子的设计图稿。"

"他花了不少心思在上面。第二天，他把文章和图稿交给了老师。两天后，发下的作业上画了一个大大的F(极差)，旁边有一行字：下课后来见我。"

"满怀梦想的年轻人去了，问道：'为什么给我F？'老师说：'对你来说，这个梦想不太现实。你没有钱，家庭条件一般，没有基础。创办马场得花一大笔钱。买地、创建投资、花大笔钱买种马，你根本没办法做到。'老师接着说：'如果你肯重新定一个现实的目标，改写这篇文章的话，我会重新考虑你的分数。'

"回到家，年轻人苦苦思考了很久。他问父亲该如何是好，父亲答到：'孩子，你得自己拿主意。我想这对你很重要。'过了一个礼拜，年轻人一字未改，把原稿又交了上去，他还写道：'你的F可以保留，我的梦想也得保留。'"

蒙丁转过身来，对大家说："说这个故事的时候，你们已经置身于我200英亩的马场中心4 000平方英尺的大房子中了。那篇文章至今我还留在壁炉上的镜框里。故事的精彩部分是，前年夏天，那位老师带了30个孩子到我的马场露营一周。临行前他说：'看，蒙丁，现在

I can tell you this now.When I was your teacher,I was something of a dream stealer.During those years I stole a lot of kids' dreams.Fortunately you had enough gumption not to give up on yours.'"

Don't let anyone steal your dreams.Follow your heart,no matter what.

CHICKEN
SOUP

我可以告诉你了。我做你老师的时候,我像是一个偷梦者,我偷走了很多孩子的梦想,幸好你有进取心,始终不肯放手。'"

别让任何人偷走你的梦想。不管发生什么事,都要追寻自己的梦想。

杰克·卡菲尔德

The Perfect Hug
完美拥抱

Please continue to look at your children as valuable treasures.Honor them and yourself.

Bernie Siegel

请一直把你的孩子们视为珍宝,尊重他们和你自己。

波涅·西杰尔

The room was filling up with teachers and administrators.It was a long room with those bare and fading painted walls that we've come to associate with schools,church rectories and other under-funded instituitions.The only details to relieve the plainness were the flag up on the front wall and the cracked slate chalkboard.This huge room served many purposes:classroom,meeting space and recreation hall for this old,small college.

I had been invited to present a workshop on innovative teaching methods to a large group of local teachers.

房间里挤满了教师们和教育管理人员,这是一间墙壁上的油漆已经陈旧剥落的狭长的大房间,这儿聚集的人来自各个学校、教区和这个基金会名下的大学。房间前面墙上挂的标志和斑驳的黑板提示,这间房间兼有多种用途:它是这所不大的古老的大学的教室、会议室和娱乐厅。

我受邀参加一项当地许多老师参与的教学方法改革的工作。

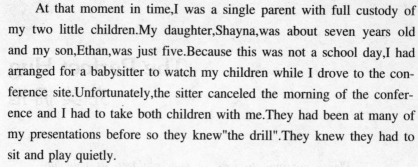

At that moment in time,I was a single parent with full custody of my two little children.My daughter,Shayna,was about seven years old and my son,Ethan,was just five.Because this was not a school day,I had arranged for a babysitter to watch my children while I drove to the conference site.Unfortunately,the sitter canceled the morning of the conference and I had to take both children with me.They had been at many of my presentations before so they knew"the drill".They knew they had to sit and play quietly.

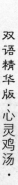

Shayna brought books and drawing materials to occupy her time. She also brought her doll collection including a box of Barbie dolls and their myriad accessories.Ethan brought a small suitcase of building blocks and soldier dolls with all their guns and equipment.

They sat at a table at the very back of the room,facing away from the front where I would be presenting,both fully engrossed in play.

The teachers group was lively and responsive.Every activity I proposed they enthusiastically made their own.Participation was nearly total as I demonstrated teaching methods and organized small groups to share ideas.

At one point,a teacher raised her hand and said,"I wonder what you'd suggest about hugging."

"Tell me more about your concern," I replied.

"Well,I teach elementary school—fourth and fifth grade combined—and sometimes I just want to hug the kids,especially the ones who are often in trouble.Do you think it's all right to do that?"

"It's a strange world,indeed,that we are living in,"I replied. "Hugging is such a natural and spontaneous display of affection.It is often the very best thing you can do when a child is hurting,depressed,crying or frightened.Yet we've learned to be worried about it.There have been, sadly enough,too many cases reported in the media,of adults touching kids inappropriately.So it is important to have guidelines and clear limits

当时我独自一人带着一对儿女,女儿莎娜7岁左右,儿子埃赛才刚5岁,因为那天不是上学的日子,我去开会时必须找人帮我照看孩子。不巧的是,开会的这个上午,照看孩子的人有事不能来。我只好把他们一起带上。以前也常有这样的事,因此,他们知道怎么做,知道必须安静地坐在那儿自己玩耍。

莎娜带了书和画画的东西打发时间,她还带了收藏的娃娃,其中有一整盒芭比娃娃和娃娃要换的各种衣服。埃赛带来一小箱积木和他的士兵玩偶,还有枪和其他装备。

他们坐在房间最后面的桌子旁,背对着前面我坐的地方全神贯注地玩。

教师们很积极,很活跃,对于我提议的每一项活动他们都热烈响应,提出自己的建议。当我演示新的教学方法时,所有的人都参加了,还组织了小组进行讨论。

谈到某一点时,一个老师举手发言:"我对你的关于拥抱的建议还不太清楚。"

"是哪些地方不清楚呢?"我说。

"是这样,我教小学四年级和五年级的一个合班,有时我很想拥抱那些孩子,特别是那些有这样那样问题的孩子,我这样做对吗?"

"我们所居住的世界确实是非常奇怪的世界,而拥抱是我们表达爱的最自然而又发自内心的行为。当孩子们受了伤害,情绪低落,伤心或者受了惊吓等,你可以做的最好的事就是拥抱。当然,我们也知道要当心。媒体已经报道了不少成人不适当地触碰孩子的事例,已经令人很伤心了。所以如何和孩子相处具有一定的指导和行为的

to how, when and where we touch kids. Yes, I think hugging is a very good thing to do."

I concluded with this comment: "You know, when adults hug each other, there's always a bit of selfconsciousness about it. Part of you is committed to the hug and part of you may be thinking something like 'I wonder if this person understands what I really mean by this hug,' or 'I wonder what this person means by his or her hug!' or 'I wonder if anyone else is watching this hug and I wonder what they think,' or—'I added for the sake of humor—even 'I wonder if I've paid my Master-Card bill.'" The group roared with laughter.

"As adults, because we've been through so many experiences, we each bring our entire personal history into the hug and all the concerns that come with that history. Further, we are worried about, thinking about, planning for, engaged in, so many, many things that it's hard to just be in the hug totally and completely. The reason I am thinking about this is that I can see my children at the back of the room."

At this, the group turned their heads to look at my children who were still sitting quietly, engrossed in play, facing away from the group. Then the participants turned back to me as I went on.

"You see, when I get home at the end of a work day, as tired as I am, one of the things I most look forward to is a hug from my children. As young as they are, they have less history and fewer complicated worries and no bills to pay. As I walk in the door, they each almost fly up my body and hug and kiss me. My son particularly nearly melts his body into mine, burying his face in my neck and just hugs me. I believe that at such moments he is fully, completely and only hugging me, without distracting thoughts and without reservation. And it's the most tender moment in my life!" The group smiled approvingly and that started a number of side conversations that went on for several minutes before we went on with the workshop.

界定,即什么方式、什么时机、什么地点去和孩子接触等,都是非常重要的。我想:拥抱是非常好的一件事。"

我总结说:"大家知道,成年人相互拥抱时,多多少少含有一些自我意识在里面。一部分意识在拥抱上,还有一部分意识正在思考,比如:'这个人是不是明白我拥抱他的真正含义呢?'或者'他或她的拥抱是什么意思啊?'又或'有没有人看见我在拥抱,他们会怎么想?'等等,甚至会想起(我增添了点幽默气氛)'我是否付过了万事达信用卡上的欠款。'"大家哄堂大笑起来。

"作为成年人,因为我们有了不少生活阅历,我们每个人都会把我们的个人经历以及所有那些与个人经历有关的东西带进拥抱中,进而还有那些我们的担忧、我们的思考、我们的打算、我们的事业等许多许多的东西,这就让我们不可能全心全意地投入拥抱。让我想到这些是因为我可以看到坐在后面的我的孩子。"

这时,所有的人都回头看我的两个孩子,他们背对着大家坐在那儿专注地玩。大家转回头时,我继续讲道:

"要知道,结束了一天的工作回到家里,我们非常疲惫,此时最盼望的就是孩子们的拥抱。他们那么小没有什么阅历,也没有复杂的担忧,更没有欠款。我一进门,他们就飞跑过来,扑到我怀里,拥抱亲吻我。特别是我的儿子几乎把他小小的身体融化到我的身体里,把小脸埋在我的脖子里,紧紧地抱着我。我相信,此刻他是全心全意地,只是拥抱我,毫无保留,也不会去想别的什么,这是我生活中最温馨的时刻。"大家都赞许地笑了,并从各个侧面讨论了几分钟,然后继续进行教学研讨。

Six or seven weeks later I was coming home from a long and exhausting day at the university where I taught educational psychology.I pulled into the garage,took my briefcase and entered the house through the kitchen door.Both children came flying down the stairs screaming," Daddy,Daddy,Daddy! "and Shayna leaped into my arms,"I missed you, Daddy.Do you know what I did?" And of course I wanted to know all about what she had done.Their nanny stood beaming in the background as Shayna told her story.Then,done with me,Shayna ran gaily out of the kitchen and returned to her latest project.

Ethan had barely contained himself.He,too,leaped up on my chest and hugged me with all his might.He buried his face in my neck and his breathing slowed.His body softened as he seemed to melt into me.Then he raised his head slightly away from my neck and whispered in my ear, "I wonder if I paid my MasterCard bill! "

Hanoch McCarty

6至7个星期后的一天,我在大学上了整整一天教育心理学课程,很晚才回家,非常疲劳。我把车停在车库,拿起公文包从厨房的门进入房间,两个孩子从楼上飞跑下来,大声喊着:"爸爸,爸爸,爸爸!"莎娜跳进我的臂膀里,"我想你,爸爸,你知道我干什么了?"当然我十分想知道所有她做的事情。莎娜叙述着她的故事,他们的保姆微笑着站在后面,然后,莎娜欢快地跑出厨房去忙她最新的"事业"了。

伊桑几乎无法控制自己,他也跳起来紧贴我的胸口,用尽全力抱着我。他把脸埋在我的颈下,放慢了呼吸,身体软软地仿佛要融入我的身体。后来,他从我颈下微微地抬起头,在我耳边轻轻地说:"我在想是否付过信用卡上的欠款!"

哈诺克·莫卡提

The Smile
微　笑

Smile at each other, smile at your wife, smile at your husband, smile at your children, smile at each other—it doesn't matter who it is—and that will help you to grow up in greater love for each other.

Mother Teresa

向对方微笑，对你的妻子微笑，对你的丈夫微笑，对你的孩子微笑，无论对方是谁，朝他微笑，这会让你在与他人更大的互相关爱中成长。

特蕾莎修女

Many Americans are familiar with *The Little Prince*, a wonderful book by Antoine de Saint-Exupery. This is a whimsical and fabulous book and works as a children's story as well as a thought-provoking adult fable. Far fewer are aware of Saint-Exupery's other writings, novels and short stories.

许多美国人都熟知安东尼·圣·伊格优普利写的那本精彩的《小王子》。这是一本十分搞笑精彩的书，既是孩子们的读物也是发人深省的成人寓言。可极少有人知道圣·伊格优普利的其他作品，长篇小说和短篇小说。

经典系列／时光的印记

11

Saint-Exupery was a fighter pilot who fought against the Nazis and was killed in action.Before World War II,he fought in the Spanish Civil War against the fascists.He wrote a fascinating story based on that experience entitled *The Smile* *(Le Sourire)*.It is this story which I'd like to share with you now.It isn't clear whether or not he meant this to be autobiographical or fiction.I choose to believe it is the former.

He said that he was captured by the enemy and thrown into a jail cell.He was sure that from the contemptuous looks and rough treatment he received from his jailers he would be executed the next day.From here,I'll tell the story as I remember it in my own words.

"I was sure that I was to be killed.I became terribly nervous and distraught.I fumbled in my pockets to see if there were any cigarettes which had escaped their search.I found one and because of my shaking hands,I could barely get it to my lips.But I had no matches,they had taken those.

"I looked through the bars at my jailer.He did not make eye contact with me.After all,one does not make eye contact with a thing,a corpse.I called out to him 'Have you got a light,*por favor?*' He looked at me, shrugged and came over to light my cigarette.

"As he came close and lit the match,his eyes inadvertently locked with mine.At that moment,I smiled.I don't know why I did that.Perhaps it was nervousness,perhaps it was because,when you get very close,one to another,it is very hard not to smile.In any case,I smiled.In that instant, it was as though a spark jumped across the gap between our two hearts, our two human souls.I know he didn't want to,but my smile leaped through the bars and generated a smile on his lips,too.He lit my cigarette but stayed near,looking at me directly in the eyes and continuing to smile.

"I kept smiling at him,now aware of him as a person and not just a jailer.And his looking at me seemed to have a new dimension,too. 'Do

圣·伊格优普利生前是一名战斗机飞行员，对纳粹作战并战死疆场。在二战前，他曾在西班牙内战中对战法西斯。根据这段经历他创作了一部极具吸引力的小说《微笑》(法语 *Le Sourire*)。我要跟你分享的正是这个故事。人们尚不清楚这部小说是自传体还是虚构的。我选择相信它是自传体小说。

他叙述他被人俘虏投入狱中一个小牢房里，他从看守轻蔑的眼神和对他的粗暴待遇中读出，明天必将处死他。我将凭我的记忆从此处开始重述这个故事。

"我确定自己将被处死。我非常害怕，心烦意乱，便在口袋里摸索着，看看有没有躲过他们搜查的香烟。找到一根烟后，却因为手抖得厉害，勉强才送到嘴边。可是火柴也被他们搜走了。

"我透过囚室栅栏向看守望去，他不拿眼看我。毕竟谁都不会和一个死物，一个尸体进行目光交流。我向他叫道："有火吗，请问(西班牙语 please)？"他看着我，耸耸肩，走过来点着我的烟。

"当他走到近前点烟时，他的目光偶然和我的相遇，在这一瞬间，我微微一笑。我不知道为什么要这么做。也许是因为紧张，也许是因为两个人之间距离很近时，很难不微笑。无论是什么原因，我微笑了，在那一刻，它就像是一星火花，跨越了两颗心，两个人类灵魂之间的鸿沟，我的微笑越过栅栏，引发了他唇间的笑意，虽然我知道他本不想笑。他点着了我的烟并呆在近前，直视着我的眼睛，继续微笑着。

"我也向他微笑着，才意识到他是个人而非仅仅是个看守。他打量着我，似乎也重新度量着我。

you have kids?'he asked.

"'Yes,here,here.'I took out my wallet and nervously fumbled for the pictures of my family.He,too,took out the pictures of his *niños* and began to talk about his plans and hopes for them.My eyes filled with tears.I said that I feared that I'd never see my family again,never have the chance to see them grow up.Tears came to his eyes,too.

"Suddenly,without another word,he unlocked my cell and silently led me out.Out of the jail,quietly and by back routes,out of the town. There,at the edge of town,he released me.And without another word,he turned back toward the town.

"My life was saved by a smile."

Yes,the smile—the unaffected,unplanned,natural connection between people.I tell this story in my work because I'd like people to consider that underneath all the layers we construct to protect ourselves,our dignity,our titles,our degrees,our status and our need to be seen in certain ways—underneath all that,remains the authentic,essential self.I'm not afraid to call it *the soul*.I really believe that if that part of you and that part of me could recognize each other,we wouldn't be enemies.We couldn't have hate or envy or fear.I sadly conclude that all those other layers,which we so carefully construct through our lives,distance and insulate us from truly contacting others.Saint-Exupery's story speaks of that magic moment when two souls recognize each other.

I've had just a few moments like that.Falling in love is one example.And looking at a baby.Why do we smile when we see a baby? Perhaps it's because we see someone without all the defensive layers, someone whose smile for us we know to be fully genuine and without guile.And that baby-soul inside us smiles wistfully in recognition.

Hanoch McCarty

"你有孩子吗？"他问道。

"有，这儿，这儿。"我拿出钱夹，紧张地翻找出家人的照片。他也拿出他几个孩子(西班牙语 children) 的照片并开始谈着对于他们的计划和寄托在他们身上的希望。我的眼中充盈着泪水。我说我害怕再也见不到家人，再也没机会看孩子们长大。泪水也渐渐涌入他的眼眶。

"突然，他一言不发地打开我这间牢房的门，无声地把我领出来，领出监狱，又无声地沿后门的路领我出了城。在那儿，在小镇边上，他放了我。仍然一言不发地，他转身走向城里。

一个微笑拯救了我的生命。

是的，微笑是人与人之间真挚的、即兴的、不做作的纽带。

在我的作品里提及这个故事是因为我希望人们重新审视在为了保护自己，保护我们的尊严、头衔、级别、地位和需要，而建立起来的所有包装之下，人们保持最真实的最根本的自我。我不顾虑称之为灵魂。我真的相信，如果你的灵魂和我的灵魂能互相认出彼此，我们就不会是敌人，我们就不可能有憎恨、嫉妒和惧怕。我很难过地得出结论，我们毕生小心建立起来的那些层层包装，使我们难以甚至无法与他人真正沟通。圣·伊格优普利的故事说到了当两个灵魂相遇时辨认出彼此的奇妙时刻。

我仅有过几次类似经历，坠入爱河便是一例。看着婴儿也是一例。为什么我们在看见婴儿时会微笑？也许是因为我们看到了一个毫无防御包装的人，一个我们知道其微笑是完全真实绝不带一丝狡诈的人。我们内心的"婴儿灵魂"在相遇相识时发出渴望的微笑。

哈诺克·莫卡提

15

The Gift

"Grandpa,please come,"I said,knowing he wouldn't.In the pale light that filtered through the dusty kitchen window,he sat stiffly in his padded vinyl chair,his thick arms resting on the Formica table,staring past me at the wall.He was a gruff,crusty,old-country Italian,with a long memory for past hurts both real and imagined.When he was feeling testy,he responded with a grunt.He gave me one now that meant no.

"Come on,Gramps,"pleaded my six-year-old sister,Carrie. "I want you to come."Twenty-one years younger than I,she had been a startlingly late addition to our family."I'm going to make your favorite cookies just for you.Mommy said she would show me."

"It's for Thanksgiving,for God's sake,"I said. "You haven't joined us for dinner for four years now.Don't you think it's about time we let the past be？ "

He glanced at me,his blue eyes flashing the same fierce intensity that had intimidated the entire family all these years.Except me.Somehow,I knew him.Perhaps I shared more of his loneliness than I cared to admit,and the same inability to let emotions show.Whatever the reason,I knew what was inside him.*The sins of the fathers will be visited on their sons,*it was written,and so they were.How much suffering occurs because of the unfortunate "gift"each male receives before he is old enough to decide if he wants it,this misguided idea of manhood.We end up hard on the outside,helpless on the inside,and the few feet that separated me from my grandfather might just as well have been measured in light years.

16

礼　物

"爷爷，来一下，"我说，明知他不会来。暗淡的灯光滤过厨房满是灰尘的窗玻璃，在灯光里，爷爷僵硬地坐在他那加了垫子的树脂椅里，粗大的胳膊搁在福米卡(家具塑料贴面的商标名称)桌子上，目光穿透我的身体，定在墙上。他是个鲁莽、粗暴的意大利乡下老人，满脑子都是对于逝去伤痛的长长的回忆，这些伤痛有些是真的，有些是他想象出来的。当他觉得烦躁时，他就咕哝一声作为回应。现在他就对我咕哝了一声以示拒绝。

"来嘛，爷爷。"我6岁的小妹妹嘉莉求道。"我要你来。"她比我小20岁，是我们家里迟到的惊人的附加品。"我要特意为你做你最爱吃的点心。妈咪说她会教我做的。"

"是为感恩节准备的，看在上帝的分上，"我说。"你已经4年没和我们一起吃饭了。难道你不认为是时候让过去随它去吗？"

他瞥了我一眼，蓝眼睛放出非常凶狠的光，这目光这些年来吓坏了家人，除了我。我稍稍了解他些。也许我比自己所说的更了解他的孤独，以及不能宣泄情感的无助。不管怎样，我知道他内心是怎样的一个人。书上说，父债子偿，的确如此。每个男人在尚未成熟到能够决定是否愿意接受之前，这个不幸的"礼物"就被送给他们了。关于男人的这个谬论导致了多少痛苦。我们这些男人外表刚强，内心无能。我和祖父只有几步之遥，但这几步恐怕得用光年来衡量。

经典系列／时光的印记

17

Carrie chattered on,still trying to convince him.She had no idea how hopeless it was.

I got up and walked to the window overlooking his backyard.In the winter light,the disheveled garden was a delicate gray,overgrown with tangled weeds and vines gone wild.Grandpa used to work miracles there—a substitute,perhaps,for his inability to orchestrate his own nature. But after Grandma died,he let the garden go,retreating even further into himself.

Turning away from the window,I studied him in the deepening gloom.From his prominent chin to his thick,rough hands,everything about him reflected the relentless discipline his life had been:work since age 13,the humiliation of unemployment during the Depression,decades of hard manual labor in the Trenton Stone Quarry.Not an easy life.

I kissed him on the cheek. "We have to go now,Grandpa.I'll pick you up if you decide to come."

He sat stone-still,staring straight ahead,sucking on his old pipe.

A few days later,Carrie asked me for Grandpa's address.

"What for? "I asked.

She was neatly folding a sheet of paper to fit into a blue envelope. "I want to send him a gift.I made it myself."

I told her the address,pausing after each line so she could get it all down.She wrote slowly,concentrating on making each letter and number neat and round.When she finished,she put her pencil down and said firmly,"I want to mail it myself.Will you take me to the mailbox? "

"We'll do it later,okay? "

"I need to do it now.Please? "

So we did.

On Thanksgiving I awoke late to the delicious smell of pasta sauce. Mom was preparing her special dinner of ravioli,turkey,broccoli,sweet potatoes,and cranberry   sauce,a wonderful amalgam of Italian and

嘉莉还在说着,试图说服爷爷。她还不知道什么叫做无药可救,我起身走到窗前俯视他的后院。在这冬日的光线下,杂乱的园子就是一片嫩灰色的荒地,长满了纠结的乱草和横生的藤蔓。爷爷过去在这片荒地上创造了奇迹——也许是把它当做一个替代品,以弥补他对协调自己本性的无能为力。但是奶奶去世后,他就不再打理园子了,而是深深地躲在自己的世界里。

　　我把目光从窗前移开,怀着深深的忧郁打量他。他那突出的下巴,他那双厚实又粗糙的手,每一处都诉说着他这一生不断遭受的残酷的磨炼:13岁参加工作,大萧条时期失业的耻辱,在特灵顿(新泽西州首府)采石场几十年的手工劳动。此生不易。

　　我吻吻他的脸颊,"我们得走了,爷爷。如果你决定来的话我会来接你的。"

　　他像石头一样静静地坐着,直视前方,吸着老烟斗。

　　几天后,嘉莉向我要爷爷的地址。

　　"干什么用?"我问。

　　她把一张纸整齐地叠起来塞进一个蓝色信封。"我要送他个礼物。我自己做的。"

　　我告诉她地址,说一句停一下好让她记下来。她慢慢写着,专心致志地把每一个字母和数字都写得整齐、柔顺。写完后她放下铅笔坚定地说:"我要自己寄,你带我去邮箱那儿好吗?"

　　"我们晚点去,好吗?"

　　"我现在就必须去,求你了。"

　　于是我们就去了。

　　感恩节那天,我醒得晚,一醒来就闻到意大利面酱的宜人香味。妈妈正在准备她的特色大餐。意大利小方饺、火鸡、山芋、蔓越橘酱,

American traditions. "We need only four places, Carrie," she was saying as I entered the kitchen.

Carrie shook her head. "No, Mommy, we need five. Gramps is going to come."

"Oh, honey," Mom said.

"He's coming," my sister said flatly. "I know he is."

"Carrie, give us a break. He isn't coming and you know it," I said. I didn't want to see her day spoiled by crushing disappointment.

"John, let her be." Mom looked at Carrie. "Set an extra place then."

Dad came in from the living room. He stood in the doorway, hands in his pockets, looking at Carrie as she set the table.

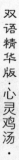

Finally we sat down to dinner. For a moment we were all silent. Then, glancing at Carrie, Mom said, "I guess we had better say grace now. Carrie?"

My sister looked toward the door. Then she set her chin, bowed her head and mumbled, "Please bless us, O ,ord, and the food we are about to eat. And bless Grandpa...and help him to hurry. Thank you, God."

Shooting glances at each other, we sat in silence, no one willing to seal Grandpa's absence and disappoint Carrie by eating. The clock ticked in the hallway.

Suddenly there was a muffled knocking at the door. Carrie leapt to her feet and ran down the hallway. She tore open the door. "Gramps!"

He stood straight in his black, shiny suit, the only one he owned, pressing a black fedora against his chest with one hand and dangling a brown paper bag with the other. "I bring squash," he said, holding up the bag.

Several months later, Grandpa died quietly in his sleep. Cleaning out his dresser, I found a blue envelope, a folded piece of paper inside. It was a child's drawing of our kitchen table with five chairs around it. One of the chairs was empty, the others   occupied by faded stick figures labeled

一顿融合意大利和美国传统食物的美味。"我们只需要4个位子，嘉莉。"我进厨房时正听她这么说。

嘉莉摇摇头。"不，妈咪，我们需要5个。爷爷会来的。"

"哦，亲爱的。"妈妈说。

"他就要来了，"妹妹毅然地说。"我知道他就要来了。"

"嘉莉，别添乱了，他不会来的，你也知道。"我说，我不想看到她这一天被巨大的失望破坏掉。

"约翰，随她去吧。"妈妈看着嘉莉。"那么，再添张位子吧！"

爸爸从起居室走进来，他站在门口，手插在口袋里，看着嘉莉摆座位。

终于我们都坐到桌前，一时间我们都没说话。然后妈妈看了一眼嘉莉，说："我想我们最好现在就祈祷，嘉莉？"

我妹妹看向门口，然后她放低下巴，垂着头喃喃自语，"请保佑我们，上帝，和我们要吃的食物，保佑爷爷……帮助他快一点，谢谢你上帝！"

我们交换了一下目光，无声地坐着，没人愿意用吃东西来肯定爷爷的不来并且让嘉莉失望。走廊里的钟嘀嗒嘀嗒地走着。

突然大门那儿传来压抑的敲门声。嘉莉跳起来跑过走廊，她拽开门。"爷爷！"

他笔直地站在那，穿着光鲜的黑西服，他唯一的西服。一手把黑色软呢帽抵在胸前，另一只手上晃荡着一个棕色的纸袋。"我带了西葫芦来。"他举起手中的袋子说。

几个月后，爷爷在睡眠中安详地死去。清理他的衣橱时，我们发现了一个蓝色的信封，里面有一张折起来的纸。是一张孩子画的图画，图上是一张围着5张椅子的餐桌。其中一张椅子是空的，其他的

Momy,Dady,Johny and Carrie.Hearts were drawn on the four of us,each cracked jaggedly down the middle.

John Catenacci

椅子上坐着褪色的简易小人，分别标着妈咪、爹地，约翰和嘉莉。图中我们4个人上都画了心，每颗心从中间呈锯齿状裂开。

约翰·凯特纳西

John
约翰

Charity sees the need, not the cause.

German Proverb

慈善只眷顾需要,而非理由。

——德国谚语

For many years now I've struggled with my purpose, working in what is a very high-crime area. I've encountered prostitutes performing sex acts on clients in the alley as I took out the trash. I've had heated discussions with the City to enforce health laws with other business owners, as transients would leave behind feces in and around trash areas. I've picketed and even faced the City Council, pleading that they close down adult bookstores in the neighborhood. I've seen the corruption and the destruction pornography can do to people's lives, especially to the children in our neighborhood. I've found myself on several occasions

多年以来,我一直为了我的目标奋斗,在一个犯罪率非常高的区域工作。出来倒垃圾时,我能看到妓女们在巷子里和顾客们从事色情交易。当看到盲流们在垃圾区里面以及附近大便,我曾经为此和市政府激烈地讨论过,要求加强生意人对于卫生法的执行力度。我叫过纠察员,甚至和市议会碰面,请求他们关闭居民区的成人书店,我已看到色情作品对人们生活的腐化和损害,特别是对附近的

driving to work in tears,asking God,"What is it that I'm supposed to be doing here?"

About a year ago I met John.He's what many people might call a street person,or a panhandler.Most might even call him crazy.

When I first met John,he came by my office selling cigarette lighters,two for a dollar.I'd probably never have thought much more about him,but a few days later he stopped in again just to ask if I minded if he drank water from our water fountain.We talked for a while.As he left he apologized for taking up so much of my time.

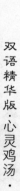
John came from a wealthy family.At one time he had it all by today's standards:a home,a boat,a business,and he even flew a plane.He stood to inherit enough money to live his retirement years comfortably anywhere in the world he would have liked to.The very sad thing about John is that he has never felt loved. Certainly he has never experienced unconditional love before.As an adult he suffered from post-traumatic stress syndrome (stemming from service in Vietnam) and depression (because of a few sad events that drew his beloved little girl away from him). John decided to walk away from his life as he had known it.

Looking at John today,you might think I am crazy to believe in him,and that he does not have much to offer this world anymore.You would be very sadly mistaken.Besides offering me practical advice on how not to go crazy in life,when he visits he pumps me with self-esteem and pride as a person.He is one of the kindest people I know.He's borrowed money to buy milk for a lady and her children that he had met on the street,and we've shared stories of how we have both helped the same elderly man that stands on a nearby corner with a sign that says, "Will work for food."(The poor soul can hardly stand with the help of his cane,much less work.)

John tells me how sad it is that people go without lunch,when he gets a free lunch every day at the park.After the school bus leaves with

双语精华版·心灵鸡汤·

孩子们。我发现自己有好几次在开车上班的路上哭起来，问上帝，"我在这里所要做的有什么意义？"

1年前我遇到了约翰，他是那种许多人称之为睡大街的或者乞丐，大多数人可能会喊他疯子。

当我第1次看到约翰的时候，他来我的办公室推销打火机，1美元两个。我原先可能没在意他，但几天后，他又来了，问我是否会介意他从我们的水龙头里喝点水。我们交谈了一会，离开时，他说很抱歉占用了我这么多时间。

约翰生于一个富裕的家庭，即使用今天的标准衡量，他也曾经拥有一切，房子，船，生意，他甚至还开过一架飞机。他继承了足够的钱，够他退休后衣食无忧，在世界上任何他想去的地方生活。令人悲哀的是，他从来没被爱过。显然他以前从未体验过无条件的爱。作为一个成年人，他受战争后遗症（服役于越战留下的）和抑郁症（因为一系列伤心的事，他心爱的小女孩被夺走了）的折磨。约翰决定逃离他所了解的往日生活。

看看今天的约翰，你可能会认为我简直是疯了，居然相信他这个人，相信这个对世界不再有多少贡献的人。那你就大错特错了，他不仅给我提出关于不要在生活中做出疯狂之举的切实可行的建议，而且当他来时，他的自尊和做人的骄傲亦鼓舞着我。他是我所认识的最善良的人之一。他借钱买牛奶送给他在街上遇到的一位女士和她的孩子。我们曾经有过帮助同一个老人的共同经历。这个老人站在附近的墙角举着个牌子，上书"将为了食物而工作，"（这可怜的人儿挂着拐杖都难以站起来，更别提去工作了）。

当他在公园里享用每天的免费午餐时，约翰告诉我，人们没有吃饭而出门是多么伤心的事。当校车把孩子们带去实地考察时，他会把

the children on their field trips,he pulls their unopened milk cartons and uneaten lunches out of the trash can.He helped get a prostitute into a home for abused women and has written a letter of recommendation to help her get her daughter back.

I can always tell when John has had a hard time fighting his depression,as I won't see him for a few days.Then he shows up looking a little tired from the wear on his body,but with a story to share about a book he has read,a new person he has met on the street,or possibly even about being beaten up by someone.

On June fifteenth the apple of his eye will graduate with honors from California State University at Santa Barbara.He has hired a taxi to drive him there.The taxi driver (who knows him) will take his own private vehicle,so that John will not embarrass his daughter in anyway.John will bathe,shave and put on an old suit to go and watch his little girl receive her degree.My heart is happy yet broken for him,as I've mentally thought of what he will be going through when he sees her walk up on stage to receive her degree.I can feel the love and pride that he feels collide with the hurt and regret.I pray that when the time comes,God will sustain him and help him get through it.I will hold my friend up in thought and spirit and once again,my heart will break with his.

"Do you know they say I'm crazy?"

I smile."I don't think you're crazy,John."

There are times I envy a part of John's life.There are no earthly things he is attached to—only the desire to love others and to be loved. Maybe someday,even unconditionally.

Tomorrow,on my way to work once again,I will struggle and ask God, "What was it I'm supposed to be doing down here,Lord?"And probably he will send another person,from whose shoes I am not worthy of wiping the dirt,and I'll do my best to love him.

Terry O'Neal

他们没打开过的牛奶和没吃的食物从垃圾筒里拿出来。他帮助过一个妓女住进受虐待妇女之家，还写了封推荐信帮她把女儿要了回来。

只要我几天看不到他，我就可以断定约翰正在同他的抑郁症作斗争。虽然他会带着一丝疲倦出现，但是他会和我分享他刚刚读的一本书上的故事，或他在街上新近遇到的一个人，甚或告诉我他又被谁打了。

6月15日，他的掌上明珠将从加利福尼亚大学圣芭芭拉分校以荣誉生毕业，他租了辆出租车到那儿去。出租车驾驶员（他认识约翰）将开着他的私家车，这样约翰就不会令他的女儿尴尬。约翰会沐浴、剃胡子，穿上他的旧西服，去看他的小女孩被授予学位。我想象着他看到女儿走上主席台被授予学位时会是什么样子，既为他高兴又替他心碎。我能感受到他的爱和自豪交织着伤痛和后悔。我祈祷，当那个时刻到来的时候，上帝支持他并帮他度过这一关。我将再次在思想上和精神上支持我的朋友，我将和他一起心碎。

"你知道他们说我疯了吗？"

我笑笑。"我认为你不疯，约翰。"

有时候我妒忌约翰的部分人生，他不染尘事，只拥有爱和被爱的愿望。也许有朝一日他会拥有，甚至是无条件的。

明天，当我又行驶在上班的路上，我会在内心问上帝，"上帝啊，我在这里所要做的有什么意义？"可能上帝将会再送一个人到我身边来，我甚至不配擦他鞋上的灰，我会尽力去爱他。

特瑞·奥尼尔

经典系列／时光的印记

27

A Story For Valentine's Day

Larry and Jo Ann were an ordinary couple.They lived in an ordinary house on an ordinary street.Like any other ordinary couple,they struggled to make ends meet and to do the right things for their children.

They were ordinary in yet another way—they had their squabbles. Much of their conversation concerned what was wrong in their marriage and who was to blame.

Until one day when a most extraordinary event took place.

"You know,Jo Ann,I've got a magic chest of drawers.Every time I open them,they're full of socks and underwear,"Larry said. "I want to thank you for filling them all these years."

This wasn't the first time Larry had done something odd,so Jo Ann pushed the incident out of her mind until a few days later.

Jo Ann stared at her husband over the top of her glasses."What do you want,Larry?"

"Nothing．I just want you to know I appreciate those magic drawers."

This wasn't the first time Larry had done something odd,so Jo Ann Pushed the incident out of her mind until a few days later.

"Jo Ann,thank you for recording so many correct check numbers in the ledger this month.You put down the right numbers 15 out of 16 times.That's a record."

Disbelieving what she had heard,Jo Ann looked up from her mending."Larry,you're always complaining about my recording the wrong check numbers.Why stop now?"

情人节的故事

拉里和柔安是一对寻常的夫妇。他们住在一条寻常街道的普通房子里。和许多其他的普通夫妇毫无二致，他们努力工作以平衡收支，努力为孩子们做一切事情。

就连他们吵架都那么普通。大部分谈话都是有关他们的婚姻出了什么问题、应该责怪谁。

直到有一天一件非同寻常的事发生了。

"你知道，柔安，我有个有许多抽屉的魔法柜子。每次我打开那些抽屉，里面都装满袜子和内衣"，拉里说，"我谢谢你这么多年来把那些抽屉装满。"

柔安抬眼从眼镜上方盯着她丈夫，说，"你想要什么，拉里？"

"不要什么。我只不过想让你知道我感激这些魔法抽屉。"

这不是拉里第一次做古怪的事，因此直到几天后柔安才去想这件事。

"柔安，感谢你在这个月的账本上记录了那么多正确的支票数字。16次中有15次你记下正确的数字。这是个纪录。"

柔安从缝补中抬头看向她丈夫，难以相信自己的耳朵。"拉里，你总是抱怨我记下错误的账目。为什么现在不这么做了？"

"No reason.I just wanted you to know I appreciate the effort you're making."

Jo Ann shook her head and went back to her mending,"What's got into him?"she mumbled to herself.

Nevertheless,the nextday when Jo Ann wrote a check at the grocery store,she glanced at her checkbook to confirm that she had put down the right check number. "Why do I suddenly care about those dumb check numbers?"she asked herself.

She tried to disregard the incident,but Larry's strange behavior intensified.

"Jo Ann,that was a great dinner,"he said one evening. "I appreciate all your effort.Why,in the past 15 years I'll bet you've fixed over 14,000 meals for me and the kids."

Then "Gee,Jo Ann,the house looks spiffy.You've really worked hard to get it looking so good."And even "Thanks,Jo Ann,for just being you.I really enjoy your company."

Jo Ann was growing worried. "Where's the sarcasm,the criticism?" she wondered.

Her fears that something peculiar was happening to her husband were confirmed by 16-year-old Shelly,who complained, "Dad's gone bonkers,Mom.He just told meI looked nice.With all this makeup and these sloppy clothes,he still said it.That's not Dad,Mom.What's wrong with him?"

Whatever was wrong,Larry didn't get over it.Day in and day out he continued focusing on the positive.

Over the weeks,Jo Ann grew more accustomed to her mate's unusual behavior and occasionally even gave him a grudging "Thank you."She prided herself on taking it all in stride,until one day something so peculiar happened,she became completely discombobulated:

"I want you to take a break,"Larry said. "I am going to do the

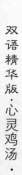

"没理由。我只是想让你知道我感激你做出的努力。"

柔安摇摇头,继续缝缝补补,"他怎么了?"她嘟囔着。

然而,第2天当柔安在杂货店开支票时,她看了一下支票簿,以便确定她写下的数字是正确的。"为什么突然之间我对这些愚蠢的支票数字在乎起来了?"她自言自语着。

她打算让这件事就这么过去,不再深究。但拉里的奇怪行为愈演愈烈。

"柔安,这晚饭真是太好吃了,"有天晚上他说。"我感激你所有的努力。哎呀,在过去15年里我确信你为我和孩子们做了超过14,000顿饭。"

后来他又说过"哇,柔安,房间好整洁呀。你真的下了工夫让它看起来这么棒。"甚至说"谢谢,柔安,只因你这个人。我真的很享受你的陪伴。"

柔安越来越担忧。她寻思,"那些挖苦、指责都到哪去了?"

她害怕丈夫身上发生了什么特殊的事情,这种担心被16岁的雪莉证实了,她抱怨道:"爸爸疯了,妈咪。他说我看起来很宜人。即使化着浓妆,穿着这身邋遢的衣服,他还这么说。妈咪,那不是爸爸。他怎么了?"

不管他怎么了,拉里没有恢复常态。日复一日,他继续赞扬着。

几个星期过去了,柔安已稍稍习惯于她的配偶反常的行为,偶尔也勉强说声"谢谢"。她很自豪自己能从容地对待拉里的古怪行径。直到有一天,发生了一件格外特别的事。她又完全乱了分寸。

"我希望你休息休息",拉里说:"我打算洗碗。所以,请把你的手

dishes.So please take your hands off that frying pan and leave the kitchen."

(Long,long pause.)"Thank you,Larry.Thank you very much! "

Jo Ann's step was now a little lighter,her self-confidence higher and once in a while she hummed.She didn't seem to have as many blue moods anymore."I rather like Larry's new behavior,she thought.

That would be the end of the story except one day another most extraordinary event took place.This time it was Jo Ann who spoke.

"Larry,"she said,"I want to thank you for going to work and providing for us all these years.I don't think I've ever told you how much I appreciate it."

Larry has never revealed the reason for his dramatic change of behavior no matter how hard Jo Ann has pushed for an answer,and so it will likely remain one of life's mysteries.But it's one I'm thankful to live with.

You see,I am Jo Ann.

Jo Ann Larsen
Deseret News

从煎锅上拿开,离开厨房吧。"

（长长的停顿。）"谢谢你,拉里。非常感谢！"

现在柔安脚步轻盈了些许,她的自信更多了一分,有时还哼着小曲儿。她似乎不再有忧伤的情绪。"我相当喜欢拉里的新做法",她想。如果不是有一天发生了一件最异乎寻常的事,故事就该到此为止了。这一次是柔安发话了。

"拉里,"她说,"我想谢谢你这些年工作供养我们。我想我从未跟你说过我有多么感激你的付出。"

无论柔安怎么追问,拉里都不曾说出他突然变化的原因。看来这将又是人生的一个秘密。但这是个我心怀感激与之共存的秘密。

你该明白,我就是柔安。

柔安·拉森

犹他新闻（Deseret——犹他州的别名）

What's in a Name?

He who raises a child is to be called its father, not the man who only gave it birth.

Midrash, Exodus Rabbah, 46:5

I was 11 when Mom remarried. When I was four or five, she and my father had divorced. We'd gone from a bright and cheery ground-floor apartment in a safe, middle-class neighborhood, to a fourth floor, cramped and darker apartment in a poorer area of New York City. My brother and I often felt lonely and frightened, listening to police and ambulance sirens piercing the night.

In the six years we lived there, I remember envying those friends who had fathers. It was my dream to get a father for myself. My own father had completely left my life—his whereabouts a mystery. I thought that, if I had a father, he would be a powerful guardian who would magically defend me against the many perils I felt that I faced in the streets. Somehow, in that childhood fantasy, my new father would not have to work. He'd just be there for me, whenever I needed him. If other boys menaced me, Super Dad would appear and chase them off. It was pure wish fulfillment, but nonetheless a powerful dream for a frightened little boy.

Suddenly, Frank McCarty appeared in our lives. He was exciting and interesting because he was a New York City police captain of detectives. He had a gold police shield and there was a gun in a holster on his belt, under his suit coat. I don't remember the day he first appeared,

姓名的意义

> 父亲是指抚养孩子长大的人，而不是仅仅给予他
> 生命的人。
>
> 圣经注释，46:5

　　我母亲再婚时，我11岁。四五岁时，我的父母离婚了，我们从中产阶级社区一个安全而又宽敞明亮的一楼住处搬到纽约市贫民区一个四楼的公寓，阴暗而狭促。我和弟弟常常听到警察或是救护车的警报器响彻夜空，这令我们感到孤单和恐惧。

　　住在那儿的6年我始终羡慕我的那些朋友都有父亲。能有个父亲是我的梦想。我自己的父亲已经无影无踪，没人知道他到哪儿去了。我想如果我有父亲，他一定是我强大的保护神，他会神奇地保护我不让我在街上遇到危险。不知何故，在我儿时的幻想中，我的父亲不必工作。我随时需要他，他都会出现，无论何时，其他的男孩子欺负我，我高大的爸爸都会赶来赶跑他们。虽然这纯粹是个愿望，但却是一个饱受惊吓的小男孩的动人梦想。

　　突然，弗兰克·莫卡提出现了，令人既兴奋又好奇。因为他是纽约市的一名侦探长，他有一件金色的警用防弹衣，警服皮带上的枪套里有枪。我不记得他是哪一天来的，但记得大致的时间，也记得当

but I do remember the general time and its feeling of excitement and drama.Police were the stuff of movies.Police weren't people you actually knew.I told all my friends about him.Their eyes widened as I described his gun and the stories that he told me about capturing some bad guys.

He didn't like to tell these stories,but my mom wanted him to be accepted by her sons and she knew what kids liked to hear. She'd cue him to tell a certain story and he'd acquiesce and patiently tell the story. As he got more deeply into the story,he became animaled and the story took on mythic proportions.

One day,Mom asked me how I would feel if she married Frank.By this time,I was really hooked.He had taken me to the Giants game at the Polo Grounds.He had taken me to Coney Island.He talked with me.He gave me advice on how to fight back when confronted with bullies in the street.His gun gleamed darkly from under his coat.I could have a dad,a protector,someone to take me to the game. "Wow! " I said, "I'd love it! "

The date came.We went to a rural resort hotel whose owner was a friend of my mother's.Another friend of Mom's,a judge,presided over the wedding.I had a dad.Everything was going to be all right now.

I didn't know,as a child of 11,how profoundly my life would change with that one moment.

A bachelor until that point,my new dad had very limited experience with children.He didn't have the opportunity to learn his new parenting job in the natural,step-by-step way that fathers usually do.He never held a baby of his own,shared in the delight of that baby's first steps,or had to take turns feeding that child,dressing him,changing diapers,or any of the countless tasks that parenting means.

He was suddenly thrust into the role of parent,and he retreated to what he knew.His experience with kids had been limited to arresting

时的激动和兴奋。警察有些神秘,不是人们真正可以了解的,我向所有的朋友炫耀他,当我谈到他的枪,讲起他告诉我的那些抓坏人的故事,他们的眼睛瞪得老大。

他并不喜欢讲这些故事,但我妈妈想让儿子们接受他,妈妈当然知道孩子们想听什么。她暗示他讲什么样的故事,而他只好同意,耐心地讲故事给我们听。当被自己叙述的故事吸引时,他讲得非常生动,故事呈现出神入化般的意境。

一天,妈妈问我如果她和弗兰克结婚,我会觉得怎么样。那时候,我已经完全被他吸引了。他带我去波罗游乐园玩巨人游戏,还带我去克耐岛玩。他和我交谈,他教给我一些在街上面对暴徒的斗争方法。他的警服下的枪闪着黝黑的光,我要有个爸爸了,一个保护者,一个带我去游戏的人。"哦!"我说:"我喜欢!"

那一天终于来了,我们一起去了乡村的一个常去的旅馆,那是我妈妈的朋友开的。妈妈的另一个朋友是个法官,他主持了婚礼,于是我有了父亲,一切都太美好了。

11岁的我不知道,这一刻将会给我的生活带来多么大的改变。

由于一直是单身汉,我的新爸爸没有和孩子相处的经验,他也没有机会像其他父亲那样一步步地、自然而然地学习如何做父亲。他自己没有孩子,从来没有带过孩子,分享孩子迈开第1步时的喜悦,也没有轮流喂孩子吃饭、穿衣、给孩子换尿布。他没做过所有那些养育子女的繁杂工作。

他突然闯进了父母的角色。他回忆他所知道的和小孩子相处的

some.His memories of parenting were of his own father's turn-of-the-century methods.He assumed that he could sit at the head of the table and issue orders that complaisant children would instantly obey.

Unfortunately for him,my mother raised us to be more independent,more participatory in dinner table discussions.We were encouraged to have opinions.She taught us to speak up as well as to listen.We weren't taught to be impolite or rude,but we were contentious.

Complicating all of this was the onset of puberty.Frank McCarty became a father,with his need to be in control,all-knowing,the leader—at the very moment that I was becoming a teen and was in the throes of the adolescent search for independence and self-authority.I was so attracted to him,I almost instantly loved him.Yet,at the same time,I was angry at him almost constantly.He stood in my way.He wasn't easy to manipulate.My brother and I could masterfully manipulate our mother. Frank McCarty was immune to our tricks.

Thus began eight years of pure hell for me and for my new dad. He announced rules and I tried to flout them.He sent me to my room for rudeness or for my attitude.I complained bitterly to my mother about his dictatorial practices.She tried hard to be the peacemaker but to no avail.

I must admit that there were many occasions in my life from age 13 until I was 20 that I was stuck in a state of anger and frustration at some perceived slight by my father.Passionate as these times were,they were punctuated by great moments with him.Going shopping with him, every week,for flowers to "surprise your mother," he'd say.Going to a ball game.Sitting in a car with him,late at night,watching a house.He'd take me on a surveillance,when he became a private detective back in New York City,if the case was an insurance fraud or something similarly nonviolent.We'd sit there in the darkened car,sipping coffee,and he'd talk about "the job," as he called his career in the police department.I felt so special,so loved,so included at these times.This was exactly what

唯一经验就是管住他们。他记忆中父母管教孩子的方法就是他自己父亲的那种百年难遇的方法。他还想着坐在餐桌的一头发号施令，而彬彬有礼的孩子们完全服从。

对他来说十分不幸的是，我的母亲把我们培养得十分独立，积极参与餐桌讨论。妈妈鼓励我们发表意见，她要我们不能光听，也要说。我们得到的是这样的教育，不允许无礼和鲁莽，但我们十分喜欢争论。

青春期的抗争使一切变得更加复杂。弗兰克·莫卡提成了父亲，他需要至高无上的权力，要知道一切，领导一切。而我是正值青春躁动期的少年，正寻求着独立和自尊。我被他深深吸引住，几乎立刻就爱上他了。但同时我也开始不断地气他，他妨碍着我，他不容易被我们操纵。我和弟弟完全可以操纵妈妈，而他能识破我们的鬼把戏。

对于我和我的新爸爸来说，接下来的8年犹如噩梦。他制定了许多规矩，而我故意违规，他因为我鲁莽的态度惩罚我，把我关在屋子里。我就向我的妈妈控诉他的独断专行。妈妈费了很大的劲去做和事佬，但是毫无用处。

我必须承认，在13岁至20岁这段时期，我常常会生气和失望，而我父亲却浑然不觉。虽然常不满意，但间或也会出现一些动人的瞬间。每星期和父亲一起去购物，他都要买花给妈妈一个惊喜。有时半夜一起坐在车子里监视某个地方，这样的事往往发生在他回到纽约充当私家侦探时，如果案子比较简单，只是一般的诈骗案或类似的非暴力的案子，他就会带着我，一起坐在黑黑的车里，父亲一边呷着咖啡，一边谈着他的警察生涯。这时我会感到如此特别、如此受宠、

my fantasy had been.A dad who loved me,who'd do things with me.

I remember many,many nights,sitting in front of him on an ottoman and he'd rub my back as we watched TV together.He gave great hugs.He wasn't afraid to say, "I love you."I found the tenderness this rough-and-ready guy was able to express remarkable.However,he could go from these intimate moments to red-faced yelling and sputtering anger if I did or said something that he thought was rude.His temper was a natural phenomenon akin to a tornado.It was a fearsome thing to watch and it was even scarier to be the target of it.

In high school,the angry moments increased and my closeness with him decreased.By the time I was in college,I was mostly alienated from him.I got a lot of mileage in terms of sympathy from my friends,if I put him down in my conversations with them.I'd tell stories of his latest "atrocity," and stuck in adolescence just as I was,they'd murmur sympathetically about how much we all had to put up with from our dads.

It was my last year in college.I don't know if there was any one event that precipitated it other than my geuting a year older and going further along on the road to maturity,but I started rethinking my relationship with him.

I thought,"Here's a guy who falls in love with my mother and he's stuck with two teenage boys as the price of being married to her.He didn't fall in love with two kids,just my mother.But we came with the package."

"And look what he does:He doesn't just relate to her and ignore us.No,he tries his very hardest to be a real father to me. He risks the relationship all the time.He tried to teach me a set of values.He made me do my homework.He took me to the emergency room at two in the morning.He paid for my education without a grumble.He taught me how to tie a tie.He did all the daddy things without thought of payback. That's really something.I guess I'm a lucky kid to have him in my life."

双语精华版·心灵鸡汤·

如此幸福,这就是我动人梦想的实现。父亲爱我,他和我在一起做共同的事情。

我记得,许多、许多晚上,我坐在他前面的扶手椅上和他一起看电视,他会抚摸着我的背,也会拥抱我,毫不畏惧地说:"我爱你。"我发现这个粗暴又急躁的男人也会表达他的不寻常的柔情。然而,他也会从柔情蜜意的瞬间转变成脸红脖子粗,咆哮着发泄愤怒,只因为他认为我做了无礼的事,或说了鲁莽的话。

他的脾气就像龙卷风一样,看着就怕,如果成了他发脾气的对象,那就更可怕了。

上高中时,随着他发脾气的次数增加,我们之间的亲密关系也渐渐淡了。上大学时就很疏远了。我的朋友们都很同情我,当我们在一起谈到父亲时,我会告诉他们父亲的残暴,那些和我一样已值青春期的朋友们就会同情地抱怨,为什么我们大家都得忍受我们的父亲。

我想情况应该是这样。一个男人爱上了我妈妈,结婚时还要带上两个十来岁的男孩子,他只是爱上了妈妈并没有爱上孩子们,因而孩子们成了他的包袱。

那么,他如何对待呢?他没有只关心妈妈而忽视我们,他尽了最大的努力要做我们真正的爸爸。他冒着有损父子关系的巨大风险,尽力地教导我们,帮助我完成家庭作业,两次一大早把我送到急诊室,毫不犹豫地替我们付学费,教我打领带,不图回报地做了所有父亲应该做的事。这就是事实。我猜我是个幸运的孩子。因为有这样一个爸爸走进我的生活。

I knew that my dad had come from an old New England Irish family.They were never famous,powerful or wealthy,but they had been here a long,long time.He felt sad that he was the last to "carry the name." "It'll die with me," he said.His brother had died without children and his sisters,having married and taken their husbands' names, wouldn't carry on that name either.

My brother and I still carried the name of our biological father;the man who sired me,but didn't stay around for the rest of the job.The thought troubled me that the man who really was my father,as I understood that word,would not be celebrated by having a son with his own name.

Ideas occur to us and gradually coalesce into behavior.The idea got stronger and stronger.My thoughts were increasingly taken over by this idea.Finally,action was inevitable.I went to an attorney and then to a court.Secretly,I had my name changed to McCarty.I told no one.I waited three months until my dad's birthday in October.

He opened the birthday card slowly.Usually when I gave him a card,it was attached to a box with his gift.This time there was no box, just the envelope.He pulled out the card and,with it,a certificate from a court.

I wrote on the card, "No store sells true gifts for father and son. You gave me roots,I give you branches."

It was one of only two or three times I ever saw my dad cry.Tears came unbidden to his eyes.He smiled and shook his head and sighed. Then he got up and enfolded me in one of his famous bear hugs. "Thank you,boy,thank you.I just don't know what to say.Thank you." My mom was stunned,too.And very happy for both of us.The war was over.I'd brought the armistice agreement,wrapped in a birthday card.

Hanoch McCarty

我知道，我的父亲出生于一个古老的新英格兰爱尔兰家族。这个家族并不出名，也不具备权力和财富，但已经存在很久很久了。父亲是这个家族最后一个具有家族姓氏的人，他常常伤心地说："这个家族要因我而灭亡了。"他的哥哥没有孩子且已去世。他的妹妹嫁了人，随夫家姓，也不能继承姓氏。

我和弟弟都继承亲生父亲的姓，而生了我们的父亲并没有待在身边尽父亲的责任。正如我对父亲这个词的理解那样，这位真正的父亲，还没有一个继承他姓氏的儿子，这让我非常忧虑。

这些想法逐渐地凝聚成行动，我的大脑被这些越来越强烈的想法完全占据，最终导致我附诸于行动。我找了律师和法院，秘密地把我的姓改成莫卡提，我没有告诉任何人，我要等到3个月后的10月份我父亲过生日时再说。

他慢慢打开生日贺卡，通常生日贺卡都是同我送他的生日礼物一起送给他，而这次没有礼物盒，只有信封。他抽出贺卡，里面夹着一份公证书。

我在贺卡上写着，"任何商店也买不到这么真诚的礼物，它是给我们父子的，你给了我根，我给你枝叶。"

我很少见到父亲流泪，这次是其中一次，泪水涌在眼眶里。他笑着，又是摇头，又是叹气。后来他站起来紧紧地拥抱着我说："谢谢你，孩子，谢谢你，我真不知该说什么，谢谢你。"我的母亲也惊呆了。

我们两人都非常高兴。战争过去了，我带来了停战协议，它夹在生日贺卡中。

哈诺克·莫卡提

经典系列／时光的印记

The Two-Hundredth Hug

Love cures people—both the ones who give it and the ones who receive it.

Dr.Karl Menninger

My father's skin was jaundiced as he lay hooked up to monitors and intravenous tubes in the intensive care unit of the hospital.Normally a well-built man,he had lost more than 30 pounds.

My father's illness had been diagnosed as cancer of the pancreas, one of the most malignant forms of the disease.The doctors were doing what they could but told us that he had only three to six months to live. Cancer of the pancreas does not lend itself to radiation therapy or chemotherapy,so they could offer little hope.

A few days later,when my father was sitting up in bed,I approached him and said, "Dad,I feel deeply for what's happened to you. It's helped me to look at the ways I've kept my distance and to feel how much I really love you."I leaned over to give him a hug,but his shoulders and arms became tense.

"C'mon,Dad,I really want to give you a hug."

For a moment he looked shocked.Showing affection was not our usual way of relating.I asked him to sit up some more so I could get my arms around him.Then I tried again.This time,however,he was even more tense.I could feel the old resentment starting to build up,and I began to think, "I don't need this.If you want to die and leave me with the same coldness as always,go right ahead."

第二百次拥抱

> 爱能治愈人的伤痛——不管是爱的施予者还是爱的接受者。
>
> ——卡尔·曼宁格博士

父亲正躺在医院的重症特护病房内,身体连着监测器和静脉输液管。他的皮肤因为疾病显出蜡黄色。正常状态下他是个身体健美的男人,但患病以来,他的体重减轻了30多磅。

父亲的病已经被诊断为胰腺癌,这是最严重的恶性肿瘤病之一。医生们尽了最大努力,然后告诉我们父亲只有3到6个月的寿命了。放疗和化疗对胰腺癌都不起作用,所以这些治疗手段带来的希望很渺茫。

几天以后,当父亲正在病床上坐着的时候,我走上前对他说,"爸爸,我对你发生的一切感受很深。这次患病不仅使我意识到我对你一直保持距离,也使我认识到我有多么爱你。"我向他倾斜想拥抱他,但是他的肩膀和胳膊都很紧张。

"来吧,爸爸。我真的想拥抱你。"

有一会儿的工夫,他显得很惊讶。表达亲密的感情不是我们之间相处的通常作法。我请他再坐起来一些,以便我能用我的胳膊环绕着他。然后我再尝试了一下,但是这一次,他比刚才还紧张。我感觉到心里的旧恨开始增长起来。我甚至想,"我不需要这些。如果你想死,并且像一直以来那样只把冷冰冰留给我,那么随你的便吧。"

For years I had used every instance of my father's resistance and rigidness to blame him, to resent him and to say to myself, "See, he doesn't care." This time, however, I thought again and realized the hug was for my benefit as well as my father's. I wanted to express how much I cared for him no matter how hard it was for him to let me in. My father had always been very Germanic and duty-oriented; in his childhood, his parents must have taught him how to shut off his feelings in order to be a man.

CHICKEN SOUP

Letting go of my long-held desire to blame him for our distance, I was actually looking forward to the challenge of giving him more love. I said, "C'mon, Dad, put your arms around me."

I leaned up close to him at the edge of the bed with his arms around me. "Now squeeze. That's it. Now again, squeeze. Very good！"

In a sense I was showing my father how to hug, and as he squeezed, something happened. For an instant, a feeling of "I love you" bubbled through. For years our greeting had been a cold and formal handshake that said, "Hello, how are you？" Now, both he and I waited for that momentary closeness to happen again. Yet, just at the moment when he would begin to enjoy the feelings of love, something would tighten in his upper torso and our hug would become awkward and strange. It took months before his rigidness gave way and he was able to let the emotions inside him pass through his arms to encircle me.

It was up to me to be the source of many hugs before my father initiated a hug on his own. I was not blaming him, but supporting him; after all, he was changing the habits of an entire lifetime—and that takes time. I knew we were succeeding because more and more we were relating out of care and affection. Around the two-hundredth hug, he spontaneously said out loud, for the first time I could ever recall, "I love you."

Harold H. Bloomfield, M.D.

双语精华版·心灵鸡汤·

多年以来，我总是用他每一次的抗拒和固执来指责他和怨恨他。并且对自己说，"看，他一点也不在乎。"但这一次，经过重新考虑我觉得拥抱对我对他都是有益的。我希望不管他接受我的关心有多么困难，我都能表现出我是多么关心他。父亲一直保有日耳曼式的性格和一切以职责为中心。在他小的时候，他的父母一定教导过他如何封闭自己的感情以便使自己成为一个男人。

把我一直持有的因我们之间的疏远而指责他的欲望抛开的同时，我希望能够面对给他更多爱的挑战。我说，"来吧，爸爸，用你的胳膊环绕着我。"

我在他的床边向他靠近一点，让他的胳膊环绕着我。"现在，抱紧。就这样。再来一次，抱紧。很好！"

在某种意义上，我正在教我的父亲如何拥抱，当他抱紧的时候，奇妙的事情发生了。一瞬间，一种"我爱你"的感觉如泡泡般涌遍全身。多年来，我们之间的问候就是一个冷冰冰的正式的握手，"喂，你好吗？"现在，我和他都在等待那一瞬间的亲密再一次来临。然而，在他开始享受到爱的感觉的那一刻，有东西使他的上身仍然很紧张，我们的拥抱仍然很笨拙很陌生。用了几个月的时间他身上的僵硬才褪去，他才能够把内心的感情通过对我的拥抱传递出来。

在父亲主动给我第1个拥抱之前，都是我主动给他很多的拥抱。我没有指责他，而是支持他；毕竟，他正在改变他一生固有的习惯——那需要时间。我知道我们一定会成功，因为我们之间的相处越来越多的来自爱和关心。大概是在第200次拥抱的时候，他自然而然地大声说出一句话，也是我可以回忆起来的第1次听到他说"我爱你。"

哈罗德·H.布鲁费尔德　医学博士

47

Nonny

CHICKEN SOUP

A single grateful thought raised to Heaven is the most perfect prayer.

Gotthold Ephraim Lessing

Johnny was three years older than me,almost to the day.I was born on August 28,and he on August 29."You were my birthday present,Sal!" he used to say.Only my brother could get away with calling me Sal.

Since both our parents worked,Johnny took care of me after school. In the winter he made sure I was dressed warmly.On rainy days,he played records and we danced around the house.

When Johnny was a high school senior,he asked me to be his prom date.We danced the night away! Though it would be years before he would tell me,I knew he was gay.All I wanted was for Johnny to be happy and loved.

And he got plenty of love from my kids.The twins,Nicholas and Matthew,couldn't get enough of him.In their tiny voices,they called him "Nonny",and the nickname stuck.

My husband,Howard,and I loved our house so full of laughter,and we wanted to fill all five bedrooms with kids.The trouble was,by the time we were ready for more,I couldn't get pregnant.At thirty-two,I was going through early menopause.

So we put our name on the long adoption waiting lists.Sometimes in the middle of the night,unable to sleep,I'd call Johnny. "I'll never have another baby,"I'd sob.Johnny's gentle voice soothed me. "Yes,you will! " he said."Never give up,Sal."

诺 尼

一个简单的感恩念头是最好的祷告。
——戈特霍德·厄弗瑞姆·莱辛

乔尼比我几乎整整大3岁，我出生在8月28日，他出生在29日，他以前总是说"你是我的生日礼物，萨儿。"只有我的兄弟可以叫我萨儿。

因为爸妈都上班，放学后就由乔尼照顾我，冬天里他确保我穿得暖和，下雨天他放唱片然后我们满屋子跳舞。

乔尼读高四时，他让我做他的毕业舞会舞伴，我们跳了一晚上舞。我知道乔尼是同性恋，虽然多年后他才告诉我。我所想要的就是让他快乐和被爱。

他从我的孩子们那里得到许多爱。尼古拉斯和马修这对双胞胎对他爱不够。他们用童音喊他"诺尼"，这个绰号就这么叫下去。

我的丈夫哈沃德和我喜欢我们的屋子充满笑声，我们想要5个卧室都有孩子，问题是当我们正准备要更多孩子时我不能怀孕了，在32岁时我患了卵巢早衰。我们就把我们的名字填在长长的排队领养单子上，有时候在半夜无法入睡，我就打电话给乔尼："我再不会有孩子了。"我啜泣着，乔尼温柔的声音抚慰着我，"不，你会有孩子的，"他说，"不要放弃，萨儿。"

Then in 1990,my world came crashing down.Johnny told me he had AIDS. "No! "I cried,tears streaming down my face.I refused to believe that my dear brother would die.I took him in my arms and we rocked and cried.If only I could hold on to him forever and protect him…

Johnny lived only a few blocks away,and I was there all the time helping out when the disease started to claim him.There were times when,with a sparkle in his eye,he'd take me in his arms and dance me around the room.But those days were fleeting.

By the fall of 1992,we knew the end was near.On a September afternoon,Mom,Dad and I gathered around his bed. "I'll miss you most of all," I whispered,bending to kiss him."When you see the bright light,you can go.It's okay."And with a last,shallow breath,he was gone.

Numb with grief,I picked up the small religious medallion that Johnny had kept at his side throughout his illness.I pressed it to my heart and cried.When I got home,I placed the medallion on a shelf.

How would I get through the rest of my life without him?I would weep and hold the medallion,praying.My big brother was gone.No more dancing.No more "Sal! "

Then one morning a few weeks later,Nicholas and Matthew ran into the kitchen,crying "Nonny is here."

I felt my legs tremble."What?"I stammered.

"He came to us,"they said."He was wearing a red shirt."

How I wanted to believe! But I knew the boys missed him and that this was their way of expressing it.

The "visits" continued for months until one day the boys just stopped mentioning them.They're okay now,I thought.Life was going on, but it was a sadder life. "We've got to have a baby,"I cried to Howard one night."We need hope in our lives."

So we stepped up our search,this time with an international adoption agency.The weeks turned into months without any word,while my

双
语
精
华
版
·
心
灵
鸡
汤
·

然后到了1990年，我的世界垮了，乔尼告诉我他得了艾滋病。"不！"我哭喊着，眼泪流淌在我的脸上。我拒绝相信我亲爱的兄弟要死了，我抱着他，我们摇晃着，哭喊着，似乎只有这样我才能永远拥有他保护他。乔尼住处离我家只有几个街区，当疾病开始夺命时，我整天都待在那里打理一切。有时候他会抱着我在屋里跳舞，眼里放着光。但这样的日子稍纵即逝。

　　到1992年秋天，我们知道最后的日子到了，9月的一个下午，妈妈、爸爸和我围在他的床前，"我会最想念你的，"我对他耳语道，弯腰吻他。"当你看到亮光时，你就可以走了，放心去吧。"伴着最后一口微弱的气息，他走了。

　　我难过得近乎麻木。拣起了乔尼患病期间一直放在身边的一个小小的宗教浮雕像，我把它按在胸口，哭起来。回家后，我把它放在架子上。

　　没有他，我该如何度过余生？我会抱着雕像，流着泪祈祷。我的大哥走了。不再跳舞，不再有"萨儿！"

　　几个星期后的一天早上，尼古拉斯和马修大叫着跑进厨房，"诺尼在这儿。"

　　我感到自己的腿在发抖。"什么？"我结结巴巴地说。

　　"他来看我们了，"他俩说。"他穿着一件红衬衫。"

　　我多么愿意相信啊！但是我知道这不过是因为孩子们想念他并以这种方式表达出来罢了。

　　乔尼的"探望"持续了几个月，有一天早上孩子们终于不再谈论此事。我想，他们现在不再想念他了。生活继续着，但反而更糟糕了。"我们得再生个宝宝，"有天晚上我对豪伍德哭诉。"我们的生活需要希望。"

　　因此我们加快寻找的步伐，这次联系了一家国际领养机构。没

heart grew eager to give a child the love I could no longer give to Johnny.In dark moments when my hope started to turn to despair,I heard Johnny's words:Never give up,Sal.

I didn't.After two years we got the call.A two-year-old Russian girl named Anna needed a family.Before I knew it,I was on a plane.Though her life had been hard,Anna was healthy,and she thrived with us.She didn't know English,but she communicated through smiles and kisses.

She'd been with us a few months,when one afternoon I came home from shopping to find Howard anxiously waiting at the door.Taking my arm,he led me over to Anna.In her hand was the religious medallion I had taken from Johnny's deathbed. Looking up at me,Anna held out the medal and said,"Nonny,"then laid it down at my feet."She's been saying his name all afternoon,"Howard said.

My eyes filled with tears and my mind was wild with wonder.Shakily,I put down my packages."We've never talked to her about him.She barely understands what we say! "I cried.And even if she'd heard the boys talk about Johnny,how did she know the medallion had been his?

Had Johnny visited her,too?Here in our home?Maybe back in Russia,keeping her safe until we could take her in our arms?Perhaps Johnny was Anna's guardian angel,and she'd seen him. That's why she called out his name.I thought I'd lost Johnny forever,but now it seemed I was wrong.

Last night,Anna stopped playing with her toys and ran up to hug me.I looked down at her sweet face and for a moment I saw Johnny in her joyful nature.The bonds of love never die.Johnny will always be with us—if only in Anna's beautiful smile.

Eva Unga
Excerpted from Woman's World Magazine

有回音的等待从数周变成几个月,而我越来越急切地要把不能再给乔尼的爱给一个孩子。在我的希望变成绝望的黑暗时刻,我听见了乔尼的声音:永远不要放弃,萨儿。

我没有放弃。两年后,我们等到了电话。一名两岁大的俄罗斯女孩安娜需要一个家。在我反应过来之前,我已经在飞机上了。虽然安娜过去的生活艰苦,可她健康,和我们生活在一起后她茁壮成长。她不懂英语,但她用微笑和亲吻来和我们交流。

她和我们共同生活了没几个月后的一天下午,我购物归来看见豪沃德急切地等在门口。他拉着我的胳膊把我带到安娜面前。她手里拿着我从乔尼临死时所卧的那张床上带回的宗教浮雕像。安娜看着我,伸出雕像,说:"诺尼。"然后把它放在我脚下。"她整个下午都在说他的名字,"豪沃德说。

眼泪一下涌出来,我的心由于惊奇而疯狂。我颤抖着放下购物袋。"我们从来没有跟她提过他。她几乎听不懂我们说的话!"我哭喊着。再说即使她听到两个男孩谈论乔尼,她又如何知道雕像是他的呢?

乔尼也探望过她吗?在我们的家这儿吗?也许远在俄罗斯,乔尼就保护着她一直到她来到我们的怀抱。或许乔尼是安娜的守护天使,所以安娜看得见他。这就是为什么她叫得出他的名字。我原以为我永远失去了乔尼,现在看来我错了。昨晚,安娜放下手里的玩具跑过来抱住我。我低头看着她甜美的脸,有那么一会儿,我在她快乐的天性中看到了乔尼。爱的纽带永不断,乔尼一直和我们在一起——真希望就在安娜美丽的笑容里。

伊芙·昂伽

摘自《女性世界》

Puppies For Sale

CHICKEN SOUP

A store owner was tacking a sign above his door that read "Puppies For Sale."Signs like that have a way of attracting small children,and sure enough,a little boy appeared under the store owner's sign. "How much are you going to sell the puppies for?"he asked.

The store owner replied,"Anywhere from $30 to $50."

The little boy reached in his pocket and pulled out some change."I have $2.37,"he said."Can I please look at them?"

The store owner smiled and whistled and out of the kennel came Lady,who ran down the aisle of his store followed by five teeny,tiny balls of fur.One puppy was lagging considerably behind.Immediately the little boy singled out the lagging,limping puppy and said,"What's wrong with that little dog?"

The store owner explained that the veterinarian had examined the little puppy and had discovered it didn't have a hip socket.It would always limp.It would always be lame.The little boy became excited. "That is the little puppy that I want to buy."

The store owner said, "No,you don't want to buy that little dog.If you really want him,I'll give him to you."

The little boy got quite upset.He looked straight into the store owner's eyes,pointing his finger,and said, "I don't want you to give him to me.That little dog is worth every bit as much as all the other dogs and I'll pay full price.In fact,I'll give you $2.37 now,and 50 cents a month until I have him paid for."

待售的小狗

有位店主在他店门上钉了个招牌,上书:"出售小狗。"这样的招牌总能吸引到小孩子,果然,一个小男孩出现在店主钉的招牌下。

"你打算以什么价钱把这些小狗卖掉?"他问道。

店主回答:"从30美元到50美元。"

小男孩伸手到口袋里拿出些零钱。"我有2.37美元",他说:"请让我看看它们好吗?"

店主笑了,吹了声口哨,兰黛便从狗群里走出来,它沿着店铺的通道走着,后面滚动着5只一点点大的毛球。有只小狗远远落在后头慢慢走着。小男孩立即上前挑出这只走得又慢又不稳的小狗,"这只小狗怎么了?"店主说兽医已经替小狗检查过了,发现它没有髋关节窝,它将永远跛行,永远残废。小男孩激动起来,"这就是我想买的小狗狗。"

店主说,"不,你不想买那只小狗。如果你真想要的话,我把它送给你。"小男孩很难过。他直视着店主的眼睛,指着店主说:"我不要你把他送给我。这只小狗值和其他小狗一样的价钱,我会付全价的。现在我先付你2.37美元,然后每月付50美分直到付清为止。"

55

The store owner countered."You really don't want to buy this little dog.He is never going to be able to run and jump and play with you like the other puppies."

To this,the little boy reached down and rolled up his pant lag to reveal a badly twisted.,crippled left leg supported by a big metal brace.He looked up at the store owner and softly replied,"Well,I don't run so well myself,and the little puppy will need someone who understands！"

Dan Clark
Weathering the Storm

店主反讥道:"你不会真的想买这只小狗。他永远也不会像其他小狗那样跑、跳、和你玩耍。"

听了这番话,小男孩弯下腰,卷起他的裤筒,露出一条严重扭曲的、残疾的左腿,腿上缚着个大的金属整形器。他抬头看着店主,轻声地答道:"哦,我自己也跑不好,这只小狗需要理解他的人！"

丹·克拉克

《风暴》

Love Never Leaves You
爱，从未离开

I grew up in a very normal family with two brothers and two sisters.Although we did not have much money in those days,I always remember my mother and father taking us out for weekend picnics or to the zoo.

My mother was a very loving and caring person.She was always ready to help someone else and she often brought home stray or injured animals.Even though she had five children to contend with,she always found time to help others.

I think back to my early childhood and I see my parents not as husband and wife with five children,but as a newlywed couple very much in love.The daytime was to be spent with us kids,but the night was their time to be with each other.

　　我成长在一个普通的家庭里，有两个兄弟和两个姐妹。虽然我们在那些日子里没有多少钱，但是我总记得爸妈每个周末都带我们去野餐或去动物园。

　　我妈妈是个非常有爱心又体贴的人。她随时准备帮助他人，她经常带回家一些流浪动物或受伤的动物。尽管她有5个孩子要对付，她也总能挤出时间帮助别人。

　　我回忆起童年的早期，我觉得我的父母亲不仅是有5个孩子的妻子和丈夫，也是非常相爱的新婚夫妇，白天和我们这些孩子共度，但夜晚是他们留给对方的时间。

经典系列／时光的印记

I remember I was lying in bed one night.It was Sunday,May 27, 1973.I woke up to the sound of my parents coming home from a night out with some friends.They were laughing and playing around and when I heard them go to bed,I rolled over and went back to sleep,but all that night my sleep was troubled by nightmares.

Monday morning,May 28,1973,I awoke to a cloudy overcast day. My mother was not up yet so we all got ourselves ready and went to school.All that day,I had this very empty feeling inside.I came home after school and let myself into the house. "Hi,Ma,I'm home."No answer.The house seemed very cold and empty.I was afraid.Trembling,I climbed the stairs and went to my parents' room.The door was only open a little and I could not see all the way inside. "Ma?"I pushed the door open all the way so I could see the whole room,and there was my mother lying on the floor beside the bed.I tried to wake her,but she would not wake up.I knew she was dead.I turned around,left the room and went downstairs.I sat on the couch in silence for a very long time until my older sister came home.She saw me sitting there and then in a flash she was running up the stairs.

I sat in the living room and watched as my father talked to the policeman.I watched the ambulance attendants carry out the stretcher with my mother on it.All I could do was sit and watch.I couldn't even cry.I had never thought of my father as an old man,but when I saw him that day he never looked so old as he did then.

Tuesday,May 29,1973.My 11th birthday.There was no singing,no party or cake,just silence as we sat around the dining room table looking at our food.It was my fault.If I had come home sooner she would still be alive.If I had been older she would still be alive.If...

For many years,I carried around the guilt of my mother's death.I thought about all the things I should have done.All the nasty things I had said to her.I truly believed that because I was a troublesome child,

CHICKEN SOUP

双语精华版·心灵鸡汤·

我记得有一个晚上我躺在床上。那是1973年5月27号,星期日,我被父母亲回家的声音吵醒,他们和朋友在外度过了一晚上。他们大笑着,嬉闹着,当我听到他们去睡觉了,我便在床上翻了个身也睡了,但是整个晚上我都在不断地做噩梦。

　　1973年5月28号,周一。早上,我醒来发现天上乌云密布,妈妈还没起床,我们就自己准备好然后去上学。那一整天我心里都空荡荡的。放学回家后我进屋就喊:"嘿,妈,我回来了。"没有回答。屋子里显得冷冷清清的。我害怕了,颤抖着上了楼,走到父母的房间。门只开了一点点,我看不到里面。"妈?"我把门推开以便能看见整个房间,只见妈妈躺在床边的地上。我试图叫醒她,但她再也醒不来了。我知道她死了,我转身离开房间下了楼。我呆呆地在沙发上了坐了好长时间,直到姐姐回家。她见我坐在那就突然冲上楼去。

　　我坐在起居室里,看着父亲跟警察说话,看着救护人员把妈妈抬上救护车。我所能做的就是坐在那儿看着,我甚至哭不出来,我从来没把父亲看做一个老人,但是那天我看到他时,他看上去显得前所未有的老。

　　1973年5月29号,星期二。我11岁生日。没有歌声,没有聚会,没有蛋糕,我们都沉默地坐在餐桌前,看着我们的食物。都是我的错,如果我早点回家,她也许还活着。如果我年长一点,她也许还活着,如果……

　　多年来,我都对妈妈的死心怀愧疚,我想着我本应该做的一切,我对她说过的粗话,我真的相信因为我是一个调皮的孩子,上帝就

God was punishing me by taking away my mother.The thing that troubled me the most was the fact I never got the chance to say goodbye.I would never again feel her warm embrace,smell the sweet scent of her perfume or feel her gentle kisses as she tucked me into my bed at night. All these things taken away from me were my punishment.

May 29,1989:my 27th birthday,and I was feeling very lonely and empty.I had never recovered from the effects of my mother's death.I was an emotional mess.My anger at God had hit its peak.I was crying and screaming at God. "Why did you take her away from me? You never even gave me the chance to say goodbye.I loved her and you took that away from me.I only wanted to hold her one more time.*I hate you*! "I sat in my living room sobbing.I felt drained when suddenly a warm feeling came over me.I could physically feel two arms embrace me.I could sense a familiar but long-forgotten fragrance in the room.It was her.I could feel her presence.I felt her touch and smelled her fragrance.The God that I had hated had granted me my wish.My mother was coming to me when I needed her.

I know today my mother is always with me.I still love her with all my heart,and I know that she will always be there for me.Just when I had given up and resigned myself to the fact that she was gone forever, she let me know that her love would never leave me.

Stanley D. Moulson

带走了我的妈妈,以此来惩罚我。最困扰我的是我都没来得及说声再见。我再也不能感受到她在晚上把我送进被窝时那温暖的怀抱,好闻的香水味和温柔的亲吻。所有这些都被剥夺了,这就是我受到的惩罚。

1989年5月29号。我27岁的生日,我感到非常孤独、空虚。我从未曾从失去妈妈的影响中缓过神来。我的情绪一团糟,对上帝的气愤达到顶峰。我对着上帝哭喊着,"为什么你把她从我身边带走?你都没有给我机会说声再见。我爱她,你却把她从我身边带走。我只想再抱她一次。我恨你!"我坐在房间里啜泣着,觉得眼泪流干了,突然,有一股温暖的感觉涌遍全身,我能真切地感觉到两条手臂拥抱着我。我闻到屋里有股熟悉而又久违的香气。是她。我能感觉到她的触摸,闻到她的芳香。我憎恨的上帝满足了我的愿望,当我需要妈妈的时候,她就来到了我身边。

如今,我知道妈妈依然一直和我在一起,我依然全身心地爱她,并且知道她会一直在那儿陪着我。就在我绝望地认为她已永远离开我时,她让我知道她的爱永远不会离开我。

斯坦雷·D.摩尔逊

A Simple Act of Love

A thousand words will not leave so deep an impression
as one deed.

Henrik Ibsen

When I was growing up,my father always stopped what he was doing and listened while I'd breathlessly fill him in on my day.For him, no subject was off-limits.When I was a lanky and awkward 13,Dad coached me on how to stand and walk like a lady.At 17 and madly in love,I sought his advice on pursuing a new student at school."Keep the conversation neutral," he counseled."And ask him about his car."

I followed his suggestions and gave him daily progress reports: "Terry walked me to my locker! " "Guess what?Terry held my hand! " "Dad! He asked me out! " Terry and I went steady for over a year,and soon Dad was joking,"I can tell you how to get a man;the hard part is getting rid of him."

By the time I graduated from college,I was ready to spread my wings.I got a job teaching special education at a school in Coachella, California,a desert town about 170 miles from home.It was no dream job.Low-income housing across the street from the school was a haven for drug users.Street gangs hung around the school after dark.Many of my charges,emotionally disturbed 10-to 14-year-old boys,had been arrested for shoplifting,car theft or arson.

"Be careful," Dad warned me during one of my frequent weekend visits home.He was concerned about my living alone,but I was 23,enthu-

爱 很 简 单

一个简简单单的小动作能胜过千言万语。

亨利克·艾伯森

在我成长的过程中,我的父亲经常停下自己正在做的事,聆听我气喘吁吁地述说。对他来说,只要是我的事,是没有禁区的。我长到13岁时,身材细长且笨拙,父亲告诉我怎样站立和走路才像个淑女。17岁时,我爱上了一个同学,我向爸爸征求意见,爸爸告诉我:"要保持中立的态度和他对话,"并告诫我:"只和他谈他的车。"

我按照他的劝告去做,每天向他汇报进展,"泰勒带我去存物柜,你猜怎么着?他拉着我的手,爸爸,他还约我出去!"泰勒和我相处了1年多,很快,爸爸跟我开玩笑:"我告诉你怎样才能抓住男人,最关键的就是欲擒故纵。"

大学毕业时,我做好展翅高飞的准备。我在加利福尼亚州的寇切拉找到一份特教教师职位,那是离家170英里的一个小镇,一片不毛之地。那不是份理想的工作。学校对面低收入者的住宅群是吸毒者的避难所,天黑后学校周围的街上聚着许多混混,在我的职责中,我大部分时间是在担心这些10~14岁的男孩子是不是因盗窃商店、汽车或是斗殴等被抓起来了。

像通常一样,一次周末回家时,父亲警告我:"一定要小心,"他是担心我一个人独自生活,但我已经23岁了,热情又质朴,我需要独

经典系列／时光的印记

siastic and naive,and I needed to be on my own.Besides,teaching jobs were tight in 1974,and I felt lucky to have one.

"Don't worry," I reassured him,as I loaded up the car to start my trip back to the desert and my job.

Several evenings later I stayed after school to rearrange my classroom.Finished,I turned out the light and closed the door.Then I headed toward the gate.It was locked! I looked around.Everyone—teachers,custodians,secretaries—had gone home and,not realizing I was still there, stranded me on the school grounds.I glanced at my watch—it was almost 6 P.M.I had been so engrossed in my work that I hadn't noticed me time.

After checking all the exits,I found just enough room to squeeze under a gate in the rear of the school.I pushed my purse through first,lay on my back and slowly edged through.

I retrieved my purse and walked toward my car,parked in a field behind the building.Eerie shadows fell across the schoolyard.

Suddenly,I heard voices.I glanced around and saw at least eight high-school-age boys following me.They were half a block away.Even in the near darkness I could see they were wearing gang insignia.

"Hey! " one called out."You a teacher?"

"Nah,she's too young—must be an aide! " another said.

As I walked faster,they continued taunting me."Hey! She's kinda cute! "

Quickening my pace,I reached into my shoulder bag to get my key ring.*If I have the keys in my hands,I thought,I can unlock the car and get in before*…My heart was pounding.

Frantically,I felt all over the inside of my handbag.But the key ring wasn't there!

"Hey! Let's get the lady! " one boy shouted.

*Dear Lord,please help me,*I prayed silently.Suddenly,my fingers

立。而且1974年时的教师工作是紧俏的,我很庆幸能成为一名教师。在我打包装车准备回到我的岗位,回到那片不毛之地时,我安慰爸爸:"不要担心。"

几天之后的一个晚上,放学后,我留在学校整理教室,忙完之后,我关上灯,关上门,向大门走去。大门上了锁,我向四周看去,所有的人都回家了,教师、管理人、秘书都走了。他们都不知道我还在里面。我被关在学校里了,我看了一下表,已经6点了,我一心在工作上,忘了时间。

检查了所有的地方后,我发现只有学校后门的下面有足够的缝隙可以钻出去。我把包先推出去,背贴地慢慢地钻了出去。

我拣起包,向停在楼后的车走去,怪诞的阴影长长地伸延在校园的广场上。

突然,我听到一些声音,我环顾左右,看到八九个高中年龄的男孩子跟着我,离我有半个街区远,虽然周围很暗,但能看到他们佩带着某个团伙的徽章。

"嗨!"一个人喊着"你是老师吗?"

"不是吧,她太小了——一定是个助理",另一个人说。我加快脚步,他们继续奚落我,"嗨,她还有点可爱哎!"

一边快行,一边把手伸到背包里去拿钥匙环,我想只要我拿到钥匙,打开车门,抢先进到车里就……我的心狂跳着。疯狂地摸遍了我的包,但没有钥匙环。

"嗨!抓住那个妞!"一个男孩高喊。

上帝啊,帮帮我,我默默地祈祷,突然我的手指在包里抓到一把

wrapped around a loose key in my purse.I didn't even know if it was for my car,but I took it out and clutched it firmly.

I jogged across the grass to my car and tried the key.It worked! I opened the door,slid in and locked it—just as the teenagers surrounded the car,kicking the sides and banging on the roof.Trembling,I started the engine and drove away.

Later,some teachers went back to the school with me.With flashlights,we found the key ring on the ground by the gate,where it had fallen as I slid through.

When I returned to my apartment,the phone was ringing.It was Dad.I didn't tell him about my ordeal;I didn't want to worry him.

"Oh,I forgot to tell you! "he said."I had an extra car key made and slipped it into your pocketbook—just in case you ever need it."

Today,I keep that key in my dresser drawer and treasure it.Whenever I hold it in my hand,I am reminded of all the wonderful things Dad has done for me over the years.I realize that,although he is now 68 and I am 40,I still look to him for wisdom,guidance and reassurance.Most of all,I marvel at the fact that his thoughtful gesture of making the extra key may have saved my life.And I understand how a simple act of love can make extraordinary things happen.

Sharon Whitley

单独的钥匙，我甚至不知道是不是我的汽车钥匙，但我还是把它拿出来，紧紧地攥在手里。

我小跑着穿过草地，到了车那儿试试钥匙，开了。

我打开车门，钻进去，锁上门。就在此时，那伙小青年围了上来，狂踢车身，猛敲车顶，我颤抖着发动汽车，开走了。

后来，几个老师陪我一起回到学校，借着手电筒的光，发现我的钥匙环在门边的地上，一定是我从那儿钻出来时弄掉的。

回到宿舍，电话响了，是爸爸打来的，我没有告诉他我经历的危险，我怕他担心。

"噢，我忘了告诉你！"他说，"我另配了一把车钥匙，放在你的手袋里，以防万一你需要它。"

现在我把那把钥匙珍藏在我梳妆台的抽屉里。只要拿起它就会想到爸爸这么多年来为我做的所有了不起的事情。

虽然他已经68岁而我也40岁了，但由于他的智慧、他的指导和他的细心，我依然很依赖他。

我特别感叹他能想到另配一把车钥匙，因而救了我一命。我明白一个因爱而生的普通小行为如何演变成非凡的壮举。

莎伦·韦特利

Just Say It!

If you were going to die soon and had only one phone call you could make, who would you call and what would you say? And why are you waiting?

Stephen Levine

One night, after reading one of the hundreds of parenting books I've read, I was feeling a little guilty because the book had described some parenting strategies I hadn't used in a while. The main strategy was to talk with your child and use those three magic words: "I love you." It had stressed over and over that children need to know that unconditionally and unequivocally that you really love them.

I went upstairs to my son's bedroom and knocked on the door. As I knocked, all I could hear were his drums. I knew he was there but he wasn't answering. So I opened the door and, sure enough, there he was sitting with his earphones on, listening to a tape and playing his drums. After I leaned over to get his attention, I said to him, "Tim, have you got a second?"

He said, "Oh sure, Dad. I'm always good for one." We proceeded to sit down and after about 15 minutes and a lot of small talk and stuttering, I just looked at him and said, "Tim, I really love the way you play drums."

He said, "Oh, thanks, Dad, I appreciate it."

I walked out of the door and said, "See you later! "As I was walk-ing downstairs, it dawned on me that I went up there with a certain mes-

说出来吧!

假设你将不久于人世并且只有一次打电话的机会,你会打给谁?你要说什么?你还等什么?

史蒂芬·赖文

一天晚上,我重温了一本养育手册,其实我已读过上百本了。读过之后,我觉得有点负罪感,因为书里写的一些育儿策略我一次也没用过。主要的方法就是和孩子们谈话并用3个有魔力的字:"我爱你!"书中一再强调孩子们有必要无条件地清楚知道你真的爱他们。

我上楼到儿子房间门口,敲敲门,当时我所能听到的只有他的击鼓声。我知道他在屋里但他就是不理敲门声。因此我打开门,果然他戴着耳塞坐在那儿,边听磁带边敲鼓。我靠过去以引起他的注意,我说:"蒂姆,你能停一会吗?"他说:"哦,当然,爸,我总是有那么会儿空子的。"接下来我们坐在那儿,乱聊了15分钟后,我看着他说,"蒂姆,我真的喜爱你敲鼓的样子。"

他说:"哦,谢谢,爸。我喜欢这句话。"

我走出房间,说:"再见!"朝楼下走着的时候,我逐渐想起来上楼去是要说某句话的,可我忘讲了。我觉得这很重要,得回去再找个

69

sage and had not delivered it.I felt it was really important to get back up there and have another chance to say those three magic words.

Again I climbed the stairs,knocked on the door and opened it."You got a second,Tim?"

"Sure,Dad.I'm always good for a second or two.What do you need?"

"Son,the first time I came up here to share a message with you, something else came out.It really wasn't what I wanted to share with you.Tim,do you remember when you were learning how to drive,it caused me a lot of problems?I wrote three words and slipped them under your pillow in hopes that would take care of it.I'd done my part as a parent and expressed my love to my son."Finally after a little small talk,I looked at Tim and said,"What I want you to know is that we love you."

He looked at me and said,"Oh,thanks,Dad.That's you and Mom?"

I said,"Yeah,that's both of us,we just don't express it enough."

He said,"Thanks,that means a lot.I know you do."

I turned around and walked out the door.As I was walking downstairs,I started thinking,"I can't believe this.I've already been up there twice—I know what the message is and yet something else comes out of my mouth."

I decided I'm going back there now and let Tim know exactly how I feel.He's going to hear it directly from me.I don't care if he is six feet tall! So back I go,knock on the door and he yells "Wait a minute.Don't tell me who it is.Could that be you,Dad?"

I said,"How'd you know that?"and he responded."I've known you ever since you were a parent,Dad."

Then I said "Son,have you got just one more second?"

"You know I'm good for one,so come on in.I suppose you didn't tell me what you wanted to tell me?"

机会说那3个有魔力的字。我又上了楼,敲敲门进去。"你有空吗?蒂姆。"

"当然,爸。我总是有那么一会儿空的。你需要我做什么?"

"儿子,前一次我上来是为了跟你分享一个信息,结果说了别的什么。但那不是我想与你分享的信息。蒂姆,你还记得你刚学驾驶那会儿吗?给我带来许多麻烦吗?我写了3个字并把它们放在你的枕头下,希望这有所帮助。我做了身为家长应做的,表达了对儿子的爱。"

聊了几句之后我看着蒂姆说:"我想让你知道我们爱你。"

他看着我,说:"哦,谢谢,爸。那是指你和妈吗?"

我说:"是啊,是我们俩。我们表达得不够。"

他说:"谢谢,你说的对我很重要。我知道你们爱我。"

我转身走出门。下楼时,我开始想:我简直不敢相信,我上了两次楼,我知道自己要说什么但说出口的还是别的话。

我决定现在就回去让蒂姆确切知道我的想法。他将直接从我口中听到这信息。我不在乎他已6英尺高了!因此我又回去,敲敲门,只听到他叫道:"等一下,不要说是谁。爸,是你吗?"

我说:"你怎么知道的?"

"自打我出生我就了解你。"

然后我说"儿子,你还有一会儿空吗?"

"你知道我有。所以进来吧。我想你还没有说你要跟我说的吧。"

I said,"How'd you know that?"

"I've known you ever since I was in diapers."

I said, "Well,here it is,Tim,what I've been holding back on.I just want to express to you how special you are to our family.It's not what you do,and it's not what you've done,like all the things you're doing with the junior high kids in town.It's who you are as a person.I love you and I just wanted you to know I love you,and I don't know why I hold back on something so important."

He looked at me and he said,"Hey,Dad,I know you do and it's really special hearing you say it to me.Thanks so much for your thoughts,as well as the intent."As I was walking out the door,he said,"Oh,hey,Dad. Have you got another second?"

I started thinking,"Oh no.What's he going to say to me?"I said,"Oh sure.I'm always good for one."

I don't know where kids get this—I'm sure it couldn't be from their parents,but he said,"Dad,I just want to ask you one question."

I said,"What's that?"

He looked at me and said,"Dad,have you been to a workshop or something like that?"

I'm thinking,"Oh no,like any other 18-year-old,he´s got any number,"and I said,"No,I was reading a book,and it said how important it is to tell your kids how you really feel about them."

"Hey,thanks for taking the time.Talk to you later,Dad."

I think what Tim taught me,more than anything else that night is that the only way you can understand the real meaning and purpose of love is to be willing to pay the price.You have to go out there and risk sharing it.

Gene Bedley

我说:"你怎么知道的?"

"自打我还在用尿布时我就了解你。"

我说:"好吧,蒂姆,这就是我一直藏在心里的。我想说你对我们全家来说多么特别。不是因为你在做什么,做了什么,比如你和镇上高中一二年级孩子们一起做的所有事情(junor high 指高中一二年级,高中有4年)。是因为你这个人。我爱你,我就是想让你知道我爱你,我不知道我为什么把这么重要的话藏在心里不说。"

他看着我,说道:"嗨,爸,我知道你爱我,但听到你亲口对我说出来是那么特别。谢谢你周到的考虑,谢谢你的良苦用心。"

当我走出房间时,他说,"哦,嗨,爸。你有空吗?"

我琢磨着,"哦不,他要跟我说什么?"我说:"当然有,我总是有那么一会儿空的。"

我不知道孩子们是从哪儿得知这点的,但不可能是从他们父母那儿得知的,他说,"爸,我想问你个问题。"

我说:"什么问题?"

他看着我说,"爸,你是不是去参加过教育孩子的短期培训或上过类似的短课?"

我想了想,"哦不,像其他18岁的孩子一样,他抓了我个现行,知道我干了啥。"我说,"没有。我正在读一本书,书里说到将你对孩子的真正感受告诉他们有多么重要。"

"嗨,谢谢你花时间看这书。爸,再聊。"

其他的不说,蒂姆那晚教给我的是:理解爱的真正含义和目的的唯一途径是愿意付出代价。你得走出心门,承担说出来的风险。

吉尼·贝德烈

Best Friends Forever

When I said good-bye to my best friend,Opal,we promised to write and vowed that we'd see each other again.At fourteen,our futures seemed full of possibilities,despite our coming separation.It was June 1957,and we had spent two and a half of the happiest years of our lives on Chitose Air Force base in Japan. Now her family was being transferred to England,mine to Florida.What hurt most about leaving each other was that she was not only my first,but my best,best friend.

Growing up with a father in the military meant moving often.The two-room schoolhouse on the northern island of Hokkaido was my ninth school—and I was only in sixth grade when I arrived.Opal's roving childhood was similar to mine,except that I was terribly,horribly, painfully,miserably shy.I loathed always being "the new girl".Once or twice I'd managed to make a friend,but before we could get to know each other well,I'd moved on to a different school.

Then one January day in 1955,when the snowdrifts were ten feet high and the wind howled around the chimney of the coal stove,I stood in the doorway of my newest classroom.As always,my stomach ached with dread,and shivers of fear ran through me like tiny sharp arrows.I hoped no one could tell I was trying to hold back tears.Twenty kids silently stared at me,and I turned red from my ears down to my toes.I kept my eyes on the floor,sneaking only quick peeks at the strange faces.Then I saw a girl beaming,her smile like warm sunshine flooding my shaking soul.She actually seemed to welcome me! When the teacher told me to take the desk next to Opal's,some of my frozen terror began

永远的挚友

当和我最好的朋友奥帕尔告别时,我们保证给对方写信,发誓我们会再见面。在14岁时,将来的一切在我们眼中充满了可能性,尽管我们即将离别。那是1957年的6月,我们在位于日本的千岁空军基地度过了一生中最快乐的两年半时光。然后她举家迁往英格兰,而我全家迁往佛罗里达州。关于分离最令人伤心的是她不仅是我的第一个朋友,还是我最好的朋友。拥有一位军人父亲意味着得经常搬家。位于北海道北部岛屿的两间房的校舍是我的第9个学校——而我到那儿才上六年级。我非常地、令人厌地、痛苦地、极其地害羞,除了这一点以外,奥帕尔流浪的童年和我相仿。我讨厌总是当"新来的女孩"。曾经有一两回,我竭力交了个朋友,但不等我们熟悉起来,我已搬到了新的学校。

1955年1月的一天, 雪积到10英尺厚, 风绕着炭炉的烟囱咆哮着,我站在新教室的门口。跟以往一样,我的胃由于害怕痛起来,寒战像锋利的小箭刺穿了我。我希望没人看出来我在试图忍住眼泪。20个孩子无声地瞪着我,弄得我从耳朵红到脚趾。我两眼盯着地面,偷偷地迅速地瞥了一眼那些陌生的面孔。然后我瞅见有个女孩正灿烂地笑着,她的笑容像温暖的阳光淹没了我颤抖的灵魂。看来她是在欢迎我!当老师要我坐在奥帕尔旁边时,我因恐惧而结的冰稍稍

to melt slightly.

"Hi,I'm Opal."Her voice carried the twang of the Midwest,her face was round,her eyes soft behind her thick glasses,her hair long and brown.And as I quickly learned,her heart was crafted of twenty-four-karat gold.

That first day,as we moved from history to math to English,she helped me find the right place in the books and filled me in on the other kids.It appeared they were all terrific,even the class pains."Don't mind about him.He likes to tease,but he sure can be funny."Or,"She acts a little snobby sometimes,but she's a real nice girl."

Because we had fourth,fifth and sixth grades in the same room,the teacher would take small groups up front while the rest of us worked at our desks,very much like the school in *Little House on the Prairie.*With only five of us in sixth grade,the angels were working overtime when they made sure one of them was Opal.

By the end of that first day,an unspoken promise had been made. Opal and I knew we would be best friends,the first either of us had found.During the next months,more and more new kids moved to the base and Opal welcomed everyone—teaching me by example to do the same.Red-haired Maureen arrived and became an especially close friend. But we all hung out together,both boys and girls,playing kickball and Red Rover,skiing on the snowy mound behind my house,exploring the woods where we were officially forbidden to go,swimming in the frigid pool when the short summers arrived,camping on what we hoped was an extinct volcano,attending the Japanese Cherry Blossom and Snow festivals.

In that large group,Opal and I were rock-solid best friends,a true Mutt and Jeff duo.She was tall and slim,I was short and plump;she was good in math,I loved reading;she wasn't athletic,but cheerfully joined the games and sports I dragged her into.Her father was a master sergeant

融化了。

"嗨,我叫奥帕尔。"她的声音带有美国中西部的鼻音,长着圆圆的脸,厚厚的眼镜片后面目光温和,棕色的头发留得长长的。我很快就了解到,她的心是24K金做的。

那一天,我们从历史课上到数学课还上了英语课,她帮助我找到所上内容在课本上的正确位置,帮助我熟悉其他孩子。显然他们都很棒,即使是班上最讨厌的人。"别介意他。他喜欢嘲弄人,但他挺有趣。"或,"她常有点势利,但她是个真正的好女孩。"

因为四五六3个年级在同一个教室里,老师每次叫几小组同学坐到前面,其他同学坐在原位上,非常像《草原上的小木屋》里的学校。因为六年级只有5个学生,天使们加班加点才把奥帕尔安排进来。

到那天放学时,我和奥帕尔之间已达成了默契。我们意识到我俩将是最好的朋友,我们各自的第一个好友。接下来的几个月里,越来越多的新生搬到基地来,奥帕尔以实际行动欢迎每一位同学的到来——给我做出了榜样,教会了我做同样的事。红发的莫琳来了并成为特别亲密的朋友。但不管男生女生,我们都聚在一起玩儿童足球(类似于棒球,但是用脚踢)和"红色海盗"(捉人游戏),在我家后面的小雪山上滑雪,去我们被明令禁止进入的树林探险。短暂的夏季一到,我们一同去寒冷的池塘里游泳。集体在山上露营,我们希望它是座休眠火山。集体参加日本的樱花节和雪景节。

在那个大队伍里,我和奥帕尔是最铁的好友,一对真正的马特和杰夫(漫画人物)二人行。她又高又苗条,我又矮又胖;她擅长数学,我喜欢阅读;她不擅长运动,却高高兴兴地参加我拽她去的比赛

(the fire chief! So romantic !),mine a lieutenant colonel.She admired my get-up-and-go;I admired her gentleness with young children,the way she always gave of herself,her ability to see the smallest rose in a thicket of thorns. Our differences meshed and never clashed.

Two years flew by—miracle years filled with fun and growth and discovery.Then the rumors began.The Air Force was closing the base, and we would all be transferred back to the States that summer,headed for different assignments,hundreds or thousands of miles apart.

As promised,Opal and I wrote occasional letters (on military salaries,long distance phone calls were out of the question)   until we were sixteen.I was in boarding school when her last letter came.She'd fallen in love with an older man—nineteen—an airman first class.She'd left her family in England and returned to the States to marry him.She had just given birth to a beautiful baby girl.

I wrote back right away but didn't get an answer.Knowing how Opal found writing an awful chore,I wrote again and again.   Finally my letters were returned:forwarding address unknown. How I worried about her! To be married and have a baby at sixteen! I knew her so well:I knew she'd be a wonderful mother,but I also knew she was too young to be married.

I graduated from boarding school and then college,was married,had three babies,divorced,remarried.My children grew up,went to college,and my daughter was now a mother.And so often I thought of Opal,wondering where she was,if she was all right,if she was happy.I'd talk about our blissful years together,and my family knew all about my best friend.

One sweaty hot August day in 1991 the telephone rang. "Is this Louise?"

"Yes."

"Is this Louise Ladd?"

"Yes."

和运动。她父亲是名二级军士长(消防队长！多么浪漫啊！)，我的父亲是陆军中校。她钦佩我行动果敢，我喜欢她对小小孩的亲切，佩服她舍己助人的方式，崇拜她能看见荆棘丛里最小的玫瑰。我们是这般互补，从没有冲突过。

两年稍纵即逝——这惊人的两年充满了欢乐、成长和发现。此时谣言开始流传。空军关闭了基地，那年夏天我们都转移回国，奔赴不同的使命，相隔数百或数千里。

如我们保证的那样，我和奥帕尔偶尔写写信(以部队的工资，打长途电话是吃不消的)，一直到16岁。当她的最后一封信来到时，我已上了寄宿学校。她爱上了一个比她大的男人——19岁的空军一等兵。为了嫁给他，她离开了在英格兰的家，回到了美国。她刚刚生了一个漂亮的小女孩。

我马上就回了信，但没收到回信。因为知道奥帕尔认为写信是非常讨厌的家务，我一再写信给她。最后我的信被退回来了：查无此人。我多么担心她啊！16岁就结婚生子！我太了解她：知道她会是一个良母，但亦清楚她太年轻，尚不适合结婚。

从寄宿学校毕业后，我上了大学，然后结了婚，有了3个孩子，离婚，再婚。孩子们长大了，上了大学，现在我女儿也做了母亲。我如此频繁地想起奥帕尔，想知道她在哪儿，她是否健康，她是否快乐。我想跟她一起说说那欢乐的往昔。我的家人知道我最好朋友的所有往事。

1991年8月的一天，天气炎热，令人汗流浃背，电话响起。"是露易丝吗？"

"是的。"

"是露易丝·莱德吗？"

"是的。"

"Is this Louise Ladd from Japan?"

"Who are you?"I roared.

"This is Opal."

I screamed.I was outside on the porch and the entire town must have heard me.Dancing around and jumping up and down,I shouted out my joy.

Thirty-four years after we said good-bye,she had found me. Sorting through piles of stuff after a recent move,she had opened an ancient box marked "papers".My letter from 1959 was in it.Immediately she called everyone named Ladd who lived anywhere near my old address in Maryland;then,refusing to give up,she called my boarding school.After much begging and pleading (she swears she was literally down on her knees),the alumnae office finally gave her my phone number.

That Christmas,Opal and her second husband drove from Omaha, Nebraska,to spend a few days with us in Connecticut. She looked exactly the same.She sounded exactly the same.She radiated the same warmth and love I'd always known.She'd missed me as much as I'd missed her. She'd been through difficult times,but as always,had managed to find the good in life. Twenty-four-karat gold does not tarnish.

And now we are together again:best friends,forever.

Louise Ladd

"是从日本回来的露易丝·莱德吗？"

"你是谁？"我吼道。

"我是奥帕尔。"

我尖叫一声，冲出门廊，想必全镇人都听见了我的叫声。我手舞足蹈，上蹿下跳，大声喊出我的欢乐。

分别34年后，她找到了我。最近一次搬家后，奥帕尔在整理一堆东西时打开了一个旧盒子，盒子上标有"文件"。里面是我自1959年写的信。她马上给住在我在马里兰州的旧址附近的每一个莱德打电话；然后，拒绝放弃，她把电话打到我求学的寄宿学校。奥帕尔百般乞求（她发誓说她实实在在地跪在地上），毕业生联谊处终于把我的电话号码给了她。

那一年圣诞节，奥帕尔和她的第2任丈夫从内布拉斯加州奥马哈开车来，和住在康奈蒂克州的我们共度了几天。她看上去还是老样子，她的声音也是老样子。她散发着我所熟悉的温暖和爱。她就像我思念她那般思念我。她吃过苦，但她一如既往，依然竭力发现生活的乐趣。24K金是不会褪色的。

如今我们又生活在一起啦：最好的朋友，永远。

露易丝·莱德

Someday

CHICKEN SOUP

*Someday when the kids are grown,*things are going to be a lot different.The garage won't be full of bikes,electric train tracks on plywood, sawhorses surrounded by chunks of two-by-fours,nails,a hammer and saw,unfinished "experimental projects," and the rabbit cage.I'll be able to park both cars neatly in just the right places,and never again stumble over skateboards,a pile of papers(saved for the school fund drive),or the bag of rabbit food—now split and spilled.

*Someday when the kids are grown,*the kitchen will be incredibly neat.The sink will be free of sticky dishes,the garbage disposal won't get choked on rubber bands or paper cups,the refrigerator won't be clogged with nine bottles of milk,and we won't lose the tops to jelly jars,catsup bottles,the peanut butter,the margarine or the mustard.The water jar won't be put back empty,the ice trays won't be left out overnight,the blender won't stand for six hours coated with the remains of a midnight malt,and the honey will stay inside the container.

*Someday when the kids are grown,*my lovely wife will actually have time to get dressed leisurely.A long,hot bath(without three panic interruptions),time to do her nails (even toenails if she pleases!)without answering a dozen questions and reviewing spelling words,having had her hair done that afternoon without trying to squeeze it in between racing a sick dog to the vet and a trip to the orthodontist with a kid in a bad mood because she lost her headgear.

*Someday when the kids are grown,*the instrument called a "telephone" will actually be available.It won't look like it's growing from a

某 一 天

某一天,当孩子们长大了,周围的事将有很多改变。

车库里不会像以前那样,挤满了自行车及纤维板作轨道的电动火车等。锯木架边零乱地堆满了小木块、钉子、锤子、锯子,及那些还没有完工的实验品、兔笼等。现在我可以让两辆汽车整整齐齐地停放在里面,再也不会被溜冰板、大堆的书本、作业(学校里用的)和从破漏的袋子里漏出的兔粮等杂物绊倒。

某一天,当孩子们长大了,厨房将会非常整洁干净,水槽里没有黏黏的污垢。垃圾筒里也没有塞满橡皮圈和纸杯。冰箱里不会有9个奶瓶。我们也不用把上层留着放果冻瓶、果酱瓶、花生奶油、人造奶油和芥末等。水瓶总是空的,晚上又总是忘了把冰盘收起来。搅拌机干净不了6个小时,上面沾满麦芽的残留物,蜜糖也残留在容器的里面。

某一天,当孩子们长大了,我可爱的妻子就有时间重新开始打扮了。可以慢慢地泡个热水澡(不会慌乱地被骚扰3次)。做做指甲(包括脚指甲)而不用回答十几个问题,不用重复拼写单词。下午可以去做个发型,而不用盘起头发急急忙忙地把生病的小狗送到兽医那里或是跑去为丢了头花正在发脾气的孩子买头花。

某一天,当孩子们长大了,那个叫做电话的设备才真正可以使用。它看起来不会像长在小家伙的耳朵上,它会挂在那里,静静地等

teenager's ear.It will simply hang there…silently and amazingly available! It will be free of lipstick,human saliva,mayonnaise,corn chip crumbs,and toothpicks stuck in those little holes.

*Someday when the kids are grown,*I'll be able to see through the car windows.Fingerprints,tongue licks,sneaker footprints and dog tracks (nobody knows how)will be conspicuous by their absence.The back seat won't be a disaster area,we won't sit on jacks or crayons anymore,the tank will not always be somewhere between empty and fumes,and(glory to God!)I won't have to clean up dog messes another time.

*Someday when the kids are grown,*we will return to normal conversations.You know,just plain American talk."Gross" won't punctuate every sentence seven times."Yuk! "will not be heard."Hurry up,I gotta go! " will not accompany the banging of fists on the bathroom door. "It's my turn"won't call for a referee.And a magazine article will be read in full without interruption,then discussed at length without Mom and Dad having to hide in the attic to finish the conversation.

*Someday when the kids are grown,*we won't run out of toilet tissue.My wife won't lose her keys.We won't forget to shut the refrigerator door.I won't have to dream up new ways of diverting attention from the gumball machine…or have to answer "Daddy,is it a sin that you're driving 47 in a 30-mile-per-hour zone?" …or promise to kiss the rabbit good night…or wait up forever until they get home from dates…or have to take a number to get a word in at the supper table…or endure the pious pounding of one Keith Green just below the level of acute pain.

Yes,someday when the kids are grown,things are going to be a lot different.One by one they'll leave our nest,and the place will begin to resemble order and maybe even a touch of elegance. The clink of china and silver will be heard on occasion.The crackling of the fireplace will echo through the hallway.The phone will be strangely silent.The house will be quiet…and calm…and always clean…and empty…and we'll

待你去使用它。上面不再沾满口红、口水、蛋黄酱、食物残渣等，上面的小洞洞里也不会插着牙签。

某一天，当孩子们长大了，我就能从车窗玻璃那儿向外看了。玻璃上的指纹、舌印、帆布鞋脚印、小狗留下的痕迹（谁也不知是怎么弄上去的）将不再存在。车后排座位不再是重灾区，我们不会坐在棋子和蜡笔画上，水箱也不会总是要么空了，要么冒烟了，而且（感谢上帝）我也不用随时清理狗弄得乱七八糟的东西了。

某一天，当孩子们长大了，我们可以像以前一样谈谈天，那只是正常的、普通的美国人的交谈，不用说每一句话被无礼的打断七八次。不会总听到大笑大叫声。也不会一边用拳头捶打着洗手间的门，一边高喊"快点，我要走了！"不用去裁决事情该轮到谁了。可以不受干扰地读完杂志的标题，再详细地讨论讨论。爸爸和妈妈不用藏到阁楼上去把话谈完。

某一天，当孩子们长大了，洗水间的手纸不会总被用完了，我妻子不会总丢钥匙。我们也不会总忘了关冰箱或大门。我也不必苦思冥想新的方法把孩子们从制糖球的机器那里吸引过来。不用回答诸如此类的问题："爸爸，在规定每小时 30 千米的区域把车开到 47 千米算不算犯罪"或者答应和小兔子道晚安并亲吻小兔子。不用永无休止地等待他们结束各种约会回家。不用在晚餐桌上套他们的话了解情况，也不用因为某个孩子不大的痛苦而承受沉重的责任。

是的，某一天当孩子们长大了，事情将变得完全不同，他们一个接一个离开我们的小窝，一切将开始有序，甚至呈现出高雅，偶尔能听到瓷器和银器丁当作响。壁炉里传出的劈劈啪啪声回荡在过道里，电话出奇地安静。房间永远都是安安静静的……没有风波……非常整洁……空空荡荡……而我们不再盼望着将来有一天会怎么

spend our time not looking forward to Someday but looking back to Yesterday.And thinking, "Maybe we can babysit the grandkids and get some life back in this place for a change! "

Charles R.Swindoll

样,而是不断地回忆昨天。我们在想:"也许,我们可以带孙子,让这儿的生活再改变一下,回到从前!"

查尔斯·R.斯温多尔

Ask, Ask, Ask
请求, 请求, 请求

The greatest saleswoman in the world today doesn't mind if you call her a girl.That's because Markita Andrews has generated more than eighty thousand dollars selling Girl Scout cookies since she was seven years old.

Going door-to-door after school,the painfully shy Markita transformed herself into a cookie-selling dynamo when she discovered,at age 13,the secret of selling.

It starts with desire.Burning,white-hot desire.

For Markita and her mother,who worked as a waitress in New York after her husband left them when Markita was eight years old,their dream was to travel the globe."I'll work hard to make enough money to send you to college,"her mother said one day."You'll go to college and

如今,世界上最伟大的女售货员不会介意你叫她女孩。这是因为从 7 岁开始卖女童子军饼的马克伊塔·安德鲁斯已赚了 8 万美元。放学后挨家挨户推销促使生性极羞怯的马克伊塔转变成了一名不知疲倦的饼干销售员,直到 13 岁那年她发现了推销的秘诀。

一切皆源于一个愿望,一个燃烧的、白热化的愿望。

马克伊塔的父亲在她 8 岁时离开了她们,从那以后,母亲就靠在纽约做女侍应谋生。这对母女梦想着周游世界。"我会努力工作,赚钱供你上大学,"有一天母亲说,"你将会上大学,毕业后你将会赚足够

when you graduate,you'll make enough money to take you and me around the world.Okay?"

So at age 13 when Markita read in her Girl Scout magazine that the Scout who sold the most cookies would win an all-expenses-paid trip for two around the world,she decided to sell all the Girl Scout cookies she could—more Girl Scout cookies than anyone in the world,ever.

But desire alone is not enough.To make her dream come true, Markita knew she needed a plan.

"Always wear your right outfit,your professional garb,"her aunt advised. "When you are doing business,dress like you are doing business. Wear your Girl Scout uniform.When you go up to people in their tenement buildings at 4:30 or 6:30 and especially on Friday night,ask for a big order.Always smile,whether they buy or not,always be nice.And don't ask them to buy your cookies; ask them to invest."

Lots of other Scouts may have wanted that trip around the world. Lots of other Scouts may have had a plan.But only Markita went off in her uniform each day after school,ready to ask—and keep asking—folks to invest in her dream. "Hi.I have a dream.I'm earning a trip around the world for me and my mom by merchandising Girl Scout cookies,"She'd say at the door. "Would you like to invest in one dozen or two dozen boxes of cookies?"

Markita sold 3,526 boxes of Girl Scout cookies that year and won her trip around the world.Since then,she has sold more than 42,000 boxes of Girl Scout cookies,spoken at sales conventions across the country,starred in a Disney movie about her adventure and has coauthored the bestseller,*How to Sell More Cookies,Condos,Cadillacs,Computers… And Everything Else.*

Markita is no smarter and no more extroverted than thousands of other people,young and old,with dreams of their own.The difference is Markita has discovered the secret of selling:Ask,Ask,Ask! Many people

的钱让你和我周游世界。对不？"

因此，当 13 岁的马克伊塔在女童子军杂志上看到卖出饼干最多的童子军将获得一次提供全部费用的双人环球旅行时，她决定尽她所能卖出所有的女童子军饼干，比世界上任何一个人曾卖出的都再多一点。

但只有愿望是不够的。马克伊塔知道要想实现梦想，她需要制定一个计划。"每次穿你的职业装，合适的套装，"姨妈建议她。"当你做生意时，穿的要像做生意的样子。穿你的女童子军制服。当你在下午 4:30 或 6:30 特别是周五，去家里向人们兜售时要多卖点。每次都要微笑，无论他们买还是不买，都要高高兴兴的。不要请求他们买你的饼干；请求他们投资。"

许多其他的童子军也许曾想拥有这次环球旅行。许多其他童子军也许曾制定过计划。但是只有马克伊塔每天放学后穿上制服出发，准备好一再请求众人投资她的梦想。"嗨，我有个梦想。我要通过出售女童子军饼干赢取我和妈妈的环球旅行。"她会站在门口说，"你愿意投资买 12 盒或 24 盒饼干吗？"

那一年马克伊塔卖出了 3,526 盒女童子军饼干，赢取了她的环球旅行。从那以后，她一共卖了 4,2000 多盒女童子军饼干，在全国销售大会上演讲，在迪士尼电影中出演她的冒险经历，合写了畅销书《如何销售更多的饼干、公寓、卡迪拉克汽车、电脑……及其他每一种物品》。

数以千计的其他人，老老少少，各自怀揣着梦想。马克伊塔跟他们一样不够聪明，不够外向。区别在于马克伊塔发现了销售的秘诀：请求，请求，请求！许多人尚未开始就已经失败，因为他们没有去要

fail before they even begin because they fail to *ask* for what they want. The fear of rejection leads many of us to reject ourselves and our dreams long before anyone else ever has the chance—no matter what we're selling.

And everyone is selling something. "You're selling yourself every-day—in school,to your boss,to new people you meet,"said Markita at 14."My mother is a waitress:she sells the daily special.Mayors and presidents trying to get votes are selling…One of my favorite teachers was Mrs.Chapin.She made geography interesting,and that's really selling…I see selling everywhere I look.Selling is part of the whole world."

It takes courage to ask for what you want.Courage is not the absence of fear.It's doing what it takes despite one's fear.And,as Markita has discovered,the more you ask,the easier(and more fun) it gets.

Once,on live TV,the producer decided to give Markita her toughest selling challenge.Markita was asked to sell Girl Scout cookies to another guest on the show."Would you like to invest in one dozen or two dozen boxes of Girl Scout cookies?"she asked.

"Girl Scout cookies?! I don't buy any Girl Scout cookies! "he replied. "I'm a Federal Penitentiary warden.I put 2,000 rapists,robbers, criminals,muggers and child abusers to bed every night."

Unruffled,Markita quickly countered, "Mister,if you take some of these cookies,maybe you won't be so mean and angry and evil.And,Mister,I think it would be a good idea for you to take some of these cookies back for every one of your 2,000 prisoners,too."

Markita asked.

The warden wrote a check.

Jack Canfield and Mark V.Hansen

双语精华版·心灵鸡汤·

90

他们想要的。不管我们销售的是什么,远在别人有机会给予我们之前由于害怕被拒绝,我们中的许多人就已否定了我们自己,否定了我们的梦想。

每个人都在销售着什么。"你每天都在学校里,向你的老板,向你新遇见的人销售你自己。"14岁时马克伊塔如是说。"我母亲是个女侍应,她卖每日特价货。市长和总统拉选票也是销售……我最喜爱的一个老师柴宾女士,她使地理变得生动有趣,这也是一种销售……处处都有销售,它是整个世界的一部分。"

请求得到你所想要的需要勇气。勇气不是害怕的缺席,勇气是去做尽管害怕也要完成的事。并且马克伊塔发现,你请求的愈多,事情就变得愈容易(且更有乐趣)。

有一次,在电视直播上,制片人决定给马克伊塔一个最棘手的销售挑战。要求她向节目里的另一位嘉宾兜售女童子军饼干。"你愿意投资买 12 盒或 24 盒女童子军饼干吗?"她问。

"女童子军饼干?!我不买什么女童子军饼干!"他回答:"我是名联邦监狱看守。每天晚上我把 2 000 个强奸犯、抢劫犯、刑事案犯、强盗、虐待儿童的犯人赶上床。"

马克伊塔沉着地立即回应,"先生,如果你买些这种饼干,或许你将不再这么小气、愤怒、凶恶。并且,先生,我以为你带些这种饼干给你那 2 000 个囚犯中的每一个人也是个好主意。"

马克伊塔请求了。

看守写了张支票。

杰克·坎菲尔德　马克·V.汉森

It Takes Courage

You gain strength,experience and confidence by every
experience where you really stop to look fear in the face…
You must do the thing you cannot do.

Eleanor Roosevelt

Her name is Nikki.She lives just down the road from me.I have been inspired by this young lady for a number of years.Her story has touched my heart and when times get tough,I reflect on her courage.

It started when she was in the seventh grade,with the doctor's report.Everything that her family had feared was true.The diagnosis: leukemia.The next few months were filled with regular visits to the hospital.She was poked and jabbed and tested hundreds and thousands of times.Then came the chemotherapy.Along with it,and a chance to possibly save her life,she lost her hair.Losing your hair as a seventh grader is a devastating thing.The hair didn't grow back.The family started to worry.

That summer before the eighth grade she bought a wig.It felt uncomfortable,it was scratchy,but she wore it.She was very popular and loved by so many students.She was a cheerleader and always had other kids around her,but things seemed to change.She looked strange,and you know how kids are.I guess maybe like the rest of us.Sometimes we go after laughter and do things even though it causes great pain in someone else.The wig was pulled off from behind about a half a dozen

需要勇气

　　你会通过每一次使你停下来并且脸上露出害怕表情的经历而获得力量、经验和自信。你必须去做你做不了的事。

——埃利诺·罗斯福

　　她的名字叫妮姬。她就住在我家的马路那头。我已经受这个年轻的女士鼓舞了好几年。她的故事感动了我的心,每当遇到困难的时候,我就回想起她的勇气。

　　故事是从她在七年级时医生的报告开始的。她家里人担心的每一件事都成了现实。诊断是:白血病。接下来的几个月被经常去医院排满了。她被戳、被刺、被检验了成百上千次。然后接下来是化疗。随着化疗和一个也许能救活她的机会而来的,是她的头发没了。七年级学生没了头发是个灾难。头发没有长回来。全家人开始担心。

　　上八年级前的夏天里她买了个假发。假发感觉很不舒服,发痒,但她还是戴着。过去她在许多学生中很受欢迎和爱戴。她是拉拉队长,总有许多学生围着她。但是现在改变了。你知道孩子们都这样,我猜像我们中间的其他人一样。有时候我们嘲笑或者恶作剧,尽管这会给别人带来很大的痛苦。八年级开始的两周,她的假发被人从后面扯掉六七次。她则会停下来,弯下腰,因为害怕和难堪而颤抖,重新

经典系列／时光的印记 ············

times in the first two weeks of the eighth grade.She would stop,bend down,shake from fear and embarrassment,put her wig back on,wipe away the tears and walk to class,always wondering why no one stood up for her.

This went on for two agonizing,hellish weeks.She told her parents she couldn't take it anymore.They said, "You can stay home if you wish."You see,if your daughter is dying in the eighth grade,you don't care if she makes it to the ninth.Having her happy and giving her a chance at peace is all that matters.Nikki told me that to lost her hair is nothing.She said,"I can handle that."She even said that losing her life is of little concern. "I can handle that,too,"she said, "but do you know what it's like to lose your friends? To walk down the hall and have them part like the Red Sea because you're coming,to go into the cafeteria on pizza day,our best meal,and have them leave with half-eaten plates? They say that they're not hungry but you know that they're leaving because your're sitting there.Do you know what it's like to have no one want to sit next to you in math class and the kids in the locker to the left and right of you have pulled out? They're putting their books in with someone else,all because they might have to stand next to the girl wearing the wig,the one with the weird disease.It's not even catching.They can't get it from me.Don't they know that I need my friends most of all? Oh,yes,"she said, "losing your life is nothing when you know that because of your belief in God you know exactly where you're going to spend eternity.Losing your hair is nothing either,but losing your friends is so devastating."

She had planned to stay home from school,but something happened that weekend.She heard about two boys,one in the sixth grade,one in the seventh,and their stories gave her the courage to go on.The seventh-grader was from Arkansas and even though it wasn't popular,he took his *New Testament Bible* in his shirt to school.As the story goes,three

戴上假发,擦掉眼泪,然后走到教室,她一直想知道为什么没有人站出来支持她。

这种情况持续了地狱般的两周。她告诉父母她再也受不了了。他们说"如果你想的话,你可以待在家里"。你看,如果你的女儿在八年级过着生不如死的日子,你不会再关心她是否能升到九年级。让她愉快并且平静地生活是最要紧的。妮姬告诉我头发没了不算什么。她说:"我能处理好那个。"她甚至说:"生命没了也没什么可关注的。我也能处理好它。"她说:"但是你知道失去了朋友是什么样的吗? 走在走廊里,他们像红海那样分开两边,因为你来了;供应比萨饼那天走进食堂,比萨饼是我们最好的伙食,他们却剩半盘子不吃就走了。虽然他们说他们不是很饿,但你知道是因为你坐在那里他们才离开的。你知道数学课没有人愿意坐你旁边和你左右两边储物柜的主人把东西搬走是什么样的感觉吗?他们把书本放到别人的储物柜里,就是因为他们本来有可能和戴假发得怪病的女孩站在一起(用储物柜)。这个病不传染的,他们不会从我这里染上。他们难道不知道我最需要的是朋友? 噢,是的,"她说:"当你知道因为信仰上帝你知道死后会去那儿,那么失去生命不算什么。失去头发也不算什么,但是失去朋友是毁灭性的。"

她原来计划待在家里不上学了,但是周末情况发生了变化。她听说了两个男孩,一个在六年级,一个在七年级,他们的故事给了她勇气。那个七年级生从阿肯色来的,尽管这个做法不流行,但他还是把圣经新约放在衬衫里带到学校。据说3个男孩走近他,抓住圣经,

boys approached him, grabbed the Bible and said, "You sissy.Religion is for sissies.Prayer is for sissies.Don't ever again bring this Bible back to school." He reportedly handed the Bible back to the biggest one of the three and said, "Here, see if you've got enough courage to carry this around school just one day." They said that he made three friends.

The next story that inspired Nikki was a six-thgrader from Ohio named Jimmy Masterdino.He was jealous of California because California had a state motto, "Eureka! "Ohio didn't have any.He came up with six life-changing words.He single-handedly got enough signatures. With his petitions full, he took it before the State Legislature.Today, because of a brave sixth grader, the official state motto for Ohio is "All things are possible with God."

With Nikki's new-found courage and inspiration, she put her wig on that next Monday morning.She got dressed as pretty and as fancy as she could.She told her mom and dad, "I'm going back to school today. There's something I've got to do.There's something I've got to find out." They didn't know what she meant and they were worried, fearing the worst, but they drove her to school.Every day for the last several weeks, Nikki would hug and kiss her mom and dad in the car before she got out.As unpopular as this was and even though many kids sneered and jeered at her, she never let it stop her.Today was different.She hugged and kissed them, but as she got out of the car, she turned quietly and said, "Mom and Dad, guess what I'm going to do today?"Her eyes were filling up with tears, but they were tears of joy and strength.Oh, yes, there was fear of the unknown, but she had a cause.They said, "What, baby? "She said, "Today I'm going to find out who my best friend is.Today I'm going to find out who my real friends are."And with that she grabbed the wig off her head and she set it on the seat beside her.She said, "They take me for who I am, Daddy, or they don't take me at all.I don't have much time left.I've got to find out who they are

说:"你这个娘娘腔。宗教是娘娘腔们的。祈祷是娘娘腔们的。不要再把圣经带回到学校来。"据说他把圣经给了3个人中最大的那个,说:"接着,看看你有没有胆量拿着圣经在校园里晃悠一天。"他们说他交到了3个朋友。

下一个激励妮姬的故事是来自俄亥俄的吉米·马斯特迪诺。他嫉妒加州因为加州有一条州标"找到了",而俄亥俄没有。他想出了6个改变他一生的词语。他一个人找到了足够的签名支持。请愿书签满了,他拿着它去了州立法机关。今天,因为这个勇敢的六年级学生,俄亥俄州官方的标语是:"上帝万事皆能"。

带着新发现的勇气和鼓舞, 接下来的星期一早晨她戴上了假发。她穿着漂亮并尽可能地花哨。她告诉爸爸和妈妈,"今天我要回到学校去。我有事要做。我要搞清楚一些事情。"他们不知道她的意思,他们很担心,害怕最坏的结果。但他们还是开车送她去了学校。过去几个礼拜的每一天,妮姬都会在下车前拥抱和亲吻她的爸爸和妈妈。这样做极不受欢迎,而且尽管许多孩子会讥笑和嘲弄她,她从来没有就此停止过。今天不同了。她依然拥抱亲吻他们,但当她从车里出来,她平静地转过身子说"爸爸妈妈,猜猜今天我会做什么?"她的眼睛充满泪水,但那是喜悦和坚强的泪水。噢,是的,以前有过对未知事物的害怕情绪,但那是有原因的。他们说:"做什么,宝贝?"她说:"今天我要发现谁是我最好的朋友。今天我要发现谁是我真正的朋友"。她拿下了假发,把它放在她旁边的座位上。她说:"要么我是什么样他们就接受什么样,爸爸,要么就完全不要接受我。我剩下的时间不多了。今天我要搞明白他们是什么样的人。"她走了两步,然

today." She started to walk, took two steps, then turned and said, "Pray for me." They said, "We are, baby." And as she walked toward 600 kids, she could hear her dad say, "That's my girl."

A miracle happened that day. She walked through that playground, into that school, and not one loud-mouth or bully, no one, made fun of the little girl with all the courage.

Nikki has taught thousands of people that to be yourself, to use your own God-given talent, and to stand up for what is right even in the midst of uncertainty, pain, fear and persecution is the only true way to live.

Nikki has since graduated from high school. The marriage that was never supposed to take place happened a few years later, and Nikki is the proud mother of a little girl that she named after my little girl, Emily. Every time something that seems impossible comes before me, I think of Nikki and I gain strength.

Bill Sanders

后转身说：“为我祈祷吧。”他们说：“我们会的,宝贝。”当她向600个孩子走去的时候,她听到她爸爸说：“那才是我的女儿。”

那天一个奇迹诞生了。她走过了操场,走进学校,没有人大声嚷嚷或者欺侮她,没有人嘲笑这个充满勇气的小女孩。

妮姬给几千人上了一课,做你自己,发挥上帝赐予的天赋,甚至是在半信半疑、痛苦、害怕、迫害中坚持正确的,这些才是唯一的真正生活之路。

妮姬后来高中毕了业。从来没想过的婚姻几年后发生了,妮姬成了一个小女孩的骄傲的母亲。小女孩的名字是她用我小女儿的名字命名的,艾米莉。每次我面对看起来不可能做到的事情时,我都会想到妮姬然后我就会获得力量。

比尔·桑德斯

The Beloved

Where love is, there is God also.

Leo Tolstoy

I was called to the delivery room one night to assist with a term infant because of a small amount of meconium that was present. Meconium is the substance within the bowels of the infant before delivery, and it can sometimes signal distress or abnormality in the infant. It generally requires a pediatrician or other qualified individual to be in attendance. However, most of the time these babies are born without complication and are healthy and normal.

In the delivery room, both mother and father were anxious yet happy as they anticipated the birth of their first baby. The pregnancy had been uneventful. But when the baby was born, it was immediately apparent that there was a significant problem. The baby was anencephalic. This means that there is essentially no upper brain, and the dome of the calvarium, or skull, is also absent. These babies generally don't survive the immediate newborn period, and often they have other significant abnormalities.

The obstetrician immediately handed the baby to me. Even the father, beside himself in anticipation and excitement, could see that the baby was not normal. The mother had not been sedated and, of course, wanted to see her baby right away. The baby did not cry significantly, but it was not in any serious respiratory distress. It did maintain a deep bluish color, indicating the possibility of severe heart disease, which is common in these infants.

双语精华版·心灵鸡汤·

心爱的人

上帝与爱同在。

雷欧·托尔斯托伊

　　有一天晚上,我被叫去分娩室助产一名足月胎儿,因为胎儿排出了少量胎便。在分娩之前,胎便是胎儿肠内的物质,它通常是胎儿有危险或是畸形的信号。一般来说,这就需要小儿科医生或是有经验的人来助产。不过,在大多数情况下,出生前排便的孩子们生下来是没有并发症的,他们是健康正常的。

　　在产房里,父母亲都在既担心又高兴地盼着他们第 1 个孩子的诞生。妊娠期里风平浪静。但是当孩子降生,问题的严重性立即很明显。孩子患有无脑畸形,这就意味着实际上没有大脑上半部,也没有头盖骨,或者说,颅骨也不存在。一般来说,这样的孩子活不过新生儿期,并且他们常常有其他严重的畸形。

　　产科医生立即把婴儿递给我。即使是由于期待和激动而欣喜若狂的父亲也能看到孩子不正常。孩子的母亲没打镇静剂,理所当然想马上就见到她的宝宝。孩子不能大声啼哭,但不存在呼吸危险。孩子的皮肤呈深蓝色,这表明孩子可能有严重的心脏病——这一类婴儿的常见病。

The almost instantaneous emotional sweep that takes place under these circumstances is impossible to describe.One moment everyone is joyous and laughing,joking and high with the expectation of a beautiful baby being born and all the possibilities that life holds.Then,in an instant,emotions sink to the abysmal depth of total disbelief,anger and despair.

I put my arm around the father as we wheeled the baby over to the mother's side.I held her hand and explained the diagnosis.No one could listen carefully at that point.I wrapped the baby up and asked the father to carry the infant to the nursery.I told the mother that we needed to do some initial evaluations,but that we would be back to talk to her soon.

As we walked to the nursery,I asked the father,"What were you going to name the baby?"

He did not respond but asked me,"Will the baby live?"

I answered,"I need to evaluate him more closely."I thought about the vigorous interventions attempted to keep these babies alive for weeks or months or even years,knowing that what we could do was,perhaps,not even morally correct.

In the nursery,the baby began to breathe rapidly.The evaluation of the heart revealed a significant heart lesion.The chest X ray and ultrasound revealed cardiac defects that could not be successfully repaired. The baby had other problems as well,including abnormalities of the kidneys,leaving him without normal renal function.

By this time,the nurses had wheeled the mother into the room where I was examining the baby.After listening to my technical explanations about the multiple problems this baby had,she simply looked up at me and said,"His name is John.It means the beloved one."Then she asked me if they could hold their child.

We went into a private room where the mother could be comfortable in a recliner and the father could sit close,and where they could

这种状况带来的瞬间情感打击无法言表。一度，人人都欢声笑语，开着玩笑，情绪高昂地期待着一个漂亮宝宝的出生和生活带来的所有可能的一切。突然之间，人们陷入深不可测的怀疑、痛苦、绝望的情绪之中。

当我们把婴儿推到母亲身边时我拥抱了一下婴儿的父亲。我握住她的手跟她解释医生的诊断。没人能在那种时候仔细听。我把婴儿包起来，让父亲把婴儿送到婴儿室去。我告诉婴儿的母亲我们先要去做些检查，稍后回来跟她谈。

去婴儿室的路上，我问这位父亲，"你们原打算给宝宝起什么名字？"

他没有回答，却问我，"宝宝会活下来吗？"

我答道，"我得给他做进一步的检查。"我想到那全力以赴的抢救——明知我们所做的也许有悖常理，还试图让婴儿存活数周，个把月，甚或几年。

在婴儿室，婴儿的呼吸开始加快。心脏检查结果显示有严重的心脏缺损。胸部 X 光透视和超声检查显示心脏缺陷不可能被成功修复。婴儿还有其他问题，包括肾脏畸形，使得他没有正常的肾功能。

此时，护士们已经把婴儿的母亲推到我给婴儿体检的房间来。听了我对婴儿的多种问题做出的专业解释，她仅仅抬头看着我说，"他叫约翰。意思是心爱的人。"接着她问我他们能否抱抱孩子。

我们转移到隔离间里，以便母亲能舒适地躺在躺椅上，父亲也能坐近点，在这儿他们既能抱着约翰还能跟他说说话。我准备离开，

both hold John and talk to him.I started to leave but they asked me to stay.

The mother prayed for the baby aloud,then sang songs and lullabies to her son.She told him all about herself and her husband,their hopes and dreams.Over and over again she told him how much they loved him.

I sat spellbound as feelings of despair and hopelessness changed to ones of intense love and caring.One of the most horrific experiences of life had been cast upon this couple,an experience that usually—and un-derstandably—results in anger,hostility and self-pity,as hopes and dreams of watching your child grow up are shattered.But somehow with-in that terrible disappointment,this couple understood that what was most important was for them to give this baby a lifetime of love in the very short time they had with him.As they talked,sang,introduced themselves, and held him tight,they did not see the physical features that often have been described as grotesque.Instead,they saw and felt the soul of one small being who had only a few short hours to live.And,indeed,John died a few minutes later.

That young couple taught me that the value of a life is not depen-dent upon length of time on this earth,but rather on the amount of love given and shared during the time,that we have. They had given all their love to their son.He had truly been their beloved.

James C.Brown,M.D.

他们却叫我留下来。

　　母亲大声地为孩子祷告，然后对着她的儿子唱摇篮曲和别的歌。她告诉他爸爸妈妈的一切，他们的希望和梦想。一遍又一遍地倾诉他们有多爱他。

　　我坐在那儿，像被施了魔咒，绝望和无望的情绪转变成了强烈的爱和关心。人生最可怕的经历降临到这对夫妇的身上。这种经历通常——也可以理解——导致气愤，仇视和自怜，因为看着孩子成长的希望和梦想被粉碎了。但不知怎么的，这对处于极大失望中的夫妇却清楚：对他们而言，最重要的是在和孩子共度的这短短时间内给孩子一生的爱。当他们谈话，唱歌，介绍他们俩时，当他们抱紧他时，他们无视孩子那可用"怪异"来形容的身体特点。相反，他们看见了，感觉到了一个只有短暂几小时生命的小人儿的灵魂。的确，约翰几分钟后就死了。

　　我从这对年轻夫妇身上学到了一个道理：生命的价值不在于在人间生活的时间长短，而在于在我们拥有的时间里接受和分享的爱的多少。他们给了儿子全部的爱。他真的是他们心爱的人。

詹姆士·C. 布朗，医学博士

Nouns and Adverbs

Hope is the parent of faith!

Cyrus Augustus Bartol

Several years ago,a public school teacher was hired and assigned to visit children who were patients in a large city hospital.Her job was to tutor them with their schoolwork so they wouldn't be too far behind when well enough to return to school.

One day,this teacher received a routine call requesting that she visit a particular child.She took the boy's name,hospital and room number and was told by the teacher on the other end of the line,"We're studying nouns and adverbs in class now.I'd be grateful if you could help him with his homework so he doesn't fall behind the others."

It wasn't until the visiting teacher got outside the boy's room that she realized it was located in the hospital's burn unit.No one had prepared her for what she was about to discover on the other side of the door.Before she was allowed to enter,she had to put on a sterile hospital gown and cap because of the possibility of infection.She was told not to touch the boy or his bed.She could stand near but must speak through the mask she had to wear.

When she had finally completed all the preliminary washings and was dressed in the prescribed coverings,she took a deep breath and walked into the room.The young boy,horribly burned,was obviously in great pain.The teacher felt awkward and didn't know what to say,but she had gone too far to turn around and walk out.Finally she was able to

双语精华版·心灵鸡汤·

名词和副词

几年前，一名公办学校的老师受聘参加一项为一家大医院住院的生病儿童提供服务的工作。她的工作是辅导他们学校里学习的功课，以便在他们痊愈后功课不至于落后太多。

一天，该老师像往常一样，接到要求援助的电话，要她去辅导一名特殊的病孩。电话那边的老师告诉了他孩子的姓名，医院的地址和房号并说："我们班现在正在上的课程是名词和副词，如果你能帮他做家庭作业，让他不要落后其他人，我将非常高兴。"

直到这位老师到了病孩的病房门口，她才发现原来是烧伤科，没有人事先告诉她这些。进入病房前，为了防止感染，她必须穿上医院消过毒的白大褂，戴上帽子。她被告知不能触碰孩子的身体和孩子的床。可以离孩子近一点，但必须戴着口罩和他谈话。

当完成了所有预先的消毒清洗，并按规定穿好消毒服后，她深深地叹了一口气，进入病房。

这个小孩子被烧得非常严重，很显然他承受着剧痛。老师感到很无奈，几乎不知该说什么，但她已经来了，又不能退回去。半天，她

stammer out, "I'm the special visiting hospital teacher,and your teacher sent me to help you with your nouns and adverbs." Afterward, she thought it was not one of her more successful tutoring sessions.

The next morning when she returned,one of the nurses on the burn unit asked her, "What did you do to that boy?"

Before she could finish a profusion of apologies, the nurse interrupted her by saying, "You don't understand. We've been worried about him, but ever since you were here yesterday his whole attitude has changed. He's fighting back, responding to treatment…it's as though he's decided to live."

The boy himself later explained that he had completely given up hope and felt he was going to die, until he saw that special teacher. Everything had changed with an insight gained by a simple realization. With happy tears in his eyes, the little boy who had been burned so badly that he had given up hope, expressed it like this: "They wouldn't send a special teacher to work on nouns and adverbs with a dying boy, now, would they?"

Excerpted from Moments for Mothers

双语精华版·心灵鸡汤·

才结结巴巴地说:"我是到医院来的特别教师,你的老师让我来帮助你学习名词和副词。"她认为自己上的这堂辅导课并不那么成功。

第2天上午,老师又来到医院,烧伤科的一名护士问她:"你昨天对那孩子做了什么?"

她开始解释并道歉,护士打断她的话说:"你没明白,我们一直很担心这个孩子,但昨天你来过之后,他的态度全都变了。他的斗志回来了,愿意配合治疗,仿佛他已下定决心要活下去。"

后来,这个孩子谈到当时的情况,他说当时觉得自己就要死了,放弃了一切的希望。当他看到特教老师时,这简单的援助行动让他醒悟过来。一切都变了,这个被烧伤得非常严重,对一切已失去希望的年幼的小孩子,眼里含着幸福的泪水说:"他们不仅仅是派来了一名特教老师来教一个垂死的孩子学习名词和副词,现在,明白他们做了什么吗?"

摘自《致母亲》

Lesson From A Son

My son Daniel's passion for surfing began at the age of 13. Before and after school each day, he donned his wet suit, paddled out beyond the surf line and waited to be challenged by his three-to six-foot companions. Daniel's love of the ride was tested one fateful afternoon.

"Your son's been in an accident,"the lifeguard reported over the phone to my husband Mike.

"How bad?"

"Bad.When he surfaced to the top of the water,the point of the board was headed toward his eye."

Mike rushed him to the emergency room and they were then sent to a plastic surgeon's office.He received 26 stitches from the corner of his eye to the bridge of his nose.

I was on an airplane flying home from a speaking engagement while Dan's eye was being stitched. Mike drove directly to the airport after they left the doctor's office. He greeted me at the gate and told me Dan was waiting in the car.

"Daniel?"I questioned.I remember thinking the waves must have been lousy that day.

"He's been in an accident, but he's going to be fine."

A traveling working mother's worst nightmare had come true.I ran to the car so fast the heel of my shoe broke off.I swung open the door, and my youngest son with the patched eye was leaning forward with both arms stretched out toward me crying, "Oh,Ma,I'm so glad you're home."

儿子给我的启示

　　我儿子丹尼儿迷上冲浪是从 13 岁开始的,每天课前课后,他都套上潜水服,蹚着水到海浪线之外,等着他那帮从 3 英尺到 6 英尺身高不等的同伴们的挑战。一个午后,丹尼儿的爱好遭受到命运的测试。

　　"你的儿子出事了。"救生员打电话给我的丈夫麦克说。

　　"有多糟?"

　　"很糟糕,他冲到浪顶时,冲浪板的尖头戳到了他的眼睛。"

　　麦克把儿子飞快送进了急救室, 然后被安排进了整形手术室。从眼角到鼻梁,丹尼儿缝了 26 针。那时候, 我已结束了外地的演讲活动,正在回家的飞机上。麦克离开医院直接把车开到了机场。在机场门口,他告诉我丹在车上等着。

　　"丹尼儿?"我问道。当时我还以为那天下午不适合冲浪。

　　"他出事了,不过很快会没事的。"

　　四处奔波的职业母亲最担心的事终于发生了。我冲到车旁,鞋跟折断一只。我打开车门,我的小儿子的眼睛包扎着,身体前倾伸着手喊道:"哦,妈妈,你回来我太高兴了。"

I sobbed in his arms telling him how awful I felt about not being there when the lifeguard called.

"It's okay,Mom,"he comforted me."You don't know how to surf anyway."

"What?"I asked,confused by his logic.

"I'll be fine.The doctor says I can go back in the water in eight days."

Was he out of his mind?I wanted to tell him he wasn't allowed to go near water again until he was 35,but instead I bit my tongue and prayed he would forget about surfing forevermore.

For the next seven days he kept pressing me to let him go back on the board.One day after I emphatically repeated "No" to him for the 100th time,he beat me at my own game.

"Mom,you taught us never to give up what we love."

Then he handed me a bribe—framed poem by Langston Hughes that he bought "because it reminded me of you."

Mother To Son

Well,son,I'll tell you:

Life for me ain't been no crystal stair.

It's had tacks in it.

And splinters,

And boards torn up,

And places with no carpet on the floor—

Bare.

But all the time

I'se been a-climbin' on,

And reachin' landin's

And turnin's corners,

And sometimes goin' in the dark

我在他怀里哽咽着,告诉他,我很抱歉,救生员打电话时我不在。

"没问题的,妈妈。"他安慰我道,"你并不懂冲浪。"

"什么?"我被弄糊涂了,问道。

"我没事的,医生说过8天我就能下水了。"

丹尼儿是不是疯了?我很想说:你不到35岁再不许沾水。可是我没开口,心里希望他会永远忘记冲浪。

接下来的7天里,他一直缠着我,要我答应他回冲浪板上。一天,我连声拒绝他的要求后,他"将了我一军"(在我布下的棋局里打败了我)。

"妈妈,你说过,永远不要放弃自己的所爱。"

说着,他递过一面镜框,里面是兰斯顿·休斯的一首诗,他说买这个是"因为它让我惦念着你。"

母亲给儿子的话

呵,孩子,听着:

生活并非为我铺就水晶灿烂的阶梯

其间总有钉刺

和碎片

木板磨损开裂

有些地方没有地毯——

裸露着

然而,

我总在攀登

走上一个又一个楼梯平台

转过一个又一个弯道

有时 走在黑暗中

经典系列／时光的印记

Where there ain't been no light.
So,boy,don't you turn back,
Don't you set down on the steps
'Cause you finds it's kinder hard.
Don't you fall now—
For I'se still goin',honey,
I'se still climbin'
And life for me ain't been no crystal stair.

I gave in.

Back then Daniel was a just a boy with a passion for surfing.Now he's a man with a responsibility.He ranks among the top 25 pro surfers in the world.

I was tested in my own backyard on an important principle that I teach audiences in distant cities:"Passionate people embrace what they love and never give up."

Danielle Kennedy

那里没有一丝光亮

孩子 不要回头

别因为困难放慢你的脚步

不要跌倒——

但我仍然前进

亲爱的，我会继续攀登

生活并未为我铺就水晶般灿烂的阶梯

我放弃了。

回首从前，丹尼儿只是一个痴迷冲浪的孩子，如今他是一个有责任心的男人。他跻身于世界职业冲浪选手的 25 强。我在自家的后院被我远赴异地宣讲的一个重要的人生原则测试了一下。那个原则就是"热情的人们拥抱他们所爱，永不放弃"。

丹妮尔·肯尼迪

Do It Now!

If we discovered that we had only five minutes left to say all that we wanted to say, every telephone booth would be occupied by people calling other people to stammer that they loved them.

Christopher Morley

In a class I teach for adults, I recently did the "unpardonable". I gave the class homework! The assignment was to "go to someone you love within the next week and tell them you love them. It has to be someone you have never said those words to before or at least haven't shared those words with for a long time."

Now that doesn't sound like a very tough assignment, until you stop to realize that most of the men in that group were over 35 and were raised in the generation of men that were taught that expressing emotions is not "macho". Showing feelings or crying (heaven forbid!) was just not done. So this was a very threatening assignment for some.

At the beginning of our next class, I asked if someone wanted to share what happened when they told someone they loved them. I fully expected one of the women to volunteer, as was usually the case, but on this evening one of the men raised his hand. He appeared quite moved and a bit shaken.

As he unfolded out of his chair (all 6′2″of him), he began by saying, "Dennis, I was quite angry with you last week when you gave us this assignment. I didn't feel that I had anyone to say those words to, and

现在就做!

如果我们只剩下5分钟可以说我们想说的话，那么人们就会占领每一个电话亭，然后给别人打电话结结巴巴地说爱他们。

——克里斯托弗·莫莉

最近在一个教成年人的课堂上，我做了"不可饶恕"的事。我给班级布置了家庭作业。作业是"下礼拜去找你爱的人，然后说你爱他们。但必须是那些你从未说过或者至少很长时间没有分享过这些话的人"。

现在看起来不是一个十分棘手的作业，但是想一下，你会发现班上大部分男性已经35岁多了，并且是被教导表达感情不是"男子汉"的一代。从未表露出感情或者哭泣(苍天不容！)。所以对某些人来说这是一个有威胁性的作业。

在我们开始上新课时，我问有没有人愿意分享他告诉别人他爱他们的结果。我满怀希望会是一个女性自愿分享，(因为通常都是这样)，但是这个晚上是一名男性举起了手。他显得相当感动并且有点儿震惊。

当他从椅子上站起来时 (直到完全展开他 6 英尺 2 英寸的身体)，他说："丹尼斯，上周当你给我们布置这个作业的时候我对你很生气。我不觉得我有可以说那些话的人选，另外，你算老几让我做那

经典系列／时光的印记

besides, who were you to tell me to do something that personal? But as I began driving home my conscience started talking to me. It was telling me that I knew exactly who I needed to say 'I love you' to. You see, five years ago, my father and I had a vicious disagreement and really never resolved it since that time. We avoided seeing each other unless we absolutely had to at Christmas or other family gatherings. But even then, we hardly spoke to each other. So, last Tuesday by the time I got home I had convinced myself I was going to tell my father I loved him.

"It's weird, but just making that decision seemed to lift a heavy load off my chest.

"When I got home, I rushed into the house to tell my wife what I was going to do. She was already in bed, but I woke her up anyway. When I told her, she didn't just get out of bed, she catapulted out and hugged me, and for the first time in our married life she saw me cry. We stayed up half the night drinking coffee and talking. It was great!

"The next morning I was up bright and early. I was so excited I could hardly sleep. I got to the office early and accomplished more in two hours than I had the whole day before.

"At 9:00 I called my dad to see if I could come over after work. When he answered the phone, I just said, 'Dad, can I come over after work tonight? I have something to tell you.' My dad responded with a grumpy, 'Now what?' I assured him it wouldn't take long, so he finally agreed.

"At 5:30, I was at my parents' house ringing the doorbell, praying that Dad would answer the door. I was afraid if Mom answered that I would chicken out and tell her instead. But as luck would have it, Dad did answer the door.

"I didn't waste any time—I took one step in the door and said, 'Dad, I just came over to tell you that I love you.'

"It was as if a transformation came over my dad. Before my eyes

么私人的事？但当我驱车回家时,我的内心开始跟我说话。它告诉我完全知道该对谁说"我爱你"。你看,5年前,我和父亲大吵了一架到现在都没有真正解决好。我们避免见到对方,除非是在圣诞节或其他家庭聚会上。即使在那些场合,我们彼此也不说话。所以,上礼拜二我一回到家,我就说服自己我要告诉父亲我爱他。

"有点奇怪,但是做了这个决定就像从我胸口移走了一块大石。

"我回到家,立刻冲进屋子告诉妻子我要干什么。她已经睡了,我还是把她叫醒。我跟她说了以后,她不仅仅下了床,还跳起来拥抱我,而且第1次在我们的婚姻生活里她看到我哭了。我们半个晚上没有睡,喝着咖啡聊着天。这简直太棒了。

"第2天我一大早就起来了。我太兴奋了都没怎么睡。我早早去了办公室,两个小时就完成了以前要一天才能做完的工作。

"9点整,我打电话给父亲看能不能下班后去看他。他拿起电话时,我说,'爸爸,今晚下班后我能去看你吗？ 我有话要对你说。'他不高兴地回答我,'现在你要干什么？'我保证不会占用很长时间,所以他最后同意了。

"5点半,我到了父母家按响门铃,祈祷爸爸会应门。如果妈妈来应门,我就会临阵退缩,并只跟她说。巧得很,爸爸来应门了。

"我没有浪费一点儿时间,一步跨到门里面,说'爸爸,我来就是告诉你我爱你。'

"爸爸好像变了一个人。在我的眼前,他的脸松弛下来,皱纹也

his face softened, the wrinkles seemed to disappear and he began to cry. He reached out and hugged me and said, 'I love you too, son, but I've never been able to say it.'

"It was such a precious moment I didn't want to move.Mom walked by with tears in her eyes.I just waved and blew her a kiss.Dad and I hugged for a moment longer and then I left.I hadn't felt that great in a long time.

"But that's not even my point.Two days after that visit, my dad, who had heart problems but didn't tell me, had an attack and ended up in the hospital, unconscious.I don't know if he'll make it.

"So my message to all of you in this class is this: Don't wait to do the things you know need to be done.What if I had waited to tell my dad—maybe I will never get the chance again! Take the time to do what you need to do and *do it now*! "

Dennis E.Mannering

消失了。他开始哭了。他伸出手来拥抱我,说'我也爱你,儿子。但我从来没能说出口。'

"这是个珍贵的时刻,我不想动。妈妈走过来,眼睛里满是泪花。爸爸和我又拥抱了一会儿,然后我就走了。我很长时间没有感觉这么棒过。

"但那还不是我要说的关键。两天后,我的爸爸,有心脏问题但是没告诉我,心脏病发作,结果在医院里不省人事。我不知道他能不能醒过来。

"所以我要告诉这个班上所有人的话是:不要等着去做你必须做的事。如果我没去和爸爸说会怎样呢?——也许我再也没有机会了。花一点时间去做你必须做的,现在就做。"

丹尼斯·E.曼纳林

121

Such As I Have

What you keep to yourself you lose,what you give away,
you keep forever.

Axel Munthe

With only two weeks before Christmas,the last place I wanted to be was in the hospital recovering from surgery.This was our family's first Christmas in Minnesota,and I wanted it to be memorable,but not this way.

For weeks I had ignored the pain in my left side,but when it got worse,I saw the doctor."Gallstones," he said,peering at the x rays. "Enough to strings a necklace.You'll need surgery right away."

Despite my protests that this was a terrible time to be in the hospital,the gnawing pain in my side convinced me to go ahead with surgery. My husband,Buster,assured me he could take care of things at home,and I called a few friends for help with carpooling.A thousand other things—Christmas baking,shopping and decorating—would have to wait.

I struggled to open my eyes after sleeping for the better part of two days in the hospital following my surgery.As I became more alert,I looked around to what seemed like a Christmas floral shop.Red poinsettias and other bouquets crowded the windowsill.A stack of cards waited to be opened.On the stand next to my bed stood a small tree decorated with ornaments my children had made.The shelf over the sink held a dozen red roses from my parents in Indiana and a yule log with candles from our neighbor.I was overwhelmed by all the love and attention.

像我一样拥有

越保守越容易失去,而一旦给予,你将会永远拥有。

——艾克瑟尔·蒙瑟

离圣诞还有两星期,我却因为做手术要在医院待着。这是我们家第 1 次在明尼苏达过圣诞,我希望是个特别的圣诞,但不该是现在这样。

几个星期来我都没在意左腹的疼痛,但是越来越严重,去了医院,医生看着 X 光片说:"胆结石,足够穿一串项链了,你需要立刻做手术。"

尽管我觉得去医院是十分可怕的,但剧痛让我相信必须得去做手术了。我丈夫布斯特保证他可以照顾好家里。我还找了几个朋友帮忙照顾那辆共用的车。其他许多事,圣诞节烘烤、购物、装饰等,只好以后再说了。

手术后整整睡了两天,当我努力睁开眼睛,吃惊地向周围看去,仿佛是到了圣诞花店,红色的猩猩木和其他花束挤满了窗台。一摞贺卡等着我打开。我的床边立着一棵圣诞树,上面挂满了我的孩子们做的饰物。水槽上方的架子上是我在印第安那州的父母送来的红玫瑰,还有邻居们送来的插着蜡烛的圣诞大蛋糕。我被所有的爱和关心淹没了。

经典系列／时光的印记

Maybe being in the hospital around Christmas isn't so bad after all,I thought.My husband said that friends had brought meals to the family and offered to look after our four children.

Outside my window,heavy snow was transforming our small town into a winter wonderland.The kids have to be loving this,I thought as I imagined them bundled in their snowsuits building a backyard snowman, or skating at Garfield School on the outdoor ice rink.

Would they include Adam,our handicapped son?I wondered.At five years old,he had just started walking independently,and I worried about him getting around on the ice and snow with his thin ankles.Would any-one take him for a sled ride at the school?

"More flowers! " The nurse's voice startled me from my thoughts as she came into the room carrying a beautiful centerpiece.She handed me the card while she made room for the bouquet among the poinsettias on the windowsill.

"I guess we're going to have to send you home,"she teased. "We're out of space here! "

"Okay with me," I agreed.

"Oh,I almost forgot these! "

She took more cards from her pocket and put them on the tray.Be-fore leaving the room,she pulled back the pale green privacy curtain be-tween the two beds.

While I was reading my get-well cards,I heard, "Yep,I like those flowers."

I looked up to see the woman in the bed beside me push the cur-tain aside so she could see better."Yep,I like your flowers,"she repeated.

My roommate was a small 40-something woman with Down's syndrome.She had short,curly,gray hair and brown eyes.Her hospital gown hung untied around her neck,and when she moved forward it ex-posed her bare back.I wanted to tie it for her,but I was still connected to

也许,圣诞节时住院并没有那么糟,我的丈夫说朋友们已经把圣诞节宴席送到家,还帮忙照顾4个孩子。

窗外,大雪已经把我们的小镇变成了孩童们十分喜爱的冬日仙境。我想,他们穿着滑雪装正在屋后堆雪人或者在加菲尔德学校的室外冰场溜冰。

孩子们中有我的残疾儿子亚当吗？5岁时他才能独立行走,在这样的冰雪天,我很担心他柔弱的脚踝,学校里有没有人用雪橇载他？

"好多花啊!"护士的声音惊醒了我,她捧着美丽的花盘走进来。递给我一张卡,并把花放在猩猩木中间。

"我想我们该送你回家了,"她试探着说,"这儿都没有空间了。"

"我也这么想,"我附和着。

"哦,差点忘了这些!"

她从口袋里拿出更多的卡放在盘子里,拉开两床之间的淡绿色帘子,走出房间。

在我读那些祝我康复的卡片时,听到有人说:"嗨,我喜欢这些花。"我抬头看到临床的女士,隔帘拉开了,她可以看清楚,她又说了一遍:"嗨,我喜欢你的那些花。"

我的室友是40岁左右个子矮小的女士,卷卷的灰白色短发,患有唐氏先天愚症。她的住院服没有系上带子,松松地挂在脖子上,往前走时,露出后背。我想替她系上,但连着氧气阀,不能起来。她用孩

an IV.She stared at my flowers with childlike wonder.

"I'm Bonnie," I told her. "What's your name?"

"Ginger," she said,rolling her eyes toward the ceiling and pressing her lips together after she spoke. "Doc's gonna fix my foot.I'm gonna have suur-jeree tomorrow."

Ginger and I talked until dinnertime.She told me about the group home where she lived and how she wanted to get back for her Christmas party.She never mentioned a family,and I didn't ask.Every few minutes she reminded me of her surgery scheduled for the next morning. "Doc's gonna fix my foot," she would say.

That evening I had several visitors,including my son Adam. Ginger chattered merrily to them,telling each about my pretty flowers.But mostly,she kept an eye on Adam.And,later after everyone left,Ginger repeated over and over,just as she had about my flowers, "Yep,I like your Adam."

The next morning Ginger left for surgery,and the nurse came to help me take a short walk down the hall.It felt good to be on my feet.

Soon I was back in our room.As I walked through the door,the stark contrast between the two sides of the room hit me. Ginger's bed stood neatly made,waiting for her return.But she had no cards,no flowers and no visitors.My side bloomed with flowers,and the stack of get-well cards reminded me of just how much I was loved.

No one sent Ginger flowers or a card.In fact,no one had even called or visited.

Is this what it will be like for Adam one day?I wondered,then quickly put the thought from my mind.

I know,I decided.I'll give her something of mine.

I walked to the window and picked up the red-candled centerpiece with holly sprigs.But this would look great on our Christmas dinner table,I thought,as I set the piece back down. What about the poinsettias?

子似的天真又惊喜的眼神盯着那些花。

"我是邦妮,你叫什么名字?"我问她。

"金洁,"她说,抿了抿嘴,眼睛看向天花板,"医生要治疗我的脚,明天我要做手术。"

我和金洁一直谈到晚饭时。她告诉我她与他人合住的家,她多么想回去参加圣诞聚会。她没有提到家人,我也没问。每隔几分钟她都会提醒我她第 2 天的手术,她总会说:"医生就要给我治脚了。"

那天晚上,有几个人来看我,其中有我的儿子亚当。金洁高兴地喋喋不休地与他们交谈,告诉每一个人关于我的那些美丽的花。但是,大多数时候她都在看着我的儿子,等客人都走了,金洁就像谈我的花那样一遍又一遍地重复:"嗨,我喜欢你的亚当!"

第 2 天早上,金洁去做手术了。护士来帮我在厅里散会儿步。我感觉好了很多。

很快,我就回屋了。一进门,屋子里两边鲜明的对比让我吃惊。金洁的床叠得整整齐齐等她手术回来。但没有贺卡,没有花,也没有人来看她。我这边花团锦簇,贺卡成堆,提示我获得了那么多的爱。

没有人送花送卡给金洁,事实上,也没有人给她打电话或来看她。我不知道这样的事是否有一天会发生在亚当身上,我的脑子里突然有了一个念头。

我明白,我做了决定,我要把我的那些分给她。

我走到窗边,拿起插着蜡烛用冬青树叶装饰的花盘。但它放在我们家的圣诞桌上看起来似乎非常好。我一边想一边把它放回去。那么猩猩木怎么样?然而,我觉得那深红色的植物可以放在我家的

Then I realized how much the deep-red plants would brighten the entry of our turn-of-the-century home.And,of course,I can't give away Mom and Dad's roses,knowing we won't see them for Christmas this year,I thought.

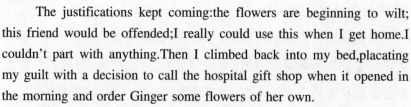

The justifications kept coming:the flowers are beginning to wilt; this friend would be offended;I really could use this when I get home.I couldn't part with anything.Then I climbed back into my bed,placating my guilt with a decision to call the hospital gift shop when it opened in the morning and order Ginger some flowers of her own.

When Ginger returned from surgery,a candy-striper brought her a small green Christmas wreath with a red bow.She hung it on the bare white wall above Ginger's bed.That evening I had more visitors,and even though Ginger was recuperating from surgery,she greeted each one and proudly showed them her Christmas wreath.

After breakfast the next morning,the nurse returned to tell Ginger that she was going home."The van from the group home is on its way to pick you up," she said.

I knew Ginger's short stay meant she would be home in time for her Christmas party.I was happy for her,but I felt my own personal guilt when I remembered the hospital gift shop would not open for two more hours.

Once more I looked around the room at my flowers.Can I part with any of these?

The nurse brought the wheelchair to Ginger's bedside. Ginger gathered her few personal belongings and pulled her coat from the hanger in the closet.

"I've really enjoyed getting to know you,Ginger,"I told her. My words were sincere,but I felt guilty for not following through on my good intentions.

The nurse helped Ginger with her coat and into the wheelchair.

进门处使我们那百年难遇的家更加美丽。当然,一想到今年圣诞我们将见不到爸爸和妈妈,那么他们送的红玫瑰也不行。

理由一个接一个,比如这束花已经开始蔫了,这个朋友不该冒犯,这个拿回家还能用的上,等等,一样也不能放弃。只好回到我的床上,为了安慰自己的内疚,决定等到第 2 天上午医院的礼品店一开门就打电话为金洁订一些属于她自己的花。

金洁手术回来时, 一个长相甜美的军官给她带来一个小小的,上面有红色彩结的绿色圣诞花环。她把它挂在床上方裸露的白墙上。那天晚上,有更多的朋友来看我。尽管金洁刚做过手术,她还是招呼着每一个人,自豪地展示她的圣诞花环。

第 2 天早饭后,护士来告诉金洁她就要回家了,"家里的车已经上路来接你了,"她说。

我知道金洁可以赶得及回去参加圣诞聚会了。我为她高兴,但当我想到医院的礼品店两个小时以后才开门我就很内疚。

我再一次环顾四周房间里的那些花。我可以割舍它们吗?

护士把轮椅推到金洁床边, 金洁收拾好为数不多的个人用品,从壁橱的衣架上拿下外衣。

"我真的很高兴能认识你,金洁,"我对她说。我的话是真诚的,但我为没能坚持自己原来的想法而感到亏欠她。

护士帮助金洁穿上外衣,坐上轮椅。把小花环从墙上的钉子上

Then she removed the small wreath from the nail on the wall and handed it to Ginger.They turned toward the door to leave when Ginger said, "Wait! "

Ginger stood up from her wheelchair and hobbled slowly to my bedside.She reached her right hand forward and gently laid the small wreath in my lap.

"Merry Christmas," she said."You're a nice lady." Then she gave me a big hug.

"Thank you," I whispered.

I couldn't say anything more as she hobbled back to the chair and headed out the door.

I dropped my moist eyes to the small wreath in my hands. Ginger's only gift,I thought.And she gave it to me.

I looked toward her bed.Once again,her side of the room was bare and empty.But as I heard the "ping" of the elevator doors closing behind Ginger,I knew that she possessed much,much more than I.

Bonnie Shepherd

拿下来递给金洁,向门口走去,金洁突然说:"等一等!"

金洁从轮椅上站起来,步伐蹒跚地走到我的床边,伸出右手很优雅的把花环放在我的膝盖上。

"圣诞快乐!"她说,"你人真好。"她拥抱了我,在我耳边说:"谢谢你。"

她又蹒跚着坐回轮椅向门口走去。

我一句话也说不出来,泪眼朦胧地低头看着手中的小花环,金洁唯一的礼物,而她却给了我。

我再次看向她的床那边,房间那边空空的,什么都没有。然而,随着金洁走后听到电梯门"砰"的关上的声音,我知道她拥有很多,比我要多得多。

邦妮·舍佛德

Neither Have I

CHICKEN SOUP

Nature cannot be tricked or cheated.She will give up to you the object of your struggles only after you have paid her price.

Napoleon Hill

It has been my experience that one stumbles across life's most profound lessons in the most unexpected places—places like a neighborhood Little League baseball diamond.

Our sons' first game of the season was scheduled for an evening in early May.Since this particular league included grades six through eight, our older son was a third-year veteran on the team,while his younger brother,a sixth-grader,was among the new recruits.The usual crowd of parents had gathered as I took my seat on a weather-beaten plank,third row from the top.Sandwiched between a cotton candy-faced youngster and somebody's mother,I checked the scoreboard.Fourth inning already. Because the boys had anticipated my late arrival,they instructed me to watch the first base and catcher positions.As my attention moved between them,I glanced at the pitcher's mound.Jason Voldner?

Jason was undoubtedly the most well-liked and good-natured boy on the team,but athletically,his participation had been limited to the alternating positions of right field or bench—the latter,unfortunately,more frequently.Having spent an uncountable number of hours as a spectator (on an equally uncountable number of varying bleachers),it is my belief that every ball field has its own version of Jason Voldner.

我也没有

大自然不会被蒙蔽。只要你付出代价,她就会向你妥协,献上你为之拼搏的物品。

————拿破仑·希尔

我们的长子在这个赛季的首场比赛排在 5 月初的一个晚上。

我有过这样的经历:一个人在最没料到的地方偶然发现生命中最意义深刻的教训——比如街道上的美国少年棒球协会球场。因为这个特殊的协会招收从六年级到八年级的学生,我们的长子是在队里待了 3 年的老手,而他上六年级的弟弟是新招募的队员之一。按惯例家长们都成群结队地来过了,我也坐在从最高排数第 3 排一块饱经风霜的木板上。夹在一个脸像棉花糖的年轻人和某个人的妈妈之间,我查看了一下记分牌。已是第 4 局了。因为孩子们预料到我来的晚,他们授意我盯住一垒和接球手。当我的目光在这两者之间移动时,我注意到了投手的投手板。杰森·沃尔德勒?

杰森毫无疑问是队里最讨人喜欢,性情最好的男孩儿。但从技术上讲,他的参与仅限于在右场和板凳队员之间交替,不幸的是,更多时候是后者。作为一个花了无数的时间的观众(在同样数不清的不同的露天看台上看),我相信每次比赛都有自己版本的杰森·沃尔德勒。

The Jasons of the world show up at a tender young age for their first Saturday morning T-ball practice,oiled glove in hand.By the end of this long awaited "chance to play ball,"the heavy-hearted Jasons return home remembering the boy who hit farther,the boy who ran faster and the boy who actually knew what he was supposed to do with the glove.

CHICKEN SOUP

Ability is not only recognized but utilized,allowing for the exceptional players to become even more so,while the Jasons wait their turn to play the seventh inning.Right field.Their allotted playing time is not only limited,it's conditional:only if the team is already winning.If not,the Jasons have simply been waiting to go home.And yet here was Jason Voldner pitching what I would say was the game of his life.

Turning to comment to anyone willing to listen,I now realized that the "somebody's mother" sitting beside me belonged to Jason."Such talent,"I offered."I've never seen your son pitch before."In a voice of quiet resolve she responded,"Neither have I."And then she told me this story.

Four weeks ago,she had chauffeured a car full of boys,her son included,to this same baseball diamond for their first spring practice.Just before dusk she had sat on her porch swing,dodging the sudden downpour and waiting for the next carpool mother to drop Jason off after practice.As the van pulled up,Jason emerged from behind the sliding door."His face was a combination of dirt smudges and rain streaks and would have masked from anyone but me that he was upset,"she said.

"My immediate concern was for an injury,"Jason's mother continued.But there was none.Probing questions led her no closer to the elusive pain.By bedtime,she knew no more than she did back on the porch. This would change shortly.

"Sometime in the hours that followed,I was awakened by choking sobs.Jason's.At his bedside,broken words were telling his story.'Waiting. Eighth grade. Sick of right field. Eighth grade.'"As Jason's mother calmed her son,he further explained that Matthew,a sixth-grader,was

双语精华版·心灵鸡汤·

这个世界上的杰森们都是在他们脆嫩的年纪第一次出现在周六早晨的儿童棒球练习场上，手里拿着油渍麻花的手套。在长长的打球等待结束后，心情沉重的杰森们一边往家走一边记住了是哪个男孩将球击得更远，是哪个男孩跑得更快，是哪个男孩知道戴着手套应该干什么。

能力不仅要被认可还要派得上用场。为了让候补队员的能力被认可并派上用场，杰森们等着轮到他们打第7局。右场。摊派给他们的打球时间不仅有限，还有条件：只有当球队占上风时。反之，杰森们只能等着回家。现在就是杰森·沃尔德勒在投球，我认为，是他一生最重要的竞赛。

在寻求愿听我评论的人时，我才发现我身边那位某人的妈妈属于杰森。"多有天分，"我主动说。"我以前从没看过您儿子投球。"她声音颇坚定地答道，"我也没有看过。"然后她跟我讲了这个故事。

4周前，她驾驶着一辆满载男孩的车，她的儿子也在其中，来到这同一个棒球场，那是他们的第1次春季练习。天黑前，她坐在门廊的秋千上，躲过了一阵大雨，等着合伙用车的另一个妈妈在练习结束后把杰森送回来。车子开走后，杰森从侧门后面冒出来。"他的脸上满是污垢和一条条雨水的痕迹，这可以在别人面前掩饰他的沮丧，但骗不了我。"她说。

"我的第1个反应就是看看他是否受伤了。"杰森的妈妈继续说着。但没有伤。她刨根问底，也没问出是什么难以捉摸的伤痛。直到睡觉时她还跟在门廊时一样一无所知。很快事情就有转机了。

"不知过了多久，我被哽咽声弄醒。是杰森在哭。我坐在他床边，他断断续续地道出了原委。'等待。八年级。讨厌右场。八年级。'"妈妈使杰森平静下来后，他又说了些：马修，六年级，打第2垒，"因

going to play second base "because his dad is coaching";John,a sixth-grader,was assigned to shortstop "because he's Matthew's friend";and Brian,yet another sixth-grader,was the new catcher "because his brother is on the team."

I found myself bristling here and wondered where her story was going.Brian was my younger son.

"Not fair.Not fair.Not fair."Listening to Jason,his mother's heart ached for him.There should be a word that takes empathy to another level;a word for the exclusive use of parents.

"While my son was waiting for me to agree with him,"said his mother,"I was making the difficult decision not to.One has to be careful when having a direct and lasting effect on another person's negative emotions.Agreement may appear to be the most caring and loyal means of help,but in reality,it can work to the contrary as you reinforce the negative feelings.

"So first I explained to Jason that until we were ready to assist the coach with his responsibilities,we would trust his judgments."

"Secondly,I reminded him how seldom we passed the vacant lot on the corner of our block without finding the three sixth-graders in question involved in a random,unscheduled game of ball.Playing infield is not about being in the sixth grade or the eighth;it's about working hard and capability,not preferential treatment.All through your life you are going to come into contact with individuals possessing a natural talent for what they are pursuing—on the ball field,in the classroom,in the workplace.Does this mean you are unable to achieve what they have? Certainly not.You simply have to choose to work harder.Resentment, blame and excuses only poison potential."

Finally,Jason's mother tucked him back into bed.As she smoothed the covers over him,she said to her son,"You're disappointed that the coach doesn't believe in you,Jason,but before you can expect others to

为他爸爸是教练"；约翰，六年级，被分派当游击手，"因为他是马修的朋友"；布莱恩，六年级的，是新的接球手，"因为他哥哥在队里"。

我发现自己毛发竖起，想知道事情的进展。布莱恩是我的小儿子。

"不公平。不公平。不公平。"听着杰森的话，母亲为他心痛。应该有个词比"同情"能表达更深一层意思，应该有个词供家长专用。

"当儿子等着我同意他的看法时，"他母亲说，"我正在艰难地做出不同意的决定。当一个人对另一个人的不良情绪有直接的持久的影响时，他得小心行事。同意也许是最体贴的最忠诚的帮助方式，但在现实中，它却起着反作用，因为你强化了不良情绪。

"因此，首先我向杰森解释在我们能帮教练当教练之前，我们要相信教练的判断。"

"其次，我提醒他在路过街区拐角的空地时很少不发现他怀疑的 3 个男孩在参与随时的计划外的球赛。上场比赛不在于是在六年级还是八年级；而是关乎刻苦练习和能力，和优待无关。终其一生，你始终会遇到一些人，天生具有从事他们的追求所需要的才能——在球场上，在教室里，在工作上。难道这意味着你不能得到他们拥有的吗？当然不是。你只得更加刻苦。憎恨，责备和借口只会毒害潜能。"

最后，杰森的妈妈把他塞回被窝里。当她为孩子将平盖被时，她对儿子说，"杰森，你很失望教练不相信你，但是在你期望别人相信你之前，你得相信自己。教练的安排基于他到目前为止观察到的表

believe in you,you have to believe in yourself.The coach is basing his placements on the performance he has seen thus far.If you truly feel you deserve a position other than right field,then prove it."With those words she kissed him goodnight.

Jason's mother laughed softly."We spoke more in those few minutes than we have pretty much in the weeks since.Our contact recently has been through notes that Jason leaves me on the kitchen table:'Gone to practice.Gone to prove it.'" She paused."And he did."

Yes,it has been my experience that one stumbles across life's most profound lessons in the most unexpected places—like the neighborhood Little League baseball diamond,while sitting on a weather-beaten plank, third row from the top.

Rochelle M.Pennington

现。如果你真正觉得你配得上除右场外的其他位置,就证明它。"说完, 她吻吻他道了晚安。

杰森的妈妈温柔地笑起来。"我们在这几分钟里说的话比之后几个 星期说的都多。我们近来通过杰森在厨房餐桌上给我留的便条联系: '练习去了,证明去了。'"她停顿了一下。"他这么做了。"

坐在从最高排数第 3 排一块饱经风霜的木板上,是的,这是我的 亲身经历,一个人在最没料到的地方偶然发现生命中最意义深刻的 教训——比如街道上的美国少年棒球协会球场。

罗切尔·M.裴宁顿

Remember, We're Raising Children, Not Flowers!
记住，我们是在养孩子，而不是养花儿！

David, my next-door neighbor, has two young kids ages five and seven. One day he was teaching his seven-year-old son Kelly how to push the gas-powered lawn mower around the yard. As he was teaching him how to turn the mower around at the end of the lawn, his wife, Jan, called to him to ask a question. As David turned to answer the question, Kelly pushed the lawn mower right through the flower bed at the edge of the lawn—leaving a two-foot wide path leveled to the ground!

When David turned back around and saw what had happened, he began to lose control. David had put a lot of time and effort into making those flower beds the envy of the neighborhood. As he began to raise his voice to his son, Jan walked quickly over to him, put her hand on his shoulder and said, "David, please remember...we're raising children, not

大卫是我的隔壁邻居，有两个5岁和7岁大的孩子。这天，他正教他7岁的儿子凯利如何在院子里操纵燃油割草机。正当他教凯利如何在草坪尽头使割草机调头时，他的妻子简唤他说要问他个问题。大卫便扭头回答她的问题，这时凯利驱动割草机径直冲过紧挨着草坪的花床——在花床中犁出一道两英尺宽的土路！

当大卫转身看见眼前的一切，他发起火来，他花了很多时间和精力使那些花床成为街坊邻居羡慕的对象。他提高嗓音冲着儿子叫时，简快步朝他走来，把手放在他肩上，说："大卫，请记住……我们

flowers！"

Jan reminded me how important it is as a parent to remember our priorities.Kids and their self-esteem are more important than any physical object they might break or destroy.The window pane shattered by a baseball,a lamp knocked over by a careless child,or a plate dropped in the kitchen are already broken.The flowers are already dead.I must remember not to add to the destruction by breaking a child's spirit and deadening his sense of liveliness.

......

I was buying a sport coat a few weeks ago and Mark Michaels,the owner of the store,and I were discussing parenting.He told me that while he and his wife and seven-year-old daughter were out for dinner,his daughter knocked over her water glass.After the water was cleaned up without any recriminating remarks from her parents,she looked up and said, "You know,I really want to thank you guys for not being like other parents.Most of my friends' parents would have yelled at them and given them a lecture about paying more attention.Thanks for not doing that！"

Once,when I was having dinner with some friends,a similar incident happened.Their five-year-old son knocked over a glass of milk at the dinner table.When they immediately started in on him,I intentionally knocked my glass over,too.When I started to explain how I still knock things over even at the age of *48*,the boy started to beam and the parents seemingly got the message and backed off.How easy it is to forget that we are all still learning.

......

I recently heard a story from Stephen Glenn about a famous research scientist who had made several very important medical breakthroughs.He was being interviewed by a newspaper reporter who asked him why he thought he was able to be so much more creative than the average person.What set him so far apart from others?

是在养孩子,而不是养花儿!"

简提醒了我,作为父母记住事情的轻重缓急有多重要,孩子们和他们的自尊比任何他们毁掉或破坏的物质的东西都重要。被篮球砸碎的窗玻璃,被一个不小心的孩子撞倒的落地灯,或掉在厨房地上的碟子,统统都已经损坏了。那些花儿也已经死了。我必须记住不能再雪上加霜地摧残孩子的精神,扼杀他们的活力。

……

几周前我到马克·麦克司的店里买一件运动外套时和他讨论育儿之道。他聊起一件事。他和妻子带着7岁的女儿出去吃饭时,女儿打翻了她的水杯。见父母没有一句责备的话就把水擦干净,女儿抬头看着他们说,"你知道,我真心谢谢你俩没有像别的父母亲那样。我大多数朋友的父母都会冲着他们大吼大叫,再给他们上一节关于如何更加小心的课。谢谢你们没有那么做!"

有一回,我和几个朋友在外聚餐,发生了一件类似的事。朋友5岁大的儿子打翻了餐桌上的一杯牛奶。马上朋友夫妇俩就瞪着儿子。这时,我故意打翻我的那杯牛奶。当我开始解释我都48岁了怎么还会打翻牛奶时,那男孩两眼开始放光,那对夫妇亦心领神会,恢复原态。人是多么容易忘记我们所有人都还在学习之中。

……

最近我听史蒂芬·格兰讲了个故事,是关于一位做出杰出医学贡献的著名科学家。他在接受一名记者的采访时被问及为何他能够远比普通人更具创造性。是什么使他远远胜过其他人呢?

He responded that, in his opinion, it all came from an experience with his mother that occurred when he was about two years old. He had been trying to remove a bottle of milk from the refrigerator when he lost his grip on the slippery bottle and it fell, spilling its contents all over the kitchen floor—a veritable sea of milk!

When his mother came into the kitchen, instead of yelling at him, giving him a lecture or punishing him, she said, "Robert, what a great and wonderful mess you have made! I have rarely seen such a huge puddle of milk. Well, the damage has already been done. Would you like to get down and play in the milk for a few minutes before we clean it up? "

Indeed, he did. After a few minutes, his mother said, "You know, Robert, whenever you make a mess like this, eventually you have to clean it up and restore everything to its proper order. So, how would you like to do that? We could use a sponge, a towel or a mop. Which do you prefer? "He chose the sponge and together they cleaned up the spilled milk.

His mother then said, "You know, what we have here is a failed experiment in how to effectively carry a big milk bottle with two tiny hands. Let's go out in the back yard and fill the bottle with water and see if you can discover a way to carry it without dropping it." The little boy learned that if he grasped the bottle at the top near the lip with both hands, he could carry it without dropping it. What a wonderful lesson!

This renowned scientist then remarked that it was at that moment that he knew he didn't need to be afraid to make mistakes. Instead, he learned that mistakes were just opportunities for learning something new, which is, after all, what scientific experiments are all about. Even if the experiment "doesn't work", we usually learn something valuable from it.

他答道,在他看来,这源自于两岁时他与母亲的一次经历。那次,他试图从冰箱里拿出一瓶牛奶,奶瓶太滑,他失手将奶瓶打碎了,泼出来的牛奶盖满了厨房的地面——真正是一片牛奶的海洋!

　　母亲闻声赶到厨房后既没斥责他或给他讲一堆道理,也没惩罚他。相反,她说:"罗伯特,你弄了多么伟大而精彩的一团糟啊!我还没见过这么巨大的一个牛奶池呢。既然损失已经造成,在我们清理之前你不想下来在这牛奶里玩会儿吗?"

　　他果真这样做了。玩了一会儿之后,他母亲说:"你知道,罗伯特,无论你何时制造了这一类的混乱,最后你都得打扫干净,把每样东西放回原位。那么,你该怎么清理呢?我们可以用一块海绵,一条毛巾,或一把拖把。你愿意用哪一个?"他选择了海绵,然后他们共同清扫了泼出来的牛奶。

　　他的母亲后来说:"看,我们做了一次失败的实验,尝试如何才能用两只小手端一大瓶牛奶。让我们到后院用水装满这个瓶子,看看你能不能找到方法来端住它不让它掉到地上。"小男孩学到了如果用双手抓住靠近瓶盖的瓶颈处,瓶子就不会掉到地上。多么精彩的一课啊!

　　这位著名的科学家接着评论道,在那一刻,他知道了他无需害怕犯错。相反,他知道了犯错只不过是学习新东西的机会罢了。别忘了,新东西就是科学实验的全部。即使实验是失败的,通常我们也会从中学到有价值的新东西。

経典系列／时光的印记

Wouldn't it be great if all parents would respond the way Robert's mother responded to him?

……

One last story that illustrates the application of this attitude in an adult context was told by Paul Harvey on the radio several years back.A young woman was driving home from work when she snagged her fender on the bumper of another car.She was in tears as she explained that it was a new car,only a few days from the showroom.How was she ever going to explain the damaged car to her husband?

The driver of the other car was sympathetic,but explained that they must note each other's license numbers and registration numbers.As the young woman reached into a large brown envelope to retrieve the documents,a piece of paper fell out.In a heavy masculine scrawl were these words:"In case of accident...remember,honey,it's you I love,not the car！ "

……

Let's remember that our children's spirits are more important than any material things.When we do,self-esteem and love blossom and grow more beautifully than any bed of flowers ever could.

Jack Canfield

如果所有的父母对孩子的行为做出反应的方式都像罗伯特的妈妈那样，该多好啊！

……

最后一个说明应用这种态度的故事是有关成年人的。保罗·哈维几年前在广播里讲述过。一位年轻女人下班后驾车回家时车子的挡泥板撞上了另一辆车的保险杠。她哭哭啼啼地念叨这是辆新车，离开陈列室才几天。她该怎么向丈夫解释撞坏的车呀？

另一辆车的车主虽然同情，仍然解释说他们必须抄下对方驾照的编号和车子的注册号。年轻女人伸手到一个巨大的棕色信封里找证件，这时，一张纸掉了出来。纸上是充满阳刚气的潦草字迹："万一遇上车祸……记住，亲爱的，我爱的是你，不是车！"

……

让我们记住：我们的孩子们的精神比任何物质的东西都更重要。一旦我们记住这点，自尊和爱便蓬勃生长，比任何花都生长的更美丽。

杰克·坎菲尔德

145

A Matter of Honor

CHICKEN SOUP

One looks back with appreciation to the brilliant teach-ers,but with gratitude to those who touched our human feel-ings.The curriculum is so much necessary new material,but the warmth is the vital element for the growing plant and for the soul of the child.

Carl Jung

Since kindergarten,the staff at Abraham Lincoln and Thomas Edison elementary schools in Daly City,California,had seen the results of my mother's alcoholic outrage.

In the beginning,my teachers gently probed me about my paper-thin,shredded clothes,my offensive body odor,the countless bruises and burns on my arms,as well as why I hunted for food from garbage cans. One day my second-grade teacher,Ms. Moss,demanded a meeting with the school principal and pleaded with him to do something to help me. The principal reluctantly agreed to intervene.The next morning Mother and the principal had a private meeting.I never saw Ms.Moss again.

Immediately after that,things went from bad to worse.I was forced to live and sleep in the downstairs garage,ordered to perform slave-like chores,and received no food unless I met my mother's stringent time requirements for her demands.Mother had even changed my name from "David" to "It", and threatened to punish my brothers if they tried to sneak me food,use my real name or even look at me.

The only safe haven in my life were my teachers.They seemed to

光荣的事

自打上幼儿园以来,加利福尼亚州戴利市,亚伯拉罕·林肯及托马斯·爱迪生小学的教职员工都看到了,我残暴的酒鬼妈妈带来的后果。

开始时,我的老师们逐步了解关于我的事,有关我单薄的身体、破旧的衣服、熏人的体味、数不清的瘀痕、胳膊上的灼伤,及为什么我要在垃圾筒里找吃的等。一天,我的二年级老师,茂斯夫人找到校长,并与其争辩,想找到帮助我的办法,校长勉强答应介入,第2天上午,妈妈和校长进行了私人交谈。从此后,我再也没见到茂斯夫人。

此事后,情况越来越糟,我只能睡在楼下的车库里做着奴隶式的工作。只有在妈妈严格的时间规定内完成工作才能吃到东西,妈妈甚至不再喊我的名字"大卫",而叫我"那东西",并威胁我的兄弟们,如果他们敢偷偷给我吃的东西,叫我的名字,甚至只是看我一眼都要受到惩罚。

我唯一的避风港就是我的老师们。他们仿佛始终都在想办法让

always go out of their way to make me feel like a normal child.Whenever one of them showered me with praise,I cherished every word.If one of my teachers brushed up against me as he or she bent over to check on my assignments,I absorbed the scent of their perfume or cologne.During the weekends,as I sat on top of my hands in the garage and shivered from the cold,I employed my secret weapon.I closed my eyes,took a deep breath and tried to picture my teacher's face.Only when I visualized my teacher's smile did I begin to feel warm inside.

But years later,one Friday afternoon,I lost control and stormed out of my fifth-grade homeroom class.I ran to the bathroom,pounded my tiny red fists against the tiles and broke down into a waterfall of tears.I was so frustrated because for months I could no longer see my saviors in my dreams.I desperately believed their life force had somehow kept me alive.But now,with no inner strength to draw upon,I felt so hollow and alone inside.　Later that afternoon,once my peers scurried from the classroom to their homes or the playgrounds at hypersonic speeds,I dared myself and locked my eyes onto my homeroom teacher,Mr. Ziegler.For a fragment of time I knew he felt the immensity of my pain. A moment later I broke our stare,bowed my head in respect and turned away,somehow hoping for a miracle.

Months later my prayers were answered.On March 5,1973,for some unknown reason,four teachers,the school nurse and the principal collectively decided to notify the authorities.Because of my condition,I was immediately placed into protective custody.　But before I left,the entire staff,one by one,knelt down and held me.I knew by the look on everyone's faces that they were scared.My mind flashed back to the fate of Ms.Moss.I wanted to run away and dissolve.As a child called "It," I felt I was not worth their trouble.

As always my saviors sensed my anxiety and gave me a strong hug,as if to form an invisible shield to protect me from all harm.With

我感觉自己和普通的孩子一样。当他们一个劲地表扬我时，每一个字都给了我温暖。当他们靠近我，弯下身检查我的功课时，我贪恋他们身上香水的香味。周末时，我坐在车库里，手冻得瑟瑟发抖，我就调动我的秘密武器。我闭上眼睛，深深吸一口气，脑子里描画着老师的脸。只有我想起老师们的笑容时，我的内心才开始感到温暖。

但是，几年之后，一个星期五的下午，我再也忍不住了，愤怒地从我上课的 5 年级教室冲出来，跑进洗手间，用我小小的充血的拳头拼命敲打着墙上的瓦砾，号啕大哭。我受到沉重的打击，因为几个月来，我在睡梦中见不到我的救世主。我坚信是他们在支持着我生存下去，然而现在我失去了内心支持的力量，感到无比的空虚和孤独，那天下午的晚些时候，我飞快地扫视着教室、老师宿舍和操场。我鼓励自己并把目光停留在我们班的老师仁格勒先生身上，片刻之后，我知道他已感受到我的巨大痛苦。过了一会儿，我移开目光向老师鞠躬表示我的崇敬，离开时心中一丝希望奇迹般地升起。

几个月后，我的祈祷有了回应，1973 年 3 月 5 号，不知因为什么，4 名老师、学校的护士和校长决定集体向上级报告此事。鉴于我目前的状况，我被立即实行了保护性监管。但是，在我离开时，学校里所有的教职员工，一个接一个蹲下身来抱着我，从他们每一个人的脸上可以看出，他们很不安。我的脑海中立刻闪现出茂斯夫人的命运。

我想逃开，作为一个被叫做"那东西"的孩子，我觉得自己不值得他们为我烦恼。

像以往一样，我的救星们感觉到我的悲痛，紧紧地抱着我，仿佛要为我筑一道屏障，以保护我不受到伤害。在每一个温暖的怀抱里，

each warm body I closed my eyes and tried to capture the moment for all eternity.With my eyes clamped shut,I heard one of my teachers gently whisper,"No matter the outcome,no matter what happens to us,this is something we had to do.As teachers if we can have an effect on one child's life…This is the true meaning of our profession."

After a round of good-byes,I stood paralyzed—I had never in all my life felt such an outpouring of emotion for me.And with tears streaming down my cheeks,I promised the staff at Thomas Edison Elementary that I would never forget them and I would do my best to someday make them proud.

Since my rescue,not a single day has passed that I have not thought about my saviors.Almost 20 years to the day,I returned to Thomas Edison Elementary and presented my teachers with the very first copies of my first book,*A Child Called* "It," which was dedicated to them,and was published on the 20-year anniversary of my rescue—March 5,1993.That evening my teachers sat in the front row of a capacity-filled auditorium, as I fulfilled my lifetime dream of making my teachers feel special.I looked at them,with tears now running down their faces,and said,"As a child I learned that teachers have but one goal:to somehow make a difference in the life of a child.In my case it was four teachers,my school nurse and my principal who fought and risked their careers to save the life of a child called 'It'. I cannot,nor will not,ever forget their courage and their conviction.Twenty years ago I made a promise to my teachers. And tonight I renew my vow.For me it is not a matter of maintaining a pledge to those who had an effect on my life.For me,it is simply a matter of honor."

Dave Pelzer

双语精华版·心灵鸡汤·

我闭上眼睛努力地想要永远抓住这一刻。我的眼睛紧紧地闭着,听到我的老师柔柔的耳语,"无论结果如何,无论什么事将会发生在我们身上,这都是我们必须做的。作为老师,如果我们能对孩子的一生起到一点作用……才是我们这个职业真正的含义。"

和所有人道别后,我呆呆地站在那里,我还从没感受到如此强烈的感情。我热泪满面,向所有爱迪生小学的老师们保证我永远不会忘记他们。我要拼命努力,总有一天让他们为我骄傲。

我得到救助后,每一天都在思念着我的救世主。至今已经20年了。我回到托马斯·爱迪生小学,向我的老师们奉献我写的第一本书的首批样书。这是专门为老师们写的,是在1993年3月5日我获救20周年纪念日出版的。那天晚上,在坐满听众的礼堂的前排,坐着我的老师们,我完成了让我的老师感到骄傲的终身梦想。我看着他们,现在他们脸上流淌着热泪。我说:"还是孩子时,我就知道老师只有唯一的一个目标,那就是想办法改变孩子们的人生。为了我,4名老师,我们学校的护士和校长,冒着失去工作的风险,为挽救一个被叫做"那东西"的孩子一生而抗争。我不能也永远不会忘记他们的勇气和坚定的信念。20年前,我给了老师们一个承诺,而今晚,我将再次保证我的誓言。对我来说,对于那些影响我一生的人,这不仅仅是一个永远的誓言,它其实是一件光荣的事。"

戴夫·培尔泽

The Little Lady Who Changed My life

She was four years old when I first met her.She was carrying a bowl of soup.She had very,very fine golden hair and a little pink shawl around her shoulders.I was *29* at the time and suffering from the flu.Little did I realize that this little lady was going to change my life.

Her mom and I had been friends for many years.Eventually that friendship grew into care,from care into love,to marriage,and marriage brought the three of us together as a family.At first I was awkward because in the back of my mind,I thought I would be stuck with the dreaded label of "stepfather".And stepfathers were somehow mythically, or in a real sense,ogres as well as an emotional wedge in the special relationship between the child and the biological father.

Early on I tried hard to make a natural transition from bachelor hood to fatherhood.A year and a half before we married,I took an apartment a few blocks away from their home.When it became evident that we would marry,I tried to spend time to enable a smooth changeover from friend to father figure.I tried not to become a wall between my future daughter and her natural father.Still,I longed to be something special in her life.

Over the years,my appreciation for her grew.Her honesty,sincerity and directness were mature beyond her years.I knew that within this child lived a very giving and compassionate adult.Still,I lived in the fear that some day,when I had to step in and be a disciplinarian,I might

双语精华版·心灵鸡汤·

改变我生活的小女士

当我第一次看见她时,她才 4 岁,正端着碗汤。她有非常非常漂亮的金发,肩上裹着一条粉色披肩。当时我 29 岁,正患感冒。我几乎没有意识到这位小小的女士将要改变我的生活。

她妈妈和我是多年的朋友,最后这段友谊变成了关心,由关心变成爱情,又由爱情变成婚姻,这段婚姻让我们 3 个在一起组成了一个家。一开始我有点尴尬,因为在我心底,我认为我会被贴上那可怕的标签"继父"。继父,在神话里或在实际意义上,是怪物也是孩子和亲生父亲之间特殊情感中的一根刺。

早先我努力自然地从光棍汉过渡到父亲,在我们结婚前一年半,我在离她家几个街区远的地方找了个公寓。当我们确定要结婚时,我尽量花时间来平稳地从朋友过渡到父亲的角色。我尽量不使自己成为我未来的女儿和她生父之间的一堵墙,不过我依然渴望在她的人生中有着特殊地位。

这些年来我对她的欣赏与日俱增,她诚实、真诚、坦率,超过她年龄的成熟。我知道这孩子骨子里其实是一个非常乐于奉献的成年人,但我依然生活在恐惧之中,担心有一天,当我不得不涉足扮演一

have it thrown in my face that I wasn't her "real" father. If I wasn't real, why would she have to listen to me? My actions became measured. I was probably more lenient than I wanted to be. I acted in that way in order to be liked, all the time living out a role I felt I had to live— thinking I wasn't good enough or worthy enough on my own terms.

During the turbulent teenage years, we seemed to drift apart emotionally. I seemed to lose control (or at least the parental illusion of control). She was searching for her identity and so was I. I found it increasingly hard to communicate with her. I felt a sense of loss and sadness because I was getting further from the feeling of oneness we had shared so easily in the beginning.

Because she went to a parochial school, there was an annual retreat for all seniors. Evidently the students thought that going on retreat was like a week at Club Med. They boarded the bus with their guitars and racquetball gear. Little did they realize that this was going to be an emotional encounter that could have a lasting impression on them. As parents of the participants, we were asked to individually write a letter to our child, being open and honest and to write only positive things about our relationship. I wrote a letter about the little golden-haired girl who had brought me a bowl of soup when I needed care. During the course of the week, the students delved deeper into their real beings. They had an opportunity to read the letters we parents had prepared for them.

The parents also got together one night during that week to think about and send good thoughts to our children. While she was away, I noticed something come out of me that I knew was there all along, but which I hadn't faced. It was that in order to be fully appreciated I had to plainly be me. I didn't have to act like anyone else. I wouldn't be overlooked if I was true to myself. I just had to be the best me I could be. It may not sound like much to anyone else, but it was one of the biggest revelations of my life.

个管教者,她可能会说我不是她真正的父亲。如果我不是真的,她为何必须听我的话呢?我的行为变得谨慎。我可能比我想象的表现的更宽容。我这样做是为了被她喜欢,自始至终我都在扮演自认为必须扮演的角色——认为我还不够好或者和我的身份不相称。

在这恼人的十来岁年纪里,从情感上我们似乎越来越远,我似乎失控了,她在寻找她的身份,我也是。我发现越来越难以和她交流,我感到失落、沮丧,因为最初我们是一个整体,现在我却离这种感觉越来越远。

因为她去了一个教会学校,那个学校里高年级学生每年都有一次静修,显然学生们把这当成随"地中海俱乐部"休假一周(club med 为 Club Méditerranée 的缩写,是一家法国度假旅游公司,组团前往世界各地名胜,通常是极具异域风情的区域)。她们带着吉他和壁球用具登上车,一点没有意识到这将是一次对他们产生持续影响的情感遭遇。作为参加者的父母,我们被要求给孩子写封信,要开诚布公诚实的写我们之间关系的积极方面。我写到了那个金发的小女孩在我需要照顾的时候,给我端来一碗汤。在这一个星期的假期里学生们更深地发掘出他们真正的自我。他们有机会读到身为父母的我们为他们准备的信。

在那一个星期里,有天晚上家长们也聚在一起,考虑如何向孩子们传输好的思想,当她离开时,我注意到有什么东西离开了我的身体,我知道那是什么,但我不曾面对,为了赢得她的赏识,我必须做回真实的自我。我不需要像其他人那样做,如果我能真实面对自己,我就不会被忽略,我只需要尽力做到最好。在其他人听来这不算什么,但却是我一生的最大发现之一。

The night arrived when they came home from their retreat experience.The parents and friends who had come to pick them up were asked to arrive early,and then invited into a large room where the lights were turned down low.Only the lights in the front of the room were shining brightly.

The students marched joyously in,all dirty-faced as though they had just come back from summer camp.They filed in arm-in-arm, singing a song they had designated as their theme for the week.Through their smudgy faces,they radiated a new sense of belonging and love and self-confidence.

When the lights were turned on,the kids realized that their parents and friends,who had come to collect them and share their joy,were also in the room.The students were allowed to make a few statements about their perceptions of the prior week.At first they reluctantly got up and said things like,"It was cool," and "Awesome week," but after a few moments you could begin to see a real vitality in the students'eyes. They began to reveal things that underscored the importance of this rite of passage.Soon they were straining to get to the microphone.I noticed my daughter was anxious to say something.I was equally anxious to hear what she had to say.

I could see my daughter determinedly inching her way up to the microphone.Finally she got to the front of the line.She said something like,"I had a great time,and I learned a lot about myself."She continued,"I want to say there are people and things we sometimes take for granted that we shouldn't,and I just want to say … I love you,Tony."

At that moment my knees got weak.I had no expectations,no anticipation she would say anything so heartfelt.Immediately people around me started hugging me,and patting me on the back as though they also understood the depth of that remarkable statement.For a teenage girl to say openly in front of a room full of people,"I love you,"took a great

他们静修完回家的那个晚上，来接他们的父母和朋友被要求早点到，然后被请到一个光线调得很暗的大屋子里，只有门廊里的灯很亮的照着。

孩子们愉快地排队进来。脸都脏兮兮，就像他们刚从夏令营回来似的，他们手拉手鱼贯而入，唱着属于这个星期的指定的主题歌。他们满是灰尘的脸放着光，充满爱和自信。

当灯光打亮的时候，孩子们发现来接他们和分享他们快乐的父母和朋友们也在屋子里。学生们被允许说几句对前一周的理解。一开始他们都不情愿站起来，只说了些诸如酷，不错的一周之类的话，但没过一会，你就能看到他们眼睛里的活力。他们开始说一些强调这次活动的重要性的事。很快他们争着去拿麦克风，我注意到女儿也急切地想说点什么，我也同样急切地想听她想说的话。

我看到女儿坚定地走向麦克风，最后她走到队前，她说了这些话："我玩得很快乐，我更了解了自己"，她继续说，"我想说，我们常常想当然地看待有些人和事，而我们不该那样看待，我只想说……我爱你，托尼。"

在那一刻，我膝盖发软，我没有想到也没指望她会说这么贴心的话。话音刚落，周围的人就开始拥抱我，拍我的背，似乎他们也懂那番话的深意。对于一个十来岁的女孩而言，在一屋子人的面前，公开说"我爱你"需要很大的勇气。如果说有什么比不知所措程度还深

deal of courage.If there were something greater than being over-whelmed,I was experiencing it.

Since then the magnitude of our relationship has increased.I have come to understand and appreciate that I didn't need to have any fear about being a stepfather.I only have to concern myself with being the real person who can exchange honest love with the same little girl I met so many years before—carrying a bowl full of what turned out to be kindness.

Tony Luna

的话,我正在体验。

从那以后,我们感情的强度增加了,我开始明白并意识到我无须担心自己是个继父,我只需关注做一个真实的人和我多年前遇见的同一个小女孩交换真实的爱——她端着满满一碗善意。

托尼·路纳

Beautiful on the Inside
内在美

Love is a wonderful thing. You never have to take it away from one person to give it to another. There's always more than enough to go around.

Pamela J.deRoy

爱是美妙的，你不必把它从某人身上拿走送给其他人，因为总有足够的爱让你去传播。

帕梅拉·J.德洛伊

Lisa,my two-year-old daughter,and I were walking down the street toward home one sunny morning when two elderly women stopped in front of us.Smiling down at Lisa,one of them said,"Do you know you are a very beautiful little girl?"

Sighing and putting her hand on her hip,Lisa replied in a bored voice,"Yes,I know! "

A bit embarrassed by my daughter's seeming conceit,I apologized

一天上午,阳光明媚,我和两岁的女儿丽莎走在回家的路上。迎面走来两位年长的女士,停下来,微笑着看着丽莎说:"你知道你是个漂亮的小姑娘吗?"

丽莎叹了一口气,小手放在屁股上不耐烦地说:"我知道。"

她们被我女儿的自负弄得有点尴尬,我连忙向两位女士道歉。

to the two ladies and we continued our walk home.All the way there,I was trying to determine how I was going to handle this situation.

After we went into the house,I sat down and stood Lisa in front of me.I gently said, "Lisa,when those two ladies spoke to you,they were talking about how pretty you are on the outside.It's true you are pretty on the outside.That's how God made you.But a person needs to be beautiful on the inside,too."As she looked at me uncomprehendingly,I continued.

"Do you want to know how a person is beautiful on the inside?" She nodded solemnly.

"Okay.Being beautiful on the inside is a choice you make,honey,to be good to your parents,a good sister to your brother and a good friend to the children you play with.You have to care about other people, honey.You have to share your toys with your playmates.You need to be caring and loving when someone is in trouble or gets hurt and needs a friend.When you do all those things,you are beautiful on the inside.Do you understand what I'm saying?"

"Yes,Mommy,I'm sorry I didn't know that," she replied. Hugging her,I told her I loved her and that I didn't want her to forget what I'd said.The subject never came up again.

Nearly two years later,we moved from the city to the country and enrolled Lisa in a preschool program.In her class was a little girl named Jeanna,whose mother had died.The child's father had recently married a woman who was energetic,warm and spontaneous.It was readily apparent that she and Jeanna had a wonderful,loving relationship.

One day Lisa asked if Jeanna could come over to play for an afternoon,so I made arrangements with her stepmother to take Jeanna home with us the next day after the morning session.

As we were leaving the parking lot,the following day Jeanna said, "Can we go see my mommy?"

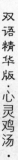

CHICKEN SOUP

继续往家走的路上，我一直在想该如何处理这种状况。

回到家，我坐在丽莎面前，轻轻地对她说："丽莎，两位女士对你说你的外表长得很漂亮。是的，这是事实，这是上帝给你的。但是，一个人也需要内在的美啊。"丽莎迷茫地看着我，我继续说道："你想知道一个人怎么才能内在美吗？"她很郑重地点点头。

"想要内在美，宝贝，需要自己去选择，要爱父母，爱兄弟姐妹，要和一起玩的小朋友做好朋友，你要关心爱护他人，宝贝。你要把玩具拿出来和小伙伴一起玩。有人遇到麻烦或受到伤害，你应该去关心和爱护他。你做了所有这些事，你就有了内在美。你明白我说的这些吗？"

"是的，妈妈，对不起，我以前不知道这些。"我把她抱在怀里，对她说我很爱她，希望她不要忘了我说的话。此后，我们再也没有谈起过这个话题。

差不多过了两年，我们从城市搬到农村。丽莎也上了学前班。她们班有一个叫吉玛的小姑娘，她的妈妈去世了，父亲再婚，其妻是一名积极、热情、自然而优雅的女人。丽莎和吉玛建立了极其友好的友谊。

一天丽莎想请吉玛来我们家玩一下午，于是我与她继母联系好第2天早市后去接她。

第2天，我们开车离开停车场时，吉玛说："可以去看我妈妈吗？"

I knew her stepmother was working,so I said cheerfully, "Sure,do you know how to get there?" Jeanna said she did and,following her directions,I soon found myself driving up the gravel road into the cemetery.

My first response was one of alarm as I thought of the possible negative reaction of Jeanna's parents when they learned what had happened.However,it was obvious that visiting her mother's grave was very important to her,something she needed to do;and she was trusting me to take her there.Refusing would send her a message that it was wrong of her to want to go there.

Outwardly calm,as though I'd known this was where we were going all along,I asked,"Jeanna,do you know where your mother's grave is?"

"I know about where it is," she responded.

I parked on the road in the area she indicated and we looked around until I found a grave with her mother's name on a small marker.

The two little girls sat down on one side of the grave and I sat on the other and Jeanna started talking about how things had been at home in the months leading up to her mother's death,as well as what had happened on the day she died.She spoke for some time and all the while Lisa,with tears streaming down her face,had her arms around Jeanna and,patting her gently,said quietly over and over, "Oh,Jeanna,I'm so sorry.I'm so sorry your mother died."

Finally,Jeanna looked at me and said, "You know,I still love my mommy and I love my new mommy,too."

Deep in my heart,I knew that this was the reason she'd asked to come here.Smiling down at her,I said reassuringly, "You know,Jeanna, that's the wonderful thing about love.You never have to take it away from one person to give it to another.There's always more than enough to go around.It's kind of like a giant rubber band that stretches to surround all the people you care about." I continued,"It's perfectly fine and

我知道她继母在上班,就很爽快地答应了她:"当然可以,你知道怎么走吗?"吉玛说知道,她来领路。我很快发现我们走在去公墓的路上。

我的第一反应是如果吉玛的父母知道了,会不会有什么不好的影响。很显然,去生母的墓地对吉玛来说非常重要,她有什么心愿必须去,因为信任我才让我带她去,如果我拒绝会让她感觉自己这样做是不对的。

虽然我已知道我们是往那儿开,我还是故作镇静地说:"吉玛,你知道你妈妈的坟在哪儿吗?"

"我知道,"她答。

我把车停在她说的地方,向四周看了一下,发现了刻有她妈妈名字的小墓碑。

两个女孩坐在墓的一边,我坐在另一边。吉玛开始谈起妈妈去世前那几个月及去世那天家里的种种。她说了有一会儿,丽莎一直泪流满面,她用胳膊搂着吉玛轻轻地拍,不停地说:"噢,吉玛,你妈妈不在了,我太难过,太难过了。"

最后,吉玛看着我说:"我一直爱着妈妈也爱新妈妈。"

我深深地感觉到这就是她要到妈妈坟上来的原因。我低头微笑地看着她,安慰她说:"吉玛,爱是美妙的,你不必把它从一个人身上拿走送给其他人,因为总有足够的爱让你去传播。它有点像一个巨大的橡皮筋,可以拉开来包容所有你爱的人。"我又说:"你爱两个妈妈

right for you to love both your mothers.I'm sure your own mother is very glad that you have a new mommy to love you and take care of you and your sisters."

Smiling back at me,she appeared satisfied with my response.We sat quietly for a few moments and then we all stood up,brushed ourselves off and went home.The girls played happily after lunch until Jeanna's stepmother came to pick her up.

Briefly,without going into a lot of detail,I told her what had occurred that afternoon and why I'd handled things as I had.To my profound relief,she was very understanding and appreciative.

After they left,I picked Lisa up in my arms,sat down on a kitchen chair,kissed her cheek and hugged her tightly and said, "Lisa,I'm so proud of you.You were such a wonderful friend to Jeanna this afternoon. I know it meant a lot to her that you were so understanding and that you cared so much and felt her sadness."

A pair of lovely,dark brown eyes looked seriously into mine as my daughter added,"Mommy,was I beautiful on the inside?"

Pamela J.deRoy

是非常好，非常正确的。你的亲妈妈知道你和妹妹有新妈妈爱你们、关心你们，她一定非常高兴。"

吉玛笑了，很满意我的回答。我们静静地坐了一会，站起来拍拍土回家了。午饭后孩子们玩得很好，直到吉玛的继母开车来接她。

我简洁地告诉她下午发生的事情以及我这样处理的原因，值得安慰的是，她非常理解，非常感激。

她们走了之后，我抱起丽莎坐在厨房的椅子上，亲亲她的面颊，轻轻拥着她说："丽莎，我为你骄傲，今天下午你对吉玛那么友好，我知道这对她意味着你的理解，你的关心，你的感同身受。"

我的女儿用她那对可爱的深棕色的眼睛严肃地看着我："妈妈，我也有内在美吗？"

帕梅拉·J.德洛伊

The Second Mile

*Somebody made a mistake,*I thought as I skimmed the Vietnam tree-tops in my unarmed Cessna.My radio had reported enemy troops below, but as I circled the site,scouring the elephant grass,I saw nothing.

My job as forward air controller with the U.S.Air Force in 1966 was to spot enemy targets and radio information back so headquarters could send attack aircraft.That morning my patrol had been uneventful. Then my radio crackled,"Airedale Pup,this is Airedale."

It was Captain Jim Ahmann,using our personal code words and calling from our forward operating base at Dong Tre.I was his junior officer,so naturally I was Pup.My little single-engine monoplane,carrying only smoke rockets to mark targets,was Bird Dog.

Ahmann continued: "We have a reported sighting of 200 or 300 Viet Cong in the open."They had been spotted by an Army forward observer plane.

"On my way,"I answered,banking Bird Dog toward the coordinates.

However,as I reached the given location,I could find no sign of the forward observer plane.I scrutinized the area,flying low,worrying about VC ground fire and remembering some bullet holes I had earlier found in Bird Dog's thin skin.I circled again. Still nothing.

"Airedale,there's nothing here."I heard our fighters checking in on the other radio frequency."Have the fighters hold high."I was about to call off the search.I had done my job.

"Have you?"demanded a gruff voice.I winced.Despite the passage of years,I could almost see his sharp features in the windshield before

再向前一里

有人出错了。坐在没有配置武器的赛斯纳飞机上环视越南树梢时，我这样想。无线电传来消息说下面有敌军，可我左右环顾，除了象草，什么也没发现。

1966年作为美国空军前进引导员，我的任务是发现敌军目标，再用无线电把消息发回空军总部，以便派遣战斗机。那天清晨，我的巡逻一无所获。突然，无线电噼啪作响："艾尔谷小狗，我是艾尔谷狗。"

是吉姆·哈曼恩上尉用我们的个人代号从同知 (注：越南地名) 前线指挥部发来的。我是他的副官，不用说，我就是"小狗"。我驾驶的单引擎飞机，只能携带发烟火箭弹来标记目标，代号"猎鸟犬"。

上尉接着说："我们接到报告在开阔地目击到200至300越军。"是陆军前线侦察机发现的。

"就到。"我答道，立即调转"猎鸟犬"飞向目标。

可到了指定位置，却不见侦察机的踪影。我仔细搜录，降低高度，一边提防越军的地面火力并想起了早先在"猎鸟犬"薄甲板上发现的弹孔。我又转了一圈，仍然没有线索。

"艾尔谷狗，这里什么也没有。"无线电另一个频率上传来其他战机上的报告，"向上攀升。"我几乎要放弃搜索，我已经尽力了。

"已经尽力了么？"一个粗哑的声音说道。我不由一怔。时光流逝，我仿佛仍能看见他的影子清晰呈现在面前：木尔瑞神父，我在纽

me:Father John Mulroy,one of my teachers at Archbishop Stepinac High School in White Plains,New York.

He had nailed me to the wall when I submitted my first class paper. I had confidently handed it in,thinking it was complete.

Father Mulroy did not.He gave me a C.I was shocked.He knew I wanted to go to the Air Force Academy,and I needed good grades.When I questioned the C,he fastened me with his dark,penetrating eyes."That's what it was worth,"he snapped.He then rattled off a list of information sources."Did you check into them?"

"I didn't think it was necessary,"I said weakly.

"You only did enough to get by,"he said."When Christ asks us to go the second mile,he means making that extra effort in *everything*." Father Mulroy tapped his desk."Out in the world,that can make a difference in getting a promotion—or saving a life.Don't try to ride Easy Street and expect to wear the stars of a general."

On my next paper I dug deeper.It still wasn't good enough for Father Mulroy."God put more into you than you think,"he said."Don't sell him short."

Try as I might,he kept sandpapering me.The more he did,the more I gritted my teeth."I'll show him,"I muttered—which was just what he wanted.

When I didn't make the starting football team as a fullback,I switched to defense,concentrated on becoming a fierce tackler and won a starting position.This,I hoped,would help me get into the Academy.

After the Academy turned me down,I went to the University of Pennsylvania,determined to put in a strong enough showing to make the Academy the next year.I earned high scores,won a starting spot on the football team,pored over Academy study guides,reapplied and got in.

After I graduated I volunteered for Vietnam,then as a forward air controller,one of the more hazardous flying assignments in the military.

约市白色平原镇的斯坦皮奈科大主教中学上学时的老师。

第1次提交课堂论文，他就让我碰了一次钉子。我自信论文不错，交了上去。

他却不以为然，给了个"C"。我呆了。他很清楚我想上空军学院，成绩对我至关重要。我质疑他时，他深邃的目光定定地看着我，断然说道："只值这个分数"，接着给出一连串资料来源。"查了这些资料了吗？"

"我想没有必要。"我怯生生地答道。

"你只是敷衍。"他说："主在《圣经》里说我们得再向前一里，是要我们做任何事情都要做出额外的努力。"木尔瑞神父敲了敲桌子"在象牙塔外的现实世界里，这往往意味着能否升迁，或是性命攸关的事。别指望不费力就戴上将星。"

第2次交论文，我尤为认真，却仍不能令木尔瑞神父满意，"主赋予你的才能超过你的想象，不要让他失望了。"

我继续努力，他继续磨砺我。他越是督促，我越是鞭策自己。"我要证明给他看。"我告诉自己，这恰恰是他所希望的。

当我不能成为橄榄球队的首发后卫时，我换当防守队员，专心做一个凶狠的阻球队员，然后赢得了一个首发位置。我希望这些能帮助我进入空军学院。空军学院把我拒之门外以后，我上了宾夕法尼亚大学。我下定决心好好表现以便来年再入空军学院。我得了高分，拿到了橄榄球队首发位置，认真学习空军学院学习指导，重新申请，终于如愿。

毕业后，我志愿赴越南参战，成为一名前线空军前进引导

Once in Vietnam,I joined Project Delta—the elite hunter-killer teams of the Green Berets who operated behind enemy lines.

Now in Bird Dog,here was Father Mulroy again.

I radioed base. "Something's wrong,"I reported. "I need some time. Give me another frequency.I've got to raise the Army forward observer."

As the new frequency came through,a swarm of Army helicopter gunships roared under me,turning in a large arc as if searching for something.

I called the Army plane on the new frequency.No response.I tried again and again to raise the mystery ship.I couldn't give up.I had to reach this guy!

Finally,a response. "This is Sundance X Ray."

"Do you have a target?"I asked.

"I've got 300 VC in the open,and I'm trying to locate our gunships."

It was obvious that Sundance was nowhere near the coordinates I had been given.But where *was* he?I had to find him.Timing was critical.

"Sundance,what do you see beneath you?"He described a meandering river,and I tried to match his description on my map. "Okay.I think I know where you are."

I shoved the throttle forward until my Cessna was making its full 115 miles per hour.Soon I spotted the observer plane high against the sky.

It was a small monoplane much like mine. "Lead me to the target,"I radioed.Glancing over my shoulder,I saw the gunships following us. "Down there,"he called, "along the light green field.They were heading west and disappeared in the trees."

I checked my map.We were six miles from the coordinates he had given us.

"Are you sure?"I asked,circling the location.

员——空军中较危险的飞行职务之一。一到越南,我就加入了德尔塔计划——在敌军后防线上活动的号称绿色贝雷帽的精锐猎杀队。

现在,在"猎鸟犬"上,木尔瑞神父又浮现在眼前。

我通知基地:"出现错误。"我报告说,"给我些时间,重新调整频率,以便联络上侦察机。"

不一会,新的频率发了过来。此时,我下方突然聚集了大批武装直升机,隆隆地响着,转了个大弯似乎在搜录什么。

我用新频率呼叫战机。没有答复。我试了一次又一次,想找到那艘神秘的潜艇(注:又名Q-ship。二战的时候英国战舰伪装成普通商船,等敌人靠近就打,德国人老被袭击,但是一直找不到这艘神秘的船。这里指找不到的那架飞机)。我不能放弃,必须找到。

终于,传来了答复:"我是圣丹斯X光。"

"是否发现目标?"我问。

"开阔地目击到300人左右的越军。正在确定我方武装直升机位置。"

显然,圣丹斯离我收到的坐标还很远。他到底在哪儿?我必须找到他。时间紧迫。

"圣丹斯,你的下方能看到什么?"他说下方有一条蜿蜒的小河。我试图在地图上找到河的位置,"好了,我知道你的位置了。"

我猛推油门,赛斯纳以115英里全速前进,不久,我发现凌空高飞的侦察机。

它是和我的飞机差不多的单翼机。"带我去目标。"我用无线电说道,一回头,身后有武装直升机跟着。"在那边下面,"他说,"沿浅绿色田地走。他们正向西前进,进了树林。"

我看了看地图。离他指定的坐标还有6英里。

"确定么?"我一边在地图上圈出位置,一边问道。

Then I saw them.A serpentine column moving through the elephant grass on the back of a knoll.Maybe 200 or 300 troops,all with packs. When I dipped closer,I saw they were in VC attire—a hodgepodge of dark uniforms.

As I moved to a safer altitude,I felt that familiar nudge.Something wasn't right.My mouth dry,I flew closer,expecting the zing of bullets and the whump of heavyweapons fire.I was about to launch my smoke rockets into the column to pinpoint it for the gunships when again something stopped me.These men didn't take cover.They *had* to see me. However,we knew that VC caught in the open often behaved like friendly troops,even to the point of waving at passing aircraft.

Now the gunships,aligned for attack,began to close in.Still something stopped me from getting out of their way.In my mind's ear I heard the distant echo of Father Mulroy's voice:*Make sure,John.Make sure.*

I had to get a closer look.I cut the Cessna's power and glided toward the elephant grass close to the column,expecting a fusillade of bullets.My heart caught.They were *our* Vietnamese troops—counterguerrilla forces who wore uniforms similar to the VC's—carrying American carbines and wearing colored scarves.*Friendlies*!

"Abort! "I shouted over the radio.But the gunships kept coming. They couldn't hear me because they were on a different frequency.

I slammed the control stick full over,jammed the throttle forward and pulled into a gut-wrenching climb.My plane shuddered into a steep bank and stalled.I rolled out to the left,completing my climbing U-turn in front of and 500 feet below the oncoming gunships,positioning myself between them and the friendlies.They couldn't fire without hitting me.

"Sundance,get the helicopters outta here! "I shouted over the radio. "They're friendlies! "

Somehow the message got through.The choppers broke off their attack.

不一会儿，我发现了他们。一条长蛇般的纵队在一座小山背面的象草丛中前行着，大约200到300人，都背着包。我靠近了一看，全穿着越军军服，黑压压的一片。

当我升到安全的高度时，我又有那熟悉的警觉感。有点不对劲。我的嘴巴很干，又飞近了些，——准备子弹呼啸或是炮声隆隆。我正要向纵队发射烟雾火箭，以便武装直升机确定位置，再次有东西阻止了我。这些人并没有隐蔽。他们看得见我。虽然我们知道，在开阔地被发现的越军往往表现的像友军，他们甚至还对路过的飞机挥手致意。

武装直升机已经排好进攻队形，准备接近。仍然有什么东西阻止我给他们让道，因为心中又响起了木尔瑞神父的声音：确认、约翰、确认……

我必须再近看一眼。关上赛斯纳油门，飞机向地面上的那队士兵滑翔过去，完全不顾可能出现的一阵弹雨。我的心紧紧地揪着。是我们的越南人部队——着装非常像越军的反游击部队——手持卡宾枪，戴着彩色的围颈。是自己人！

"取消！"我用无线电喊道。可武装直升机还在向这边靠拢。他们听不见我的话——他们在其他频率上。

我猛推操纵杆，油门踩到底，进入了一个使内脏翻腾的爬升。机身震颤着爬了个陡坡，然后停止。飞机翻滚着向左，在武装直升机编队的500英尺前下方完成了个U转爬升，恰好在机群和地面的友军中间。他们要开火，不可能不打中我。

"圣丹斯，快让直升机离开这里！"我用无线电吼道，"他们是自己人！"

无论如何，消息传出去了。直升机中止了袭击。

The Army pilot followed me back to Dong Tre.He turned out to be a lieutenant new to the country,visibly upset as he realized what had transpired.It was an honest mistake.

The Distinguished Flying Cross I was awarded for that mission meant more to me than all the other decorations I got for performance during combat.

After I returned from Vietnam,I received a note from Father Mulroy."I had the greatest confidence in you and that God would guide and protect you,"he wrote.

Today I serve on the alumni association and,like Father Mulroy,I teach school,demanding of my students in St.Francis College in Brooklyn,New York,that they go the second mile and write papers to my—and Father Mulroy's—standards.Father Mulroy died in 1994 at seventy-seven,but his message lives on.My students know they can't ride Easy Street and expect to reach the stars.

John F.Flanagan Jr.

陆军飞行员(注:army 特指陆军,陆军也有自己的飞机)随我返回了同知基地。他是一个新到这个国家的中尉。当他意识到发生的一切,他显得很是沮丧。他犯了一个诚实的错误。

对我而言,因为这次任务而颁给我的"空战有功十字勋章",远远超过参战以来所获得的所有荣誉。

回国后,我收到木尔瑞神父的一封信。他写道:"对你,我信心百倍。主会永远引领你,保佑你。"

如今,我服务于校友联谊会,像木尔瑞神父一样,从事教学活动。我要求在纽约布鲁克林区的圣弗西斯学院的学生"再向前走一里",按我和木尔瑞神父的要求写论文。1994年,木尔瑞神父去世,享年77岁。他的信念永存。我的学生们都知道,没有人可以不费力就指望触到星星。

约翰·F.小弗莱纳根

Tommy's Shoes

I had in my mind to give those shoes to Cameron and Christy if I could just remember where I'd put them.Already having looked everywhere obvious that an old pair of track shoes were likely to be,I was straining for new possibilities.Even though I'd kept them for the better part of twenty-five years,they seemed a pretty lame remembrance to give to the thirteen-year-old twins whose father had just died at the age of forty.

I'd met Cameron and Christy probably on half a dozen occasions when they were little,but I'm sure they were too young then to recognize me now.Oh,Great Gift Bearer of Worn-out Shoes.How could I explain it to them?Their father meant so many firsts in my life.Some of which I can say and others I never will.

The first time I seriously considered running away,I called Tommy. He and his brother and two sisters were all adopted.I thought it was just amazing that people would adopt four kids and actually have a functional family.I still do.I figured he might have some perspective to offer me that I hadn't imagined,and of course he did.Tommy was never short on perspective,and at times his view of the world confused me,but that night I appreciated it because I didn't run away.

Tommy was part magician.If he went out and caught a twelve-inch catfish,it'd be eighteen inches by the time it flopped into the pan,and two feet long when the butter sizzled in the skillet to fry it up.I don't think I did right by Tommy in this regard when we were teenagers. Sometimes I defended him and other times I doubted.But to Tommy,it

汤米的鞋子

　　我拿定主意,如果我想起那些鞋在哪儿的话,就把他们给卡麦隆和克里斯蒂。尽管把跑鞋可能在的地方翻了个遍,我还不肯罢休。我一直把它留着当做25年来生活中美好部分的见证,但要说把它送给那对刚刚失去40岁父亲的13岁双胞胎作为纪念,有些勉强。

　　这对双胞胎年幼时,我少说也见过六七次。但我想,他们也许不太记得我了。那时他们还小。呵,精美的礼盒里包着一双旧鞋子。我怎么对他们说呢?他们的父亲对我的生活有说不清的重要。有些能说出来,有些却永远不能。

　　第1次我想离家出走时,我给汤米打了电话。他和他的兄弟,两个姐妹都是被领养的。一个人领养4个孩子并能组成像样的家庭,多少有些让人吃惊。如今想来还是如此。我猜,他一定有我想不到的点子,事实如此。汤米有的是点子。很多次,他让我弄不明白他在想什么,不过,那一晚我很感激他,因为我没有离家出走。

　　汤米讲话有点不着调。假如他出门捉了条12英寸的猫鱼回来,扔进平底锅时就变成了18英寸,当煎锅里的牛油把鱼煎得嗞嗞作响时,又变成了2英尺。就这件事来说,我认为十几岁时我对汤米做的不对。有时候我站在他一边,有时又质疑他。可汤米却满不在乎。他

appeared to make little difference.He was not afraid of things like ridicule that kept many of us that age in a wasteland,too nearsighted to catch even a glimpse of his vision.

Tommy loved challenges. "Yeah,right,Tommy.You can get me a summer job."The next Saturday I was in the fields picking watermelons. And when the land was picked clean he got me my second job,as a painter's helper.The summer after that I was a landscaper,thanks to Tommy.

To say that we were best friends wouldn't be exactly accurate,but to say we had a whole boat load of best times together wouldn't be a lie.I guess Tommy always made me feel like his best friend when we were together.I'm sure I wasn't the only one.

He used to wear these blue running shoes made out of some kind of parachute canvas when he'd do the mile and the half-mile in high school.He wasn't the greatest long-distance runner in the state,but for a boy with a bad heart,he placed respectably in quite a few meets.I'd holler at him from inside the track all the way around,telling him where his closest competitor was. "Dig in,Tommy! Stretch it out! You're the man! "And when it was my turn to run my quarter of the mile relay, there was no one in the stadium shouting louder or harder for me than him.

When I had my first near-death experience,he was there.We were on our way home from the beach.I was driving,my girlfriend's head resting on my lap.Tommy had pulled the back cushions out of his red Barracuda convertible so he could get to the trunk from the inside,where he was sleeping.Everyone in dreamland with me cruising along at about eighty-five miles an hour in a drizzly rain.When I hit that curve,I could feel the air swirling around me thick and fast,lifting the car completely off the surface of the pavement,as if a huge window had been cracked open and then slammed shut in almost the same instant.The four tires

从不惧怕别人认为荒唐的事，而我们在那个年纪却往往避之不及。我们太短视，甚至看不清他的一星半点。

汤米喜欢挑战。"嗯，汤米，给我介绍份暑期工吧。"下周六时，我就在地里摘西瓜了。西瓜摘完时，我又接到第2份工作，做一位画师的助手。暑假过后，我成了庭园设计家。多亏了汤米。

要说我们是最好的朋友，兴许不妥，说是曾经共度过许多好时光，却不假。跟汤米在一起，让我觉得自己是他最好的朋友。但我知道，我不是唯一的。

上高中时跑一英里和半英里的项目，他总穿着用蓝色降落伞帆布做的跑鞋。他算不上我们州最好的长跑选手，但对他这样一个心脏不好的孩子来说，却着实参加过很多比赛。我会在操场内圈全程为他呐喊，告诉他最近的对手的位置。"坚持，汤米！跑起来！你是真正的男子汉！"当轮到我跑1/4英里接力时，赛场上的呐喊声从没比汤米比赛时热烈过。

当我第1次经历生命危险时，汤米也在身边。从海滩回家途中，我开着车，女友头枕着我的膝休息。汤米把后座靠垫从他的红色"梭鱼"敞篷车里拉出来，以便后座和车后的行李厢从里面连成一体，然后在里头睡。所有人都进入梦乡，和我一起在毛毛细雨中以每小时85英里的速度前行着。当我撞上弯道时，我觉得周围的空气急速旋转着，把车抬起来，完全离开了路面。就像一扇巨大的窗户被猛地撞开，随即又猛地关上。眨眼间车轮又紧贴着柏油路面了。但我明

grabbed the asphalt road again.But I know we'd have all been dead if God had wanted it so.

It was three days later before Tommy ever acknowledged the event. He came up to me in the locker room,popped me with a towel and said, "You nearly lost it on the beach road Saturday,didn't ya?"

"I thought you were asleep,"I said.He laughed at me,and I punched him in the arm as many times as I could before he got even.

Punching was a big thing for us.I remember Tommy nearly broke his hand punching out a stop sign,he was so upset over a fight he'd had with his girlfriend.He married Melanie a short while after that.She was a country girl who matched his spirit fine.Sweet and pretty,but not inclined to take any sass from the likes of Tommy.He cried so much saying his wedding vows I didn't think he was going to make it,he was so happy to get her.

The twins were born and as the seasons passed,we seemed to drift in and out of each other's lives with less frequency.The last times that represented any consistency for us were during the University of Florida Gators' home football games.Tommy was in charge of the crew that supplied hot dogs for the entire stadium,and I was his lieutenant.Part of that responsibility meant meeting at the field by 4:00 A.M.to prepare for the assembly of ten thousand hot dogs.Let me tell you,when you get up in the middle of a weekend night to work your buns off alongside a guy passing you weenies all day just for the sheer pleasure of punching him in the arm every once in a while—well,you love him.

I think why I did so much is because when I was with him,we shared things.Partly because we were pretty close to the same size,and maybe too because sometimes it wasn't easy to feel like we fit anywhere.

I guess that's why passing back the shoes feels important.He gave me many things,including these running shoes,and I'm frustrated from

白,如果上帝决定了,我们该已经全完了。

3天后,汤米才对我提这件事。他走进衣柜间,递给我一条毛巾,说:"星期六在海滩的路上你几乎搞砸了,不是么?"

"我以为你睡着了,"我说。他取笑我,我就不住地用手捶他胳膊,捶得他来不及还手。

捶击对我们而言,意义非浅。记得汤米因为捶击一个停车标志几乎把手弄伤。他为和他女友的一场争斗很是心烦。不久,他娶了梅兰妮。她是一个乡下姑娘,和他的劲头挺相配。她长得甜美,从来不在汤米喜欢的事情上顶嘴。婚礼上,汤米哭得太厉害以至于我以为他的誓言都说不下去了。能得到她,他太高兴了。

双胞胎出世了,日子一天天过去。我们彼此似乎再也不来往频繁。我们对于友谊的最后固守在佛罗里达大学短吻鳄队主场的橄榄球赛期间得以体现。汤米是负责供给全场观众热狗队伍的头,我是副手。这就意味着我得早晨4点和他在球场会合,准备上万只热狗。当你在周末的半夜里起床准备热狗面包,而身边的这个家伙一整天把热狗香肠不停地递给你,做这些的乐趣仅仅是为了可以不时捶他的胳膊,那么让我告诉你,你爱他。

我觉得我做这么多,是因为我们在一起有很多东西可以分享。部分理由是我们性情相近,或许也因为有时还真难找到像我们这样的。

我想,我之所以觉得把旧鞋还回去重要,不过于此吧。他给过我很多,包括这双跑鞋。找却找不着,我很是恼火。翻来覆去,最终在谷

looking and not finding.Rummaging through the final box in the back corner of the barn,I see a shoe toe that I recognize instantly.I pull it out like a prize from a cereal box and brush away the cockroach that has taken up residence inside.But there's only one shoe.The left mate is missing.How can I give the offspring of my old friend one beat-up, worn-out shoe that belonged to their father a quarter of a century ago? Feeling deflated,I close my eyes and ask Tommy what he thinks I should do.His response,as usual,is quick and decisive."Give the kids the dang shoe and move on."

Tommy never did steer me in the wrong direction.

Samuel P.Clark

仓的拐角看见一只鞋尖,我一眼就认出来了。我把它拖了出来,就像是在速食谷物盒子找到一件促销奖品。我把已经占据了这只鞋子的蟑螂扫除干净。可惜只有一只鞋了,左脚那只已经找不着了。我怎能把这只又破又烂、我这位老友25年前的鞋子赠送给他的孩子们? 我觉得灰心丧气。闭上眼,我想问问汤米:我该怎么办? 他的回答该和以往一样迅速、肯定:"那破玩意儿就给他们,继续生活下去。"

汤米从来不把我往错路上领。

塞缪尔·P.克拉克

The Kindness of Strangers
陌生人的善意

We have committed the Golden Rule to memory.Now let us commit it to life.

Edwin Markham

黄金法则,我们曾留给记忆;如今,让我们把它留给生活。

——爱德文·马可汉姆

One summer I was driving from my hometown of Tahoe City,California,to New Orleans.In the middle of the desert,I came upon a young man standing by the roadside.He had his thumb out and held a gas can in his other hand.

I drove right by him.

Someone else will stop for him,I reasoned.Besides,that gas can is just a ploy to flag down a car and rob the driver.

Several states later,I was still thinking about the hitchhiker. Leaving

一年夏天,我开车从老家加州太好市到新奥尔良去。在沙漠区中间,我看见路边有位年轻人。他一手打出要求搭乘的手势,一手提着一罐汽油。

我没有停车。

有人会让他搭载,我这样想。再说,那只罐子不过是拦车抢劫的幌子罢了。

开出去几个州以后,我还在想着那个搭便车的人。让他孤零零

经典系列／时光的印记

183

him stranded in the desert didn't bother me as much as how easily I'd reached the decision.I never even lifted my foot off the accelerator.*Does anyone stop anymore?I wondered.*

There was a time in this country when you'd be considered a jerk if you passed by somebody in need.Now you're a fool for helping.With gangs,drug addicts, murderers,rapists,thieves and car-jackers lurking everywhere,why risk it?"I don't want to get involved"has become a national motto.

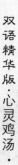

I thought of my destination—New Orleans,the setting for Tennessee Williams's play *A Streetcar Named Desire*.I recalled Blanche Dubois's famous line:"I have always depended on the kindness of strangers."

The kindness of strangers.It sounds so quaint.Could anyone rely on the kindness of strangers these days?

One way to test this would be for a person to journey from coast to coast without any money relying solely on the goodwill of his fellow Americans.What kind of America would he find?Who would feed him, shelter him,carry him down the road?

The idea intrigued me.But who'd be crazy enough to try such a trip?Well,I figured,why not me.

The week I turned thirty-seven,I realized I'd never taken a gamble in my life.So I decided to make a leap of faith a continent wide—to go from the Pacific to the Atlantic without a penny.If I was offered money, I'd refuse it.I'd accept only rides,food and a place to rest my head.It would be a cashless journey through the land of the almighty dollar.As my final destination I chose the region of Cape Fear in North Carolina,a symbol of all the fears I'd have to conquer to go the distance.

I rose early on September 6,1994,hoisted a fifty-pound pack onto my back and headed from the Golden Gate Bridge.Then I took a sign from my backpack,displaying my destination to passing vehicles:"America."

Drivers mouthed the word through windshields,then smiled.Two

留在沙漠里，我没有多少犹豫。我的脚始终没有离开过加速器。会有人停车么？我很怀疑。

一度有人认为撇下急需帮助的陌生人不管不顾是混蛋。如今，出手相助却会被当成傻瓜。合伙袭击，毒品、谋杀、强奸、偷盗、劫车……这类事随处可见，为什么要冒这个险？"不关我的事"成为全国上下的座右铭。

想到我的目的地新奥尔良——田纳西·威廉姆斯(注：剧作家托马斯·拉尼尔·威廉姆斯的笔名)的《欲望号街车》的原型地——我记起了布兰奇·札波依斯(注：剧中人物，影片中由费雯丽扮演)的名言："我总会依赖陌生人的善意。"

陌生人的善意。听起来漂亮。如今还有人指望陌生人的善意么？

要证明这一点，最好的办法是让一个人身无分文地横穿整片国土，全指靠着美国同胞的善意。他将碰到什么样的美国人，谁会提供食宿，谁会给他指路？

这个想法触动了我。可谁敢轻易动这个念头？不过，想了想，我愿意做这个人。

到了我37岁生日的那一周，我觉得自己人生中还从未赌过一把。于是，决定做一次大陆那么宽的信念的跨越——从太平洋海岸走到大西洋海岸，不带分文。如果有人资助我，我会谢绝。我只接受搭便车、食宿方面的帮助。这是在金钱至上的国土上进行的一次身无分文的旅行。最终的目的地，我选择了北卡罗来纳州的"恐怖角"区，以此象征我这番远足就是为了征服恐惧。

1994年9月6日清晨，我起了个大早，背起55磅的背包，开始朝金门大桥进发。我在背包上树了一块标识："美国"，以明去向。

沿途，司机从挡风玻璃里念叨着背包上的字，笑着。两个骑自行

women rode by on bicycles. "It's a bit vague," said one. A young man with a German accent wandered up and asked, "Where is this 'America'?" Indeed.

For six weeks I tried to find out. I hitched eighty-two rides and covered 4,223 miles across fourteen states. As I traveled, I discovered that others shared my fear. Folks were always warning me about someplace else. In Montana they said watch out for the cowboys in Wyoming. In Nebraska they told me people aren't as nice in Iowa.

Yet I was treated with kindness in every state I traveled. I was a mazed by the stubborn capacity of Americans to help a stranger, even when it seemed to run contrary to their own best interest. One day in Nebraska a four-door sedan pulled to the road shoulder. When I reached the window, I saw two little old ladies dressed in their Sunday finest.

"I know you're not supposed to pick up hitchhikers, but it's so far between towns out here, you feel bad passing a person," said the driver, who introduced herself as Vi. She and her sister Helen were going to see an eye doctor in Ainsworth, Nebraska.

I didn't know whether to kiss them or scold them for stopping. This woman was telling me she'd rather risk her life than feel bad about passing a stranger on the side of the road. When they dropped me at a highway junction, I looked at Vi. We both spoke at the same time: "Be careful."

Once when I was hitchhiking unsuccessfully in the rain, a trucker pulled over, locking his brakes so hard he skidded on the grass shoulder. The driver told me he was once robbed at knifepoint by a hitchhiker. "But I hate to see a man stand out in the rain," he added. "People don't have no heart anymore."

I found, however, that compassion was the norm. A middle-aged Iowa couple shepherded me around for an hour, trying to help me find a campground. In South Dakota a woman whose family had given me a

车的妇女经过,其中的一个说:"那有些含糊。"一个有德国口音的年轻人踱过来问道:"这个美国在哪?"问的在理。

在哪?我足足找了6个礼拜。我搭乘便车82次,穿越14个州,走了4223英里地。旅途中,我发现别人也有恐惧感。当地居民总提醒我注意一些地方。在蒙大拿州,他们说要我留意怀俄明州的牛仔。在内布拉斯加州,他们说衣阿华州的人不够友好。

然而,每到一处,我都受到了善待。美国人乐于助人的坚定天性着实让我吃惊,即便在自己不顺路的情况下依然如此。一天,在内布拉斯加州,一辆四门轿车行驶到路边停下。我走到车窗边,看见里边坐着两位年长妇女,穿着星期天宗教活动的正装。

"你知道,我不想让人搭便车,可这地方离城镇远着呢,不管不问可不好。"司机说道。她说她名叫薇,她和姐姐海伦要去内布拉斯加州的安斯沃斯看眼科医生。

我不知道该感激她们还是怨她们。眼前这个女人说,她宁可冒生命危险停下车来,也不肯从我面前疾驰而过。到了高速路口,我下车时看了一眼薇,我们几乎同时说道:"保重。"

有一回,下雨天我没能搭上便车。这时,一辆卡车开过来,司机刹车过猛,车子在路边草地上还打了个滑。司机告诉我,有一回他被搭车者持刀抢劫过。"不过我还是不想看见别人站在雨里淋着。"他接着说,"人们不再冷漠了。"

然而,我觉得怜悯之心是一种道德。一对中年衣阿华州夫妇领着我转悠了一个小时,帮我寻找野营地。在南达科他州,一家人提供

night's lodging handed me two stamped postcards:one to let her know how my trip turned out,the other to send the next day,telling her where I was so she wouldn't worry about me.

Hearing I had no money and would take none,people in every state bought me food or shared whatever they happened to have with them.A park ranger in Ukiah,California,gave me some carrots.A college student handed me sacks filled with organic tomatoes,zucchini and melons.A woman in Iowa gave me two bundles of graham crackers,two cans of soda,two cans of tuna,two apples and two pieces of chicken—a veritable Noah's Ark sack of lunches.

The people who had the least to give often gave the most.In Oregon,a house painter named Mike noted the chilly weather and asked if I had a coat.When I replied,"a light one,"he drove me to his house,rummaged through his garage and handed me a bulky green Army-style jacket.

Elsewhere in Oregon a lumber-mill worker named Tim invited me to a simple dinner with his family in their dilapidated house. He gave me a Bible.Then he offered me his tent.I refused,knowing it was probably one of the family's most valuable possessions.But Tim was determined that I have it,and finally I agreed to take it.

I was grateful to all the people I met for their rides,their food,their shelter,their gifts.But the kindest act of all was when they merely were themselves.

One day I walked into the local Chamber of Commerce in Jamestown,Tennessee.A man inside the old stone building jumped up from his cluttered desk. "Come on in,"said Baxter Wilson,fifty-nine.He was the executive director.

When I asked him about camping in the area,he handed me a brochure for a local campground. "Would you like me to call for you?" he asked.

给我一夜的食宿,临行前,女主人递给我两张贴好邮票的明信片,说是:一张让她知道我的旅行最终如何,另一张第2天就寄,告诉她我在哪儿好让她不担心。

听说我不带分文,并且不接受资助,所到之处,人们都给我买来食物,或是自己有什么就分些给我。加州乌可哈斯一位公园管理员给过我一些胡萝卜。一位大学生递给我好几口袋的"绿色食品",西红柿、绿西葫芦,还有瓜。衣阿华州的一位妇女给过我两客全麦脆饼、两罐苏打、两听金枪鱼、两个苹果、两块鸡肉。这些,差不多快赶上诺亚方舟上的午餐了。

最贫穷的人往往给予我的最多,在俄勒冈州,一个名叫麦克的刷漆工人提醒我,天气凉了,问我是否有外套。我说:"有件薄的。"他便开车带我到他家,在车库里翻了半天,递给我一件硕大的绿色军式大衣。

在俄勒冈州的另一个地方,一位叫提姆的木材厂工人曾请我在他那破旧的家里吃过简单的晚餐。他递给我一本圣经,还给我一顶帐篷。我坚决不肯收,因为那可能是他们最值钱的家当。可提姆执意要我拿着。最终我让了步。

我感激所有让我搭车,给我食宿,送我礼物的人们。但他们最有善意的行为是当他们这样做时纯粹出于本性。

一天,我走进田纳西州詹姆斯敦的地方商业局。在一座古老的石材建筑里杂乱的办公桌边突然蹦出个名叫巴克斯特·威尔森的人,59岁。"进来吧。"他说。他是那儿的执行主任。

当我询问在本地区的野营事宜时,他递给我一本当地野营场所的小册子,说,"需要我为你联系么?"

Seeing that it cost twelve dollars,I replied,"No,that's all right.I'm not sure what I'm going to do."

Then he saw my backpack."Most anybody around here will let you pitch a tent on their land,if that's what you want,"he said.

*Now we're talking,*I thought."Any particular direction?"I asked.

"Tell you what.I've got a big farm about ten miles south of here.If you're here at 5:30,you can ride with me."

I accepted,and we drove out to a magnificent country house.Suddenly I realized he'd invited me to spend the night in his home.

His wife,Carol,was cooking a pot roast when we walked into the kitchen.A seventh-grade science teacher,she was the picture of Southern charm.

Baxter explained that local folks were "mountain stay-at-home people,"and he considered himself one of them."We rarely entertain in our house,"he said."When we do,it's usually kin."The revelation made my night there all the more special.

The next morning when I came downstairs,Carol asked if I'd come to her school in Allardt and talk to her class about my trip.I told her I didn't want to encourage a bunch of seventh-graders to hitchhike across the United States (in fact,in some states it's illegal).But Carol said the kids should be exposed to what else is out there—the good and the bad. "They need to know,"she said.

I agreed,and before long had been scheduled to talk to every class in the school.All the kids were well-mannered and attentive. Their questions kept coming:Where were people kindest?How many pairs of shoes did I have?Had anybody tried to run me over?Were the pigs' feet as good in other parts of the country?Had I fallen in love with anyone? What was I most afraid of?

And my favorite,from a meek little girl with glasses and freckles, "You wanna eat lunch with us?"

双语精华版·心灵鸡汤·

我知道那得花费12美元,便说:"噢,不用了。我还没拿定主意。"

他看了看我的背包,说:"如果你愿意的话,这儿的大多数人都会允许你在他们的地盘上扎营休息。"

恰合我意。于是我问道:"能带个路么?"

"跟你说。我有片大农场,离这儿10里地。如果你5点半钟到这儿来的话,我可以带你去。"我答应了。我们开车出城,来到一座很漂亮的乡村住宅前。突然间我意识到:他这是邀请我在他家过夜。他的夫人凯偌正在烤肉。她是一位七年级自然课教师,典型的南方丽人。

巴克斯特解释道,当地人都是"居家山民",他认为自己也是如此。"我们很少在家招待客人,"他说,"除非是至亲。"这么一说,令我觉得在他家度过的那一晚上尤为特别。第2天早上下楼时,凯偌问我是否愿意去她在阿拉德的学校跟孩子们谈谈我的旅行。我告诉她我可不愿意让一帮七年级学生像我一样搭便车走遍美国(事实上,这在有些州是违法行为)。但凯偌坚持说孩子们应该了解外面的世界,不论它是好是坏。"他们需要了解。"凯偌说。

我答应了。不久,我便被安排在那所学校的每一个班级都作一次报告。所有的孩子都很有礼貌,也很专注。问题接二连三:哪儿的人最友好?你带了多少双鞋子?有人想用车轧你么?其他地方的猪蹄也和我们这儿一样好么?你爱过谁么?你最害怕什么?最有趣的问题是一位带着眼镜,脸上有雀斑的温顺小女孩提的,"你打算和我们一起吃午餐么?"

Afterward Carol told me that one of the kids I spoke to was ordinarily quite shy.After class he came up to her and announced,"I want to grow up to be a journalist and go to all the places he's been."

I was touched.When I left San Francisco,I was thinking only of myself.I never considered that my trip might affect a child in Tennessee. This reminded me that no matter how hard we try,nothing we do is in a vacuum.

Although I hadn't planned it this way,I discovered that a patriotic tone ran through the talks that I gave that afternoon.I told the students how my faith in America had been renewed.I told them how proud I was to live in a country where people were still willing to help out a stranger.

Then with only one more state to go and my journey almost over,a realization hit me:It took giving up money to have the richest experience of my life.I knew that wherever I might go,I would always remember my continental leap of faith and the country that caught me.

Mike McIntyre

随后，凯偌告诉我，我刚刚与之谈话的有一个孩子平时是很腼腆的。下课后，他走到凯偌面前说："长大了，我要做记者，去他走过的地方。"

我被触动了。离开旧金山时，我想到的都是自己。我从来没想过我的旅行会影响到田纳西州的一个孩子。这让我明白，无论我们付出多少，都不是无谓的。

尽管无心显示我的爱国热情，但在那天下午的整个谈话过程中它无处不在。我告诉孩子们，我对美国的信念已经复燃，我很骄傲自己生活在一个人人乐于向陌生人伸出援手的国度。

还有一个州，我的行程就要结束了。突然意识到：放弃金钱却使我获得人生最丰富的经历。我想，无论我将去何方，这次跨越国土的信念之旅和感动我的这个国度会永远铭记在我心中。

麦克·麦因泰尔

A Simple Act

CHICKEN SOUP

When our family—my wife Maggie,our four-year-old Eleanor,and I—drove through Messina,Sicily,to our hotel in the early hours of the morning one day last September,I felt I had never been in a bleaker place.We didn't know a soul,the streets were deserted,and we were leaving the hospital where our seven-year-old son lay in a deep and dreadful coma.

We wanted only to go home,to take Nicholas with us,however badly injured,to help nurse him through whatever he faced,to hold his hand again,to put our arms around him.

It had been the worst night of our lives.

The next morning we took a bus back to the hospital.There had been no deterioration but no improvement either."You know,there are miracles,"said the man who had been appointed to act as our interpreter,but the doctors looked grave.In lives that only a few hours before had been full of warmth and laughter,there was now a gnawing emptiness.

Within days our intensely personal experience erupted into a worldwide story. Newspapers and television told of the shooting attack by car bandits,Nicholas's death and our decision to donate his organs.Since then streets,schools,scholarships and hospitals all over Italy have been named for him.We have received honors previously reserved largely for kings and presidents,prizes that go mainly to Nobelists and awards usually given to spiritual leaders of the stature of Mother Teresa.Maria Shriver,who all her life has been told by people where they were when

简单的举动

去年9月的一天凌晨，当我们一家(我妻子麦琪，我们4岁的儿子埃里纳，还有我)开车去西西里的迈斯纳回旅馆时，我想我平生从未路过这样萧瑟的地方。谁也不认识，满街荒凉。我们刚离开医院，在那儿，7岁的儿子正在深度昏迷中。

我们只想赶回家，把尼古拉斯带回家，不论他伤得多重。我们只想照顾他渡过难关，只想再次握着他的手，把他抱在怀里。

那是我们从未经历过的暗夜。

第2天清晨，我们乘公共汽车回到医院。他的病情既没有恶化也没有好转。"总会有奇迹的。"医院派来的翻译说。但医生们表情很是严肃。就在几小时前，我们的生活还满是温馨和笑声，如今却是令人痛苦的空虚。

几天后，我们强烈的个人悲苦爆发成了家喻户晓的新闻。报纸和电视报道了汽车劫匪的枪击、尼古拉斯的死、还有我们捐献器官的决定。从此以后，意大利的很多街道、学校、奖学金，以及医院都以他的名字命名。我们接受了那些原本只有国王和总统才享有的荣誉，以及那些原本只属于诺贝尔奖获得者和像特瑞萨嬷嬷那样的精神领袖才能获得的奖项。玛丽亚·师日福，这位平生只有当肯尼迪遇刺这样的大事发生时才肯露面的人物，告诉我们她已经听说了我儿

President Kennedy was shot,told us where she was when she heard about Nicholas. Strangers come up to us on the street still,tears in their eyes.

We have received letters from about a thousand people around the world,written with a simple eloquence possible only when it comes straight from the heart.A forty-year-old American,who recently became blind,said our story had given him the strength to resist despair.One man who was close to death now has a new lung because someone was moved by what happened to Nicholas.A woman who lost her four-year-old daughter imagines the two children playing happily together in a place where there is no violence.

All this for a decision that seemed so obvious we've forgotten which of us suggested it.

I remember the hushed room and the physicians standing in a small group,hesitant to ask crass questions about organ donation.As it happens, we were able to relieve them of the thankless task.We looked at each other. "Now that he's gone,shouldn't we give the organs?"one of us asked."Yes,"the other replied.And that was all there was to it.

Our decision was not clouded by any doubts about the medical staff.We were convinced they had done everything in their power to save Nicholas.To be sure, we asked how they knew his brain was truly dead,and they described their high-tech methods in clear,simple language.It helped.But more than that,it was the bond of trust that had been established from the beginning that left no doubt they would not have given up until all hope was gone.

Yet we've been asked a hundred times:How could you have done it?And a hundred times we've searched for words to convey the sense of how clear and how right the choice seemed.Nicholas was dead.He no longer looked like a sleeping child. By giving his organs we weren't hurting him but we were helping others.

子的事。街上的陌生人含着眼泪，默默走到我们面前。

　　我们收到的来自世界各地的信件达1 000余封。所有信件的言辞都是从内心流淌出来的朴素话语。一位40岁的美国人最近失明了，他说我们的故事让他恢复了勇气。有人濒临死亡，却因为有人被我儿子的事而感动，捐献自己的肺给他，使其重获新生。一位失去4岁女儿的母亲告诉我，她能想象两个孩子在没有暴力的乐土上愉快嬉戏。

　　这一切都因一个当时看来如此理所当然的决定。我们已忘了是我俩中哪一个建议的。

　　我记得，在寂静的病室里，一小群医生迟疑地问有关器官捐献这个不那么友好的问题。实际上，我们让他们从这个不讨好的任务中解脱了。我们互相看了一眼对方，"他已经走了，不该捐赠么？"我俩中的一个问，"应该。"另一个答道。事情就是如此。

　　我们的决定，丝毫没有受到怀疑医务人员的不利影响。我们相信，他们已经尽力去抢救尼古拉斯了。为了确认，我们问医生如何知道我们的儿子已经脑死亡。他们用平实的语言把复杂的高科技方法解释得非常清楚。我们理解。不仅如此，我们双方已经建立了互信的纽带。从一开始我就没有怀疑他们会永不放弃直到所有的希望都破灭。

　　但我们被问了上百次："你们如何做出这样的决定的？"我们也上百次地寻找词藻来表达我们的选择是多么明白、多么正确。尼古拉斯已经死了。他看上去不再是一个睡着了的孩子。捐献他的器官不会伤害他，却有利于他人。

For us,Nicholas will always live,in our hearts and our memories.But he wasn't in that body anymore.

His toys are still here,including the flag on his log fort,which I put at half-staff when we returned home and which has stayed that way ever since.We have assembled all his photographs,starting with the blur I snapped a few moments after he was born.Nicholas now lies in a peaceful country churchyard in California,dressed for eternity in the kind of blue blazer and neat slacks he liked and a tie with Goofy on it.

Donating his organs,then,wasn't a particularly magnanimous act.But not to have given them would have seemed to us such an act of miserliness that we don't believe we could have thought about it later without shame.The future of a radiant little creature had been taken away.It was important to us that someone else should have that future.

It turned out to be seven people's future,most of them young,most very sick.One nineteen-year-old within forty-eight hours of death ("We'd given up on her,"her physician told me later) is now a vivacious beauty who turns heads as she walks down the street.The sixty-pound fifteen-year-old who got Nicholas's heart had spent half his life in hospitals;now he's a relentless bundle of energy.One of the recipients,when told by his doctors to think of something nice as he was taken to the operating theater,said, "I am thinking of something nice.I'm thinking of Nicholas."I recently visited him at school;he's a wonderful little fellow any father would be proud of and,I admit,I did feel pride.The man who received one of Nicholas's corneas told us that at one time he was unable to see his children.Now,after two operations,he happily watches his daughter fencing and his son play rugby.

We are pleased the publicity this incident has caused has led to such a dramatic arousal of interest in organ donation.It seems unfair, however,to the thousands of parents and children,who,in lonely hospital waiting rooms around the world,have made exactly the same decision.

对我们来说,尼古拉斯永远活着,活在我们心里和我们的记忆里,但却不在他的身体里。

他的玩具还在那儿,包括他玩的木头碉堡上的那面小旗子。我们回家后降了半旗。如今,还是那样。我们把他的照片收集在一起,从我在他刚出生不久时拍的模糊照片开始收集。尼古拉斯正安宁地躺在加州的一个乡村教堂墓园里,穿着蓝色运动上衣,他喜欢的干净的便裤,和一条印有古非狗的领带,一成不变的打扮。

捐献器官并非什么特别慷慨之举。对我们而言,不捐献才是吝啬之举。我们不相信这样吝啬会让我们事后心安理得。一个活泼小生命的前程已经不复存在。我们关心的是,其他的孩子应享有美好的前程。

最终,7个人得到了那样的前程。大多年幼,大多病笃。一个19岁的孩子已经死亡了48小时("我们已经放弃了。"她的医生事后对我们说),如今,她成长为一个活泼的美女,当她沿着街道走时,她的美丽让人侧目。

一个60磅重的15岁孩子接受了尼古拉斯的心脏。之前,他有一半时间是在医院里度过的。如今,他总是充满活力。接受捐赠的人中有一位在进手术室前,医生要他想象美好的事情。他说:"我正在想美好的事。我在想尼古拉斯。"最近我去学校看他。这个小家伙很棒,足以令为父者自豪。我承认,我也感到自豪。接受眼角膜捐赠的那位告诉我,他曾经看不见自己的孩子。经过两次手术后,他能愉快地看着女儿击剑,看着儿子打英式橄榄球了。

我们很欣慰,这件事的宣传居然极大地激起了人们对于器官捐赠的兴趣。不过,对于其他千万个家长和孩子来说,这也许不公平。他们在世界各地的医院等待室里,作了和我们一模一样的决定。他

Their loss is indistinguishable from ours,but their willingness to share rather than to hoard life has remained largely unrecognized.

I imagine that for them,like us,the emptiness is always close by.I don't believe Maggie and I will ever be really happy again;even our best moments are tinged with sadness.But our joy in seeing so much eager life that would otherwise have been lost,and the relief on the families' faces,is so uplifting that it has given us some recompense for what otherwise would have been just a sordid act of violence.

Reg Green

们的损失和我们没有两样。但他们乐于分享而不愿贮藏生命的意愿却大多不为人所知。

我在想,他们和我们一样,空虚永远不会远离。我不相信,麦琪和我会再有真正的欢乐, 即便最美好的时分也带有一抹哀伤的色彩。但是看到那么多渴求生命的人们因此而不会丧生,看到家人们脸上的欣慰,我们心中也充满了欢乐。这种欢乐是如此振奋人心,它带给我们些许慰藉,因为如果不这么做,这件事情就只剩下无耻的暴行。

瑞格·格林

Hope
希望

Someday all you will have to light your way will be a single ray of hope and that will be enough.

Kobi Yamada

终有一日,需要照亮前程的只是一缕希望,而且有它便足够。

——考比·雅马达

The air was thick with heat and the whimpers of children as Lori Weller,nineteen,stood in an orphanage far away from home.

"Bonjour,"voices chimed as Lori reached for small hands. Then her eyes met those of a little girl seated in a corner.*God brought me here for a reason,she thought.Is that reason you?*

Growing up in Walnut Bottom,Pennsylvania,Lori had a typical life: school,friends,church on Sundays.But it became a little less typical when

当19岁的劳瑞·威勒站在离家甚远的孤儿院里的时候,空气显得凝重而燥热,还夹杂着孩子们的啜泣声。

"早安,"劳瑞和那些孩子们的小手相握时,一一说道。她的视线碰到一个坐在角落里的女孩的手。她想,上帝因为某个理由把我带到这儿。那个理由就是你吗?

劳瑞从小在宾夕法尼亚州的沃纳特·伯顿长大,生活再平常不过:学校、朋友、周末的教堂。但是,当她加入教堂的青年组织,去洪

she joined her church youth group on a trip to build a new church in Honduras.

"I felt so *good* being able to help,"Lori told her parents.But even more than that,Lori felt different.*It's as if my heart is wide open,*she thought.This is what I want to do—help people.

So when,in nursing school,Lori heard of a semester-break trip to work at a medical clinic in Haiti,she leaped at the chance.

Each morning,braying donkeys woke her.Then she'd climb onto a flatbed truck and ride a bumpy path to spend her day taking blood pressure readings and bandaging scrapes.

But it was the orphaned children who tore at her heart."They will never be adopted,"she was told at one orphanage. "They're just too sick."

The walls there were bare,the few toys,broken.There were so many hands reaching up—and too few caretakers to reach back.

Then her eyes fell on a child of about three who was alone,with cereal smeared across her cheeks.Below a tangle of black curls,Lori saw her forehead pulsating. "She was left with us when she was about six months old,"the orphanage director said. "She has a hole in her skull from abuse.One fall could kill her."

"Poor baby! "Lori gasped. "Nothing can be done?"she asked.

"We don't have the money,the equipment…or the experience,"the director answered.

"What's her name?"asked Lori.

"Agat Espoire.In Creole,her last name means 'hope'."

*The child with the least hope,*Lori thought sadly.A child beaten and abandoned.But when Lori pulled Agat into her lap,the toddler surveyed her with dark,soulful eyes.*You deserve someone to love you,Agat,*she thought.

Day after day,Lori made dolls dance for Agat.But Agat was unre-

双
语
精
华
版
·
心
灵
鸡
汤
·

都拉斯新建一座教堂时，她的生活变得有一点不寻常。

"能帮助别人，感觉真好！"劳瑞对父母亲说。不仅如此，劳瑞觉得还有些不同。我的心胸似乎一下子开阔起来，她这么想。这正是她想做的——帮助他人。

因此，当劳瑞在护校上学时听说学期中间的假期有去在海地的医疗机构工作的机会，她赶紧抓住这个机会。每天清晨，驴叫声把她唤醒。接着她得爬上平板货车，一路颠簸着去把时间花在量血压和给伤口打绷带上。

然而，最让她难过的是那些孤儿。"没人会领养他们。"她在一个孤儿院里听人说。"他们病得太重了。"

孤儿院的墙上什么也没有，玩具很少，还是坏的。有那么多手向上伸着求助，却只有少得可怜的管理员伸手去拉。

她的目光落到一个孤孤单单的孩子身上，这孩子3岁上下，脸蛋上还抹着麦片。劳瑞看见她乱蓬蓬的黑卷发下，额头的筋跳动着。"她6个月大就被丢到这儿来了。"院长说，"来时脑壳上有个窟窿，被人打的。摔一跤都会送了她的命。"

"可怜的孩子！"劳瑞倒吸一口凉气。"没法治好么？"她问。

"我们没钱，没有设备……也没遇到过这种情况。"院长答道。

"她叫什么名字？"劳瑞问。

"阿伽·埃斯普瓦赫。在克利奥尔语中，她的姓是希望的意思。"

劳瑞哀伤地想，这孩子的希望最小。一个被毒打被抛弃的孩子。但是当劳瑞把她拉进怀里时，这个孩子激动地用黑眼睛打量着劳瑞（注：toddler现在特指1~3岁的孩子）。你该有人来爱，阿伽，她想。

日子一天天过去，劳瑞经常摆弄木偶逗阿伽。可她毫无反应。如

经典系列／时光的印记

sponsive.*If only I could see her smile,*Lori thought.

On her last night in Haiti,Lori lay sleepless.*How can I leave Agat here,where no one has the time to sit for hours and tell her stories? Where no one can afford to help her heal?How can I leave her...when she's already in my heart?*

Back at home,Lori couldn't stop thinking of the sad-eyed little girl. *If I never try to help,*she thought,*I'll never stop worrying about her.*

She called doctor after doctor,saying, "I have a child who needs surgery,but there's no money."

"Why don't you call..."came the usual reply.Finally,she was directed to neurosurgeon Joel Winer."When can she get here?"he asked.

Lori couldn't believe her ears."I want to repeat:There is no money," she said.

"I went into medicine to help,"the doctor explained softly.

*You sent me to Dr.Winer,Lord,didn't you?*Lori silently asked.

And as she dialed the orphanage,she looked up to see her mother smiling."I'm proud of you,honey,"she said.

Lori's church friends were proud,too. "You're doing a wonderful thing,"they said,digging into their pockets to help.A month later,with Agat's medical visa in hand,Lori flew back to Haiti.

Her heart pounded as she neared the orphanage."Agat! "Lori called, scooping her up as the director explained to the little girl that a doctor far away would make her better.Agat looked at Lori,her wide eyes full of hope.

"I'll take care of you,"Lori cooed.As Agat smiled,Lori's heart melted.

At home in Walnut Bottom,Agat was so overwhelmed by all the strange sights that she clutched the ragged toy she had brought with her. But by the second day of songs and stories,Agat—giggling—knocked down a castle Lori's dad had built from blocks.

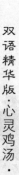

果我能看到她笑就好了,劳瑞心想。

在海地的最后一个晚上,劳瑞躺在床上睡不着。我怎么能把阿伽丢在这儿不管,这个地方没人有时间坐下来给她讲几个小时的故事,没人承担得起帮她治疗。我怎能弃她而去……当她已经进入我的内心。

回家后,劳瑞一直想着那眼神忧郁的孩子。劳瑞想,如果我不试着帮她,我将永远为她担心。

她给一个又一个医生打电话,说:"我有个孩子,她需要手术。可是没有钱。"

"为什么你不打电话给……"通常都是这样的答复。最后,有人指引她去找神经外科专家约欧·维纳。"她什么时候能来?"他问。

劳瑞不敢相信她的耳朵。"我想重复一下:我们没有钱,"她说。

"我学医是为了助人,"医生轻声说明。

主啊,是你让我找到约欧医生的,难道不是么? 劳瑞在心中问道。

每次她给孤儿院打电话时, 抬头总能看到母亲在微笑。"亲爱的,我为你而自豪。"她说。

劳瑞的教会朋友们也为之骄傲。"你在做一件了不起的事。"他们边说边倾囊相助。一个月后,劳瑞带着阿伽的医疗签证飞往海地。

快到孤儿院时,劳瑞心跳加速。"阿伽!"劳瑞一边喊,一边急忙抱起阿伽。院长在一旁对阿伽解释说,很远的地方有一位医生可以治她的病。阿伽望着劳瑞, 大大的眼睛里满是希望。"我会照顾你的。"劳瑞低声细语。阿伽笑了,劳瑞的心化了。

在沃纳特·伯顿的家里,陌生的景物让阿伽昏了头,她紧抓着从孤儿院带来的破烂玩具。但是到了充满歌声和故事的第2天,阿伽——咯咯笑着——推倒了劳瑞父亲用积木搭成的城堡。

"Listen! "Lori marveled."She's *laughing*! "

Soon,Agat was full of laughter—until the day Lori handed her to the doctor.Agat shrieked in fear as he listened to her heart.*She thinks I'm betraying her*! Lori thought.

During a six-hour operation,Dr.Winer closed the fracture in Agat's skull.And though she woke from anesthesia crying,the moment she heard Lori,she stopped.

Soon,Agat was healing at home with the Wellers.

"Apples,"Lori taught Agat,pointing to the fruit."Bicycles,"Lori said as kids rode by."Mashed potatoes! "Agat said herself."I…like mashed potatoes! "

Then one night,tucking Agat into bed,Lori said,"I love you."And a sleepy little voice echoed back,"I love you! "

Tears spilled down Lori's cheeks.She wished she could keep Agat forever.*But,I'm not even out of school yet.She sighed. Agat deserves a family.*

And that's exactly what Agat got.A few days later,the Wellers' phone rang.There had been a newspaper story about Agat's surgery. Looking at her smiling little face,a family who'd read the story said, "We'd love to open our hearts and home to her."

"They want to adopt her! "Lori cried jubilantly.And best of all,they lived only two hours away!

The day Lori finally had to say good-bye,she held Agat close."I'll always love you,"she promised.Today,Lori spends weekends sharing mashed potatoes and music with Agat's new family.

"Now Agat is going to grow up happy,healthy and loved,"beams Lori,who's still in nursing school."And I know I'll always keep in touch with her,wherever our lives take us."

Meg Lundstrom

Excerpted from Woman's World

双语精华版·心灵鸡汤·

206

"听啊！"劳瑞惊叫道。"她在大笑。"

很快,阿伽的生活就充满了欢声笑语——直到劳瑞把她递给医生。当医生用听筒听她的心跳时,她害怕得大喊大叫。劳瑞想,她以为我欺骗了她。

经过6个小时的手术,维纳医生闭合了阿伽脑壳上的裂口。从麻醉中醒来后,阿伽大哭。但一听到劳瑞的声音,她就停止了哭泣。

不久,阿伽到威勒家里养病。

"苹果。"劳瑞指着水果,教阿伽。"自行车。"骑自行车的孩子路过时,劳瑞说。"土豆泥！"阿伽主动说,"我……喜欢土豆泥！"

一天晚上,把阿伽塞进被窝里时,劳瑞说:"我爱你。"一个带着睡意的稚嫩的声音回应道:"我爱你。"泪水顺着劳瑞脸颊而下。她希望能把阿伽永远留在身边。可是我还没从学校毕业呢,劳瑞叹了叹气。阿伽需要一个家。

阿伽真的有了家。几天后,威勒家的电话响了。有报纸报道了阿伽的手术。有一户人家读了这则报道,看到报纸上阿伽微笑的小脸儿,他们说:"我们愿意向她敞开心扉,我们的家门也向她敞开。"

"他们想领养她！"劳瑞欢呼道。最让人高兴的是,他们家离这里只有两小时路程。

分别的那一天,劳瑞紧紧搂着阿伽。"我永远爱你,"她承诺。如今,劳瑞的周末都和阿伽的新家人共度,一起吃土豆泥,听音乐。

"现在阿伽正在关爱中健康快乐地成长,"劳瑞笑着,她还在护校上学。"我想,无论生活把我们带到何处,我都会一直和她保持联系。"

麦格·朗兹特洛姆
选自《女性世界》

My Name Is Mommy

I've said it a thousand times and I'll say it again:There is no job more important than that of being a parent.

Oprah Winfrey

It's only been ten years.Yet,as I stand in the vestibule of the posh country club,staring at the picture,all I can think is *where did the time go*?The girl in the picture is smiling.A wide I'm-ready-to-take-on-the-world smile of an eighteen-year-old with her whole life ahead of her.I read the caption under the picture: "Cheerleading,Varsity Track,DECA, Choir."And under that,the phrase "In Ten Years I Will Be..."The hand-writing that completes the phrase is still the same.It says, "I will have a doctorate in marine biology and be living in either North Carolina or California."

That's it.

Nowhere does it say, "I will be pregnant with my sixth child and getting ready to celebrate my tenth wedding anniversary."Yet,that's what it ought to say because that is where I am ten years after high school graduation.

The girl in the picture is me.A hardly recognizable me.Over the years,I traded in the eighties "big"hair for a more easily maintained style.I exchanged the now outdated,but then trendy,clothes for never-go-out-of-style jeans and whichever-my-hand-grabs-first-out-of-the-drawer shirts.I somehow lost the fullness to my face and the tight skin around my eyes.As I creep toward twenty-nine,these things don't bother me—

我的名字叫妈咪

> 我已经说过一千遍可我还要说一次：没有一份工作比为人父母更重要。
>
> ——奥普拉·温弗瑞

只不过10年。然而，当我站在华丽的乡村俱乐部的走廊里，注视着这幅照片时，我所想的是时间都溜到哪儿去了？照片中的女孩在微笑。一个"我准备好征服世界"的微笑，18岁女孩的微笑，她的人生路还长着呢。我读着照片下方的文字："领导拉拉队，大学径赛代表队队员，国际市场学学生组织（注：DECA 为 Distributive Education Clubs of America 的缩写），唱诗班。"下面还有一句话"10年后我将成为……"写完这句话时的笔迹还是一样的。她写道，"我将获得海洋生物学博士，并住在北卡罗莱那州或加利福尼亚州。"

就这些。

绝对不会提到，"我将怀着我的第6个孩子并正在准备庆祝我的第10个结婚周年纪念日。"这些也该加上去，因为这就是我中学毕业10年后的现实。

照片里的女孩就是我。一个几乎认不出来的我。这些年里，我不再梳理80年代流行的爆炸头，换成了好护理的发型。我换掉了以前入时但现在过时了的衣服，改穿永不过时的牛仔和我随意从抽屉里抓出来的第一件衬衫。不知怎么搞的，我的脸颊不再圆润，眼睛周围的皮肤也松弛了。当我渐渐接近29岁，这些事情都不再让我烦

经典系列／时光的印记……

209

the inevitable,the getting older.But the caption does bother me for some reason—"I will have a doctorate in marine biology…"

What was I thinking?Did I really think I could accomplish such an extravagant goal?I guess I must have.Ten years ago. Funny,I remember loving science in high school—anatomy,chemistry,botany,the whole nine yards—but marine biology?I don't even have pet fish!

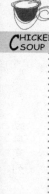

I enter the main room,where the class of '87 high school reunion is already in full swing.I am wary,uncomfortable in the outrageously expensive maternity outfit I bought especially for the occasion.I search the crowd of some two hundred people for a familiar face,but I moved six hundred miles away just after graduation,married and hadn't seen these people for ten years.When I received the invitation,it hadn't seemed so long ago.For some reason,now it feels like an eternity.

At first,faces look vaguely familiar,then names start popping in my mind like kernels of popcorn.A girl from my cheerleading squad,Debbie, yes Debbie! Gosh,she looks so chic! And…It's all coming back to me now.Over there is Brett What's-His-Name. He still looks the same,just older,just like the rest of us. Somewhere in this crowd are the girls I'd been best friends with,the girls I had once confided my deepest secrets to,my dreams,my desires.Here are the boys I once dated and fancied myself in love with for a few days or weeks.

Memories I didn't know I remembered surface,one by one,dripping a name to match a face here,then trickling more there,then flooding me with snapshot memories of classes,football games in the rain,dates and dances,musicals and plays,lunches at McDonald's on one dollar and ten cents,my first car,parties and friends.Suddenly,I don't feel so out of place.I even see a few protruding bellies that rival mine.

I take a deep breath and smile at the first girl,or should I say woman,who catches my eye.I remember her.We never did get along well,but what the heck,it has been ten years.We are all grown up now,

心——无法阻止地，我正在变老。但是由于某种原因，这照片下的文字说明的确让我烦心——"我将成为海洋生物学博士……"

我当时在想什么？我真的认为我能完成这么高的目标？想必我的确这么认为。10年前。有趣的是，我记得上中学时我爱理科——解剖学、化学、植物学，所有的领域——但海洋生物学？我甚至都没养过宠物鱼。

我进入主室，在这里，87级中学同学的团聚活动已经进入高潮。我穿着特意为这次活动买的贵得出奇的孕妇装，小心翼翼，感到不适。我在这有两百号人的人群里寻找，想找张熟悉的面孔。但是毕业后我就搬到600英里远处，结了婚，有10年没见过这些人了。收到邀请函的时候，我感觉这一切似乎不是发生在这么久之前。不知为何，现在的场景恍如隔世。

一开始，面孔隐约有点熟，然后名字像爆米花里的谷粒一样从我心中一个一个蹦出来。这是我的啦啦队里的一个女孩，戴碧，是的，戴碧！天哪，她看上去如此小资！还有……我都想起来了。那边是布瑞特。他叫什么名字？他看上去还是那样，只是跟其他人一样，老了一点。人群中有一处的那些女孩们曾是我最好的朋友。我曾经推心置腹地告诉她们我最大的秘密、我的梦想、希望。这边是我曾经约会过的男孩，我曾幻想会与他相爱几天或几周。记忆浮上心头，我以为自己都忘了。名字一个一个出现，来匹配一个一个面孔。一会儿，记忆又慢慢流淌。然后，记忆的片断淹没了我：班级，雨中的球赛，约会和跳舞，音乐剧和戏剧，花1美元10美分在麦当劳吃的午餐，我的第一辆车，聚会和朋友们。突然，我不再觉得不自在。我甚至看到了几个突出的肚子，都可以匹敌我的肚子了。

我深深地吸了一口气，冲着第1个女孩——或者应该说是女人——展露微笑，她抓住了我的目光。我记得她。我们以前处得不好，可是见鬼去吧，都10年了。我们现在都是成年人了，可不是？我向

right?

I take a step closer and yell over the eighties music and chattering noise,"Hi,Kirsten! "

She searches my face,trying to place me in her own memories. Maybe I have changed that much.She finally gives up,and her eyes float down to my name tag,then snap right back to my face as her mouth drops open."Oh,my gosh! "

I say,"How are you?"with a huge smile I practiced for just such an occasion as this.

"Oh,my gosh! "she repeats and calls me by my maiden name,a name I haven't thought of as belonging to me for nearly ten years."You look *sooo* different! "she exclaims,looking me over,the way a female will do only to another female."Are you pregnant?"she asks.

I nod and say,"Six months."

"Don't you already have like a *million* kids?"

Do I detect a condescending note in her voice?"Just five,"I answer, my eyes dancing over the crowd for a more friendly reception.I spot a girl I'd known since grade school."Nice seeing you again,Kirsten,"I call over my shoulder as I move away.

I start having fun,reminiscing with old friends I'd once shared everything with.Each conversation started with, "Oh,my gosh! You've changed *sooo* much,blah,blah,blah.You look *fabulous*! "And then,"What have you been doing?"

I listen as these once-great friends—now strangers—gush on and on about fun-filled college years,fantastic careers,outstanding salaries, dreams of corporate ladder climbing,travel,big-city life in Chicago,New York,Los Angeles,Atlanta.I am reacquainted with friends who have become doctors,lawyers,engineers,teachers,accountants,scientists,actors,etc.

And then they turn back to me and say,"What have you been doing?Where did you go to college?"

前走了一步，以盖过这80年代的音乐和嘈杂谈话声的声音喊，"嗨，科斯汀。"

她研究着我的脸,试图在记忆中找到我的位置。也许是我的变化太大,她终于放弃了。她的目光下移到我的姓名标签上,接着突然移回到我脸上,嘴张得老大。"噢,天哪!"

我说,"你好。"伴着一个大大的微笑,我特意为今天这种场合练习过。

"哦,天哪!"她重复着,用我的闺名喊我。我以为这个名字不属于我已近10年。"你看上去和从前太太太不一样了!"她惊叫着,用一种只有女人对女人才会用的方式上下打量着我。她问,"你怀孕了?"

我点点头说,"6个月了。"

"你不是已有一大群孩子了吗?"

我察觉到她声音里有种优越感吗?"只有5个。"我回答,目光移到人群里,欲找寻一个更友好的聆听者。我发现了一个女孩,从小学起我就认识她。"克斯汀,很高兴又看到你。"我头也不回地离开。

我开始找乐子,和老朋友一起追忆往事,我曾经愿与之分享每一件事。每一次对话的开头都是"哦,天哪!你的变化真真真大啊,等等,等等。你看起来好极了。"然后就是"你一直在做什么?"

我聆听这些了不起的往日朋友——现在的陌生人——滔滔不绝地谈着充满乐趣的大学生活、很棒的职业、格外高的工资、公司里向上爬的梦、旅游、大城市的生活比如芝加哥、纽约、洛杉矶、亚特兰大。我重新认识这些已经成为医生律师工程师,教师会计师科学家演员等的朋友。

然后他们转过身问我:"你一直在做什么? 在哪儿上的大学?"

This is where my smile starts to feel forced. "I didn't go to college," I say. "I got married. We started a family right away." They tell me how great they think it is that I am what they call a stay-at-home mom. How they can't believe I have five kids, am expecting a sixth and still have my sanity. How I must really have my hands full and how busy I must be.

I smile and think, *They have no idea what they are talking about.* I smile through their caustic teasing about birth control and planned parenthood. I smile through their sly speculation of what a stud my husband must be. I smile and smile and smile. I feel myself sinking. I entered the room as a mom, but now I am nothing but a mom. I never thought of myself that way before.

I return to the vestibule and stare at the picture again. What happened to the girl I once was? Or better yet, where is the woman I almost was? The marine biologist, living on the ocean, sun-kissed face, salt-bleached hair?

At one time, I was filled with such dreams, such goals. I wanted to make a difference; I wanted to be successful; I wanted to be rich…I wanted to have it all.

I think about this all the way back home on the plane to Maryland, where I now live, getting more of that awful sinking feeling in the pit of my stomach, the kind that makes you want to cry in self-pity. Then I see something.

I see a woman holding a baby.

The baby is not yet a year. He's wild-eyed, clutching his ear with one hand, the other hand wrapped around his mother's neck in a white-knuckled grip. The mother is rocking gently back and forth in her seat, singing softly, patting lightly, face calm, soothing her baby. I watch. I can't take my eyes off her. The baby's eyes begin to droop, then close; his body relaxes.

听到这里，我感觉我的笑容开始像是挤出来的。"我没上大学，"我说，"我结了婚。很快就组织了一个家庭。"他们告诉我：我是他们称之为全职妈咪的那种人，他们认为这很伟大。他们怎能相信我有5个孩子，正在期待着第6个，还依然保持精神正常。他们怎能相信我两手如何腾不开以及我必须忙到什么程度。

我笑着想，他们不知道自己在说什么。他们刻薄地谈着生育控制和有计划地做家长，我一笑而过。他们滑头地胡猜我丈夫想必是匹种马，我一笑而过。我微笑，微笑，再微笑。我觉得自己很虚弱。我以妈咪的身份进来的，但现在我什么也不是，除了是个妈咪。以前我从未这样看待过自己。

我回到走廊里重新注视着那张照片。曾经是我的这个小女孩身上到底发生了什么？或者更理想的，我就要变成的那个女人现在何方？那个海洋生物学家生活在大洋边，阳光亲吻着脸颊，海盐漂白了头发？

曾经，我满怀这样的梦想、这样的抱负。我想有所改变；我想成功；我想富有……我想拥有一切。我现在住在马里兰州，在回家的飞机上，我一直在想这个问题，越发心乱如麻。这种自怜的感觉让你想哭。然后我看到了什么。

我看到一个抱着婴儿的女人。

这婴儿还不到1岁。他目光纯净，用一只手揪着自己的耳朵，另一只手环绕着妈妈的脖子，手握得太紧连手指关节都发白了。母亲坐在椅子上轻柔地前后晃悠着，柔声地唱着歌，轻轻地拍着，表情平静地哄着宝宝。我盯着她，无法把目光从她身上移开。婴儿的眼皮开始下垂，然后合上；他的身体放松下来。

It's something I've done a hundred times,a thousand,maybe,rocking my baby,one of them,any of them,all of them.An earache,a stomachache, a nightmare,a boo-boo,a fight,something I could always fix with my rocking chair and my arms.

Suddenly,I realize I do still have dreams,just different ones.I dream of seeing the bottom of my laundry basket,an empty kitchen sink,a freezer that is always stocked,a toothpaste-free bathroom counter,a bathroom without a miniature potty right next to the big one,stairs that don't have a gate at the top and bottom,every sock in my house reunited with its mate.And I know when I have accomplished these goals,I'll sit down and cry.It occurs to me that,over the years,I have gone through an unseen but tremendous transformation.I have learned to love construc- tion paper;crayon-colored birthday cards;sun catchers made from wax paper;autumn-colored leaves;Christmas decorations of cotton balls,glitter and too much glue;Dixie cups full of dandelion tops and assorted weeds on my table;refrigerators covered in papers,and pictures with "I Love U Momy"scrawled beneath.

I've learned to see swing sets as lawn ornaments,exclaim with gen- uine enthusiasm at the sight of a hot-air balloon or a helicopter flying low in the sky,offer up a cheek for a sticky-faced kiss and then beg for another.

I *do* make a difference—in the lives of my children.I have awe- some responsibility—making major decisions that will shape the lives of five—almost six—individuals.I am rich—in love and family.

I do have it all.Or all I need to have.

The plane lands,and the passengers make their way down the gate- way.I walk slowly,waddling really,lugging my carry-on,while my mind switches back into mommy mode,as my thoughts race through all I must do once I get home.The dishes and the laundry and the groceries and the...

双语精华版·心灵鸡汤·

这是我做过上百次，也许是上千次的事情。轻轻摇晃我的宝宝，也许是宝宝中的某一个，任何一个，或者是所有人。耳朵疼、胃疼、噩梦、小错、打架、以及能凭我的摇椅和我的怀抱都能搞定的事。

　　突然，我意识到我依然有梦想，只是梦想不同。我梦想看见洗衣篮的底、空空的厨房水池、总是装满食品的冰箱、上面没有牙膏的浴室台面、没有小坐便器紧挨着大坐便器的浴室、在顶端和底部没有保护门(防孩子摔)的楼梯，梦想看见每一只袜子都和它的伴侣在一起。我也知道完成这些目标后，我会坐下来哭。这些年来，我经历了看不见却巨大的转变。我学会了爱上彩色美术纸；蜡笔上色的生日贺卡；蜡纸做的捕捉阳光的挂饰；秋天色彩的树叶；用作圣诞节装饰的棉球、亮晶晶的小饰物和大量的胶水；放在我桌子上的Dixie牌纸杯里装满蒲公英头和各种杂草；贴满了纸条的冰箱；和底下涂着"妈咪我爱你"字样的照片。

　　我学会了把秋千架当做草坪的装饰，看到热气球和直升机从低空飞过时真诚的欢呼；伸出脸颊接受黏糊糊的吻然后请求再得到一个吻。

　　我的确有很大变化——在我的孩子们的生活中。我有了不起的责任——做出重大决定，引导5个——几乎是6个——独立的个体的人生。我是富有的——在爱和家庭上。我的确拥有一切。或者说拥有我所需要的一切。

　　飞机着陆了，乘客们沿着门道行进。我慢慢地走着，实际上是摇摇摆摆地走，吃力地拖着随身行李往前移，同时头脑又调回妈咪的模式，例如快速思考一回到家我必须做的所有事情。要做饭，要洗衣服，要整理杂物，还要……

"Excuse me, ma'am." I turn toward the voice behind me, a gentleman, his hand outstretched. He asks, "Can I give you a hand with that bag?"

I smile broadly. "I'd rather you carry this baby. My back is killing me."

He laughs. "Is this your first?"

We are coming through the gate now, and I spot my family waiting to meet me, five little faces lighting up at the sight of me, and my heart swells with love. "Not hardly," I say and gesture with my free hand.

He says, "Your life must be pretty hectic."

To this I respond, "It's pretty wonderful."

Stacey A.Granger

"打扰一下,女士。"我转向背后的这个声音,是一位先生,伸着他的手。他问:"我可以帮你拿那只包吗?"

我开怀大笑。"我宁愿你抱这个宝宝。我的背疼得要命。"

他大笑。"这是你的第1个孩子吗?"

此时我们已经走出门。我认出等着接我的家人,5张因为看到我而放着光的小脸,我的心里也随之充满了爱。"不是,"我回答,并用没拿东西的那只手打着手势。

他说,"你的生活想必非常忙碌。"

对此,我的回答是,"它非常精彩。"

斯塔西·A.格兰杰

Gramma's Blanket from Heaven
外婆的天堂毯

I couldn't have been more than seven years old the night I climbed out of bed and tiptoed downstairs to look for my grandmother.Gramma liked to sit up watching *Marcus Welby,M.D.*,and sometimes I'd sneak down in my pajamas,stand quietly behind her chair where she couldn't see me and watch the show with her.Only tonight,Gramma wasn't watching TV.Nor was she in her room when I returned upstairs to look for her.

"Gramma?"I called,my young heart pounding with alarm.I couldn't ever remember wanting my grandmother when she wasn't right there to answer the call.Then I remembered Gramma had gone on an overnight trip with some friends.That made me feel better,but there were still tears in my eyes.

那时我还不到7岁,那天晚上我从床上爬下来,踮着脚下楼去找我的祖母。外婆喜欢熬夜看《马克斯·韦尔伯医生》,我常常穿着睡衣溜下楼,不出声地站在她椅子后面和她一起看电视,我在那儿她看不见。只有今晚,外婆不在看电视。我回到楼上去找她时发现她也不在自己房间里。

"外婆?"我叫道。我幼小的心惊恐地剧跳着。我从不记得发生过我需要外婆的时候,她不在那里回答我的要求。然后我想起来外婆和朋友们出行,在外面过夜了。想到这,我觉得好受些,但是眼里依然含着泪。

I dashed back to my room and burrowed beneath the afghan Gramma had crocheted,as snug and warm as one of her hugs.*Gramma will be home tomorrow,I comforted myself.She wouldn't ever go away and not come back.*

Since before I was born,Gramma Rosie had lived with our family: my mom and dad and my older brother,Greg.We lived in Holland, Michigan,and when I was in the fifth grade,we bought a big new house. My mom had to go to work to help with the mortgage.

Lots of my friends went home to empty houses after school because both their parents worked.But I was one of the lucky ones.My mom's mom was always at the back door waiting for me with a glass of milk and a thick slice of buttery banana bread piping hot from the oven. Sitting at the kitchen table,I'd tell Gramma all about my day.Then we'd play a few hands of rummy.Gramma always let me win—at least until I got good enough to put up a real challenge on my own.

Then,one day when I was seventeen,everything wasn't fine anymore.Gramma had suffered a heart attack,and the doctors said she might never get well enough to come home.

How many nights had I fallen asleep to the muffled sounds of Gramma praying in her bedroom next door and mentioning me to God by name?Well,that night I talked to God myself.I told him how much I loved my grandmother and begged him not to take her away from me. "Couldn't you wait until I don't need her anymore?"I asked with youthful selfishness,as though there'd ever come a day when I would have stopped needing my grandmother.

Gramma died a few weeks later.I cried myself to sleep that night and the next,and for many more after that.One morning,I carefully folded the afghan my grandmother had crocheted and carried it to my mom. "I can't bear feeling so close to Gramma without being able to talk to her and get a hug,"I sobbed.My mother packed the blanket away for

我冲回自己房间,藏到外婆织的阿富汗毛毯下面,温暖舒适,就像她的拥抱。外婆明天就回来,我安慰自己。她不会走了而不回来的。

　　在我出世前,外婆柔茜就和我的家人住在一起。他们是:我的妈妈、爸爸和哥哥戈瑞格。我们住在密歇根州的荷兰德,我上5年级时,家里买了新的大房子。我妈妈不得不出去工作来帮助家里还抵押贷款。

　　我的许多朋友放学后回到家里时屋里都空荡荡的,因为他们的父母都上班去了。但我是幸运者之一。我妈妈的妈妈总是拿着一杯牛奶和厚厚一片涂了黄油的香蕉面包在后门等我, 面包刚出炉,冒着热气。我坐在厨房的桌子旁,告诉外婆我今天遇到的事。然后我们玩几盘拉米纸牌。外婆总是让我赢——至少在我玩得够好能独自经受真正的挑战之前是这样。

　　然而,我17岁时的一天,每一件事都不再好。外婆患了严重的心脏病,医生说她也许不会好转到能回家的地步。

　　有多少个夜晚我是听着外婆在隔壁的卧室里低声祷告并向上帝提及我的名字声中入睡?唉,那个晚上我自己对上帝说了话。我告诉他我有多爱我的外婆,求他不要把外婆从我身边带走。"你不能等到我不再需要她时吗?"我怀着年轻人的自私问,似乎会有那么一天我将不再需要我的祖母。

　　几周后外婆死了。那天晚上和第2天晚上,我都哭到睡着,此后许多个夜晚都是如此。一天早晨,我仔细叠好外婆织的阿富汗毛毯,并把它抱给妈妈。我呜咽着说:"我不能忍受感觉离外婆很近却不能对她说话也不能得到一个拥抱。"母亲把毯子包裹起来妥善保管。直

safekeeping,and to this day it remains one of my most cherished pos
sessions.

I missed Gramma terribly.I missed her joyous laughter,her quiet
words of wisdom.She wasn't there to help me celebrate my high school
graduation,or the day eight years ago when I married Carla.But then
something happened that let me know Gramma had never really left me,
that she was watching over me still.

A few weeks after Carla and I moved to Paris,Arkansas,we learned
that Carla was pregnant.It turned out to be a difficult pregnancy with serious complications.We spent so much time in the hospital that I lost my
job mere weeks before Carla's due date.

Near the end,Carla developed toxemia,and the day our son was
born the doctors wouldn't allow me in the delivery room because they
were afraid that neither Carla nor the baby was going to survive.I paced
the waiting room,praying as the baby's vital signs plummeted and Carla's blood pressure rocketed sky high.My mom and dad were on their
way south from Michigan,but they weren't there yet. I'd never felt so
helpless and alone.Then,suddenly,I felt Gramma's arms embracing me in
one of her hugs."Everything's going to be just fine,"I could almost hear
her saying.Then as quickly as Gramma had come,she was gone again.

Meanwhile,in the next room,the doctors completed the emergency
C-section.The instant our son was born,his heartbeat grew strong and
steady.Within minutes Carla's blood pressure began to drop,and she,too,
was soon out of danger.

"Thank you,Gramma,"I whispered as I stood staring through the
nursery window at our beautiful new baby,whom we named Christian."I
only wish you could be here to give my son half of the love and wisdom you passed on to me."

One afternoon,two weeks later,Carla and I were home playing with
Christian when someone knocked at our door.It was a deliveryman with

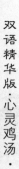

到今天,它一直是我最珍惜的财产。

我极度思念外婆。我想念她快乐的笑声、她温和而智慧的话语。她没去帮我庆祝中学毕业,8年前我和卡拉的婚礼上她也不在。但后来发生了一件事让我相信外婆从未真正离开我,她仍然看守着我。卡拉和我搬到阿肯萨斯州的派瑞斯后数周,我们得知卡拉怀孕了。这次怀孕很艰难,有许多严重的并发症。我们花了太多时间待在医院以至于在卡拉的预产期前我失去了工作。

临近最后,卡拉得了血毒症。我们的儿子出世的那天,医生不让我进产房因为他们担心卡拉和孩子都活不成。当婴儿的生命迹象骤然减弱,卡拉的血压直冲天空时,我在等待室走来走去,祈祷着。妈妈和爸爸正在从密歇根州南下的路上,他们还没到。我感到从没有过的无助和孤单。这时,突然,我感觉到外婆的手臂环绕着我,就像她的某一个拥抱那样。我几乎听到她在说:"每件事都会好转的。"正如她突然出现,外婆又突然消失了。

同时,在隔壁房间,医生们完成了紧急剖腹产。儿子出生的那一刻,他的心跳变得强劲而稳定。几分钟后,卡拉的血压开始下降,她也很快脱离了危险。

"谢谢你,外婆。"当我站在那儿透过婴儿室的窗玻璃盯着我们漂亮的新生儿时,我低声地说道。我们给孩子起名为克里斯汀,"我只希望您能在这儿把您赋予我的爱和传授给我的智慧分一半给我的儿子。"

两周后,一天下午,卡拉和我在家逗克里斯汀玩。这时有人敲门。是来送包裹的邮递员——给克里斯汀的礼物。盒子上写着"给一

a package—a gift for Christian.The box was addressed to "a very special grandbaby".Inside,there lay a beautiful hand-crocheted baby blanket and a pair of booties.

My eyes filled with tears as I read the card."I knew I wouldn't be here for the grand day of your birth.I made arrangements by proxy to make this blanket for you.The booties I made before I left on my journey."The note was signed "Great-Gramma".

Gramma's eyesight was so weak near the end that she'd had to ask my Aunt Jeanette to help out with the blanket.But she'd struggled to finish the booties herself,and she did it all during those few brief weeks before she died.

Bill Holton

Excerpted from Woman's World

个非常特殊的曾孙"。盒子里,平放着一块漂亮的手编婴儿毯和一双小毛线鞋。

当我看到卡片时,眼泪溢满了眼眶。"我知道在你出生的重大日子我将不在这儿。我委托他人为你织了这块毯子。小毛线鞋是在我上路前做的。"便条署名"曾祖母"。

在最后的日子里,外婆的眼神是如此差以至于她得要简娜特姨妈帮忙织完这块毯子。但她挣扎着自己完成了小毛线鞋。她在去世前的短短几周做完了这一切。

比尔·霍顿

选自《女性世界》

Angels All Around
天使在身边

Dorothy Wright's husband,Forrest,shook her hard, "Wake up, Dorothy! Get up! There's smoke everywhere! "

Dorothy coughed,opened her eyes to a gray haze in their bedroom, bolted upright and screamed,"Get the kids! "She grabbed the phone to call 911 but before she could tell them where they lived the line went dead.

*Oh Lord,help us,*Dorothy prayed as she and Forrest ran in opposite directions to wake their children,Forrest Junior,sixteen;Danielle,fifteen; Leonard,thirteen;Dominique,twelve;Joe,eleven;Anthony,ten;Marcus,eight; Vinny,seven;Curtis,five;Nicholas,three;and Ja-Monney,three. (Ja-Monney is her nephew that they've raised since his birth.)

多萝茜·瑞特的丈夫,弗瑞斯特,使劲地摇晃着她,"醒醒,多萝茜! 起来! 到处都是烟啦! "

多萝茜咳着,一睁眼就看到他们卧室里的灰色烟雾,猛地跳起来,尖叫着,"把孩子们找到!"她抓起电话拨了911,但还没来得及告诉他们自己家住在哪儿线就断了。

哦,主啊,帮帮我们,多萝茜祈祷着,和丈夫分头跑去唤醒他们的孩子:小弗瑞斯特,16岁;丹尼尔,15岁;列奥纳多,13岁;多米尼格,12岁;乔,11岁;安东尼,10岁;马库斯,8岁;威尼,7岁;柯提斯,5岁;尼古拉斯,3岁;嘉·莫尼,3岁。(嘉·莫尼是她的侄儿,出生后即由他们抚养。)

225

Scared and confused,the children rubbed their eyes and stumbled down the stairs and out the front door.Dorothy counted heads.

"Someone's missing! "she screamed."Who?Curtis! Forrest,Curtis is missing! "

Forrest,ran back into the house and up the steps as smoke poured out the front door.Five-year-old Curtis,who'd been hiding under his bed, struggled into the smoky hallway when he heard his Daddy's voice.He couldn't see Forrest in the thick smoke but he ran right into his Daddy's arms.Forrest grabbed him and tore back down the stairs.Halfway down Forrest fell,sprained his ankle and stumbled outdoors.

Dorothy dashed to the neighbor's house.The woman who lived there had been studying all night and had just gone to bed when Dorothy banged on the door.The neighbor finally saw the orange glow through the Wright family's windows and called 911.Within minutes the fire trucks arrived.By now the flames had spread between the walls of the old wood frame house and moved to the second floor.Neighbors took the children into their homes.But Dorothy couldn't move.As fire-fighters slammed their axes into the roof,she stood there and watched her dream evaporate.Everything inside that house went up in flames. Fur niture,clothing,housewares,linens,photo albums,cash,jewelry,the only picture she had of her mother who died when Dorothy was a teenager. Everything was gone.

*Our dream,*Dorothy thought,*How can it end like this*?She and For-rest had wanted so much more for their eleven children than was offered in the inner-city.They'd just moved to the suburb of New Milford,out-side Hackensack,New Jersey four years earlier. They didn't want the kids growing up around drugs,alcohol abuse,fighting and gangs.They didn't want the sub-standard education or the run-down neighborhoods.

What a blessing when they found the big frame house and met Di-ana,their landlord.They convinced her that they were hard workers and

孩子们吓坏了,慌乱地揉着眼睛,跌跌撞撞地下楼梯,出了前门。多萝茜清点人数。

"有人不见了！"她尖叫。"谁,柯提斯！弗瑞斯特,柯提斯不见了！"

弗瑞斯特冲回屋里,上了楼,烟雾从大门喷涌而出。5岁大的柯提斯一直躲在床下,听到爸爸的声音后挣扎着跑进烟雾迷漫的过道。在浓烟中,他看不见弗瑞斯特,但他径直跑进爸爸的怀里。弗瑞斯特抓住他,顺着楼梯快速往回跑。半途中弗瑞斯特跌倒了,扭伤了脚踝,踉踉跄跄地出了门。

多萝茜冲进隔壁的房子。当多萝茜猛敲门时,住在里面的那个女人学习了一晚上刚刚上床。邻居终于透过瑞特家的窗户看到橘色的火光,并拨打了911。几分钟后,消防车就到了。这时,火舌已经在这老式木头框架房子的墙壁间蔓延开并烧到了二楼。邻居们把孩子们带到自己家里。但多萝茜动不了。当消防员们使劲地把长柄斧砍进屋顶时,她就站在那儿,看着她的梦消失。房子里的每一件东西都在火中烧毁。家具、衣服、家用器皿、家用纺织品、影集、现金、首饰、她仅有的一张在她十来岁时去世的母亲的照片。每一样都没了。

我们的梦,多萝茜想,它怎能就这样结束呢?她和弗瑞斯特对11个孩子寄予的希望比在城里时还多。4年前,他们从新泽西州的海肯塞克搬出来,搬到新米尔福特的郊区来。他们不希望孩子们在毒品、酗酒、闹事打斗和犯罪团伙周围成长。他们不喜欢低标准的教育水平和破旧的居民区。

当他们找到这框架结构的大房子、遇见他们的房东戴安娜是多么幸运啊。他们让她相信他们是努力上班的人,孩子们是有礼貌的

that their children were polite,good kids and that they'd take care of her home.The rent was reasonable and the Wright family moved in.

Now as Dorothy stood there four years later watching their dream evaporate into smoke,all she could think about was two things:*Thank You,God,my family is safe! And then,Where will we ever find another house for our big family*?

After visiting the hospital to make sure the kids were okay and to get a cast on Forrest's sprained ankle,Dorothy went directly to Social Services in her blue pajamas and sneakers a neighbor had given her.As she stood in line people looked at her like,*What's your problem,lady*?

Dorothy didn't care what she looked like.She was a woman on a mission.The only thing the emergency assistance program could do was to put them into a family shelter back in the inner city.Thirteen people crowded into four tiny rooms.

"It was awful,"Dorothy told a friend,"So much goes on in a shelter like that.People moving in and out every day.Drugs.Yelling.Women getting beat up by boyfriends.No play area. Nothing for the children to do."

That's when the guardian angels started to arrive.Dorothy's friend Lisa,who owns Alfredo's restaurant brought food for the family every night for dinner for four months.Pizza,spaghetti,garlic bread,fresh salads, lasagna,eggplant parmesan…all the foods kids love.Their neighbors from the old neighborhood,Jerry and Cynthia,brought a TV to the shelter. Strangers brought brand new clothes.The kids' teachers brought school supplies,coloring books,crayons.Other teachers from New Milford high school,middle school and grammar school had fund-raisers for the family.

The whole town adopted the Wright family and the gifts continued all summer.But Dorothy continued to worry about how they'd ever get out of the shelter and back into the wonderful neighborhood they'd worked so hard to get into four years earlier.How would they ever find another house big enough for their family that they could afford?

好孩子,以及他们会照看好她的屋子。租金合理,瑞特一家就搬过来了。

现在,当多萝茜4年后站在那儿看着他们的梦化成烟,她所能想的是两件事:感谢你,上帝,我的家人是安全的!以后,我们到哪儿去找另外一座房子来容纳我们的大家庭?

多萝茜去了医院以确保孩子们一切都好,弗瑞斯特扭伤的脚踝打了石膏,之后她穿着邻居给她的蓝色睡衣和拖鞋径直去了社会服务部。当她站在队伍里,人们都看着她,似乎在问"你怎么了,女士?"

多萝茜不在乎她看起来什么样子。她是负有使命的女人。紧急救助计划所能做的就是把他们送回到城里的一个家庭避难所。13个人挤在4间很小的屋里。

"太可怕了,"多萝茜告诉朋友,"这么多人到一个那样的避难所里。每天都有人进进出出。毒品。叫嚷。被男友揍的女人。没有玩耍的地方。孩子们无事可做。"

这时,守护天使们开始到来。多萝茜的朋友里萨,拥有阿尔佛莱多饭店,每晚给这家人送饭,一直送了4个月。比萨、通心粉、大蒜面包、新鲜的沙拉、卤汁面、茄子意大利干酪……所有孩子们爱吃的食物。从老街区来的邻居杰瑞和辛西娅,给这个避难所买了台电视。陌生人带来崭新的衣服。孩子们的老师带来学校用品,涂色书和蜡笔。其他来自新米尔福特的初中、高中和小学的老师也为这家人募捐。

全镇人领养了瑞特家人,并且,馈赠持续了整个夏天。但多萝茜继续担心他们如何才能离开这儿,回到他们4年前努力进入的那个美好的居民区。他们如何才能找到另外一座他们能买得起的大房子容纳他们一家?

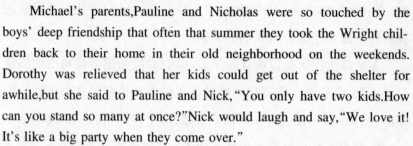

One day,one of Vinny's classmates came to visit.When little Michael Kontomanolis and Vinny saw each other they just hugged and started crying.Michael said,"Mommy,can Vinny come live with us?We have to help him.He's my friend."

Michael's parents,Pauline and Nicholas were so touched by the boys' deep friendship that often that summer they took the Wright children back to their home in their old neighborhood on the weekends. Dorothy was relieved that her kids could get out of the shelter for awhile,but she said to Pauline and Nick,"You only have two kids.How can you stand so many at once?"Nick would laugh and say,"We love it! It's like a big party when they come over."

Then the biggest surprise of all.One day Pauline said,"Dorothy,Nick and I have decided to buy a house in our neighborhood and rent it to you for four years.Then you can buy it from us.We want you to have your own home.We want you to come back to the neighborhood where you belong."

Dorothy and Forrest couldn't believe it.Why would this couple who hardly knew them before the fire do such a thing for them?Pauline just smiled and said, "We connect through our hearts,Dorothy."Together Dorothy and Pauline found a two-story Cape Cod with six bedrooms,a huge living room,big dining room and finished basement.The thirteen members of the Wright family moved in in October,just five months after the fire. On moving day the family opened the doors to discover huge "Welcome home! "banners taped everywhere.The neighbors had supplied the house with everything from toothpaste and toilet paper to laundry soap and paper towels;even make-up for the girls.

One couple,Agnes and Ralph,bought eight expensive twin beds and pillows for all the children.Others brought quilts,sheets,and bedspreads for everyone.

Since then, "Aunt Pauline and Uncle Nikkolas"as the children call

一天，威尼的一个同学来看望他们。当小米歇尔·篓图马纳利斯和威尼看到对方时，他们拥抱在一起哭起来。米歇尔说："妈咪，威尼能到来和我们一起生活吗？我们必须帮助他，他是我的朋友。"

　　米歇尔的父母，宝琳和尼古拉斯为这两个男孩的深厚友谊所触动，那个夏天，他们常常在周末带瑞特家的孩子回到他们在老居民区的家中。多萝茜很欣慰孩子们可以走出避难所一会儿，但是他对宝琳和尼古说："你们只有两个孩子，你们怎能忍受一下子有这么多孩子？"尼克就会大笑着说："我们喜欢这样！当他们过去时就像在举行一个大聚会。"

　　接着，最大的惊喜来了。一天，宝琳说："多萝茜，尼克和我决定在我们居住区附近买一所房子，然后把它租给你们4年。之后你可以从我们手里买走它。我们希望你们有自己的家。我们希望你们回到你们所属的居民区来。"

　　多萝茜和弗瑞斯特简直不敢相信。火灾发生前他们几乎不认识这对夫妇，为什么他们要为弗瑞斯特家做这件事呢？宝琳微微一笑，说："我们的心灵相通，多萝茜。"多萝茜和宝琳一同找到了一栋两层的科德角建筑（注：Cape Cod 是一种起源于17世纪的新英格兰的房型。它的传统特点是矮、阔的框架建筑。一般为一层半高，屋顶陡峭倾斜，斜屋顶两端为三角墙，中央有一个巨大的烟囱），有6个房间、一个巨大的起居室、一间大餐厅和装修好的地下室。火灾后仅5个月，瑞特家的13个人便在10月份搬了进去。搬家那天，瑞特一家打开门就发现每一处都贴着巨大的标语："欢迎回家"。邻居们已经把屋子里摆满了东西，从牙膏和卫生纸到洗衣皂和纸巾；甚至还有女孩子的化妆品。

　　一对夫妇，阿锦思和拉夫，给所有的孩子买了8张昂贵的单人床和枕头（注：美国床分为twin, full, queen, king，其中 twin最小，只能睡单人）。其他人给每个人带来了被子、床单和床上用品。

　　从那以后，"宝琳姨妈和尼古拉斯叔父"，孩子们这么称呼，就

them,have become like brother and sister to Dorothy and Forrest. They cook out together,share things,spend time together.

Every day as Dorothy watches her children come home from volleyball or basketball practice or a yearbook meeting,she thanks God that they have their dream back.Danielle wants to speak eight languages and go to Harvard to be a lawyer.One of the boys wants to be a fighter pilot. Three of them want to be doctors. Dominique wants to be a nurse. Leonard wants to be a technician for NASA.

Dorothy Wright says it best,"With as many guardian angels as this family has,and with the love we have for each other,the dreams of the entire Wright family will continue for generations."

Patricia Lorenz
Excerpted from Woman's World

变得像是多萝茜和弗瑞斯特的兄弟姐妹。他们一道在室外烹调,共享物品,共度时光。

每天,当多萝茜看到孩子们练过排球或篮球后回家,或是从年鉴会议回家,她就感谢上帝让他们找回了他们的梦。丹尼尔想要学8种语言,去上哈佛,成为一名律师。男孩子中有一个想成为战斗机驾驶员,有3个想成为医生。多米尼格想成为护士。列奥纳多想成为美国国家航空和宇宙航行局的一名技术人员。多萝茜·瑞特说得最好:"有这个家庭拥有的那么多守护天使,有我们相互之间的爱,整个瑞特家族的梦想将一代代延续下去。"

帕德里萨·娄仁兹
选自《女性世界》